SOUTH
SK

D1180681

'If you agree to come here and play the piano for me I can create another story.'

He smiled with all the charisma he employed to woo patrons in London, hoping she wouldn't dismiss the idea outright.

She laced her arms beneath her breasts and stepped back, the cynical schoolmarm returning. 'And what instrument do you hope I'll play afterwards? I'm not Madame de Badeau, a woman to be hired as a mistress.'

He didn't blame her for being cautious. Once he'd achieved fame, the number of people he could trust had shrunk significantly.

'I don't want a mistress but a muse.'

It was difficult to look at her and not think of twining his hands in her golden hair, tasting her pink lips as they parted beneath his and freeing those glorious breasts from their prim confines. He'd better not concentrate on them if he wanted to win her co-operation and keep himself free from distraction and bankruptcy.

'I need you.'

Author Note

Miss Marianne's Disgrace is about overcoming the past to build a better future. Marianne, who made her first appearance in *Rescued from Ruin*, is a talented piano player, and I wanted to explore how music allows her to cope with a difficult life. To help me craft her scenes I dipped into my childhood piano lessons experience. I never mastered the instrument, but all the hours I spent at my parents' antique Bösendorfer finally came in handy.

My inspiration for Sir Warren came from reading about Sir Walter Scott, the famous novelist, and from medical history.

Scott teetered on the verge of losing everything he'd earned when he became entangled in a publishing scheme and sank into crippling debt. He was determined to pay it off through his writing, and achieved his goal mere months before he died. Unlike Scott, Sir Warren's near bankruptcy is the result of another's scheming, but his desire to pay back investors on his own is similar to Sir Walter Scott's. I modelled Priorton on Scott's beloved Abbotsford.

Sir Warren's background as a Navy surgeon was inspired by my research for a historic battlefield medicine class that I teach. Life as a Navy surgeon in the time before anaesthesia was bloody and nerve-racking, and it seemed like a good way to torture an artistic soul.

Through their burgeoning love Marianne and Warren help each other overcome their pasts and build a future together. I hope you enjoy *Miss Marianne's Disgrace*.

MISS MARIANNE'S DISGRACE

Georgie Lee

All rights reserved including the right of reproduction in whole
or in part in any form. This edition is published by arrangement with
Harlequin Books S.A.

This is a work of fiction. Names, characters, places, locations and
incidents are purely fictional and bear no relationship to any real
life individuals, living or dead, or to any actual places, business
establishments, locations, events or incidents. Any resemblance is
entirely coincidental.

This book is sold subject to the condition that it shall not, by way of
trade or otherwise, be lent, resold, hired out or otherwise circulated
without the prior consent of the publisher in any form of binding or
cover other than that in which it is published and without a similar
condition including this condition being imposed on the subsequent
purchaser.

® and TM are trademarks owned and used by the trademark owner
and/or its licensee. Trademarks marked with ® are registered with the
United Kingdom Patent Office and/or the Office for Harmonisation in
the Internal Market and in other countries.

First published in Great Britain 2016
By Mills & Boon, an imprint of HarperCollins*Publishers*
1 London Bridge Street, London, SE1 9GF

Large Print edition 2016

© 2016 Georgie Reinstein

ISBN: 978-0-263-26328-2

Our policy is to use papers that are natural, renewable and recyclable
products and made from wood grown in sustainable forests.
The logging and manufacturing processes conform to the legal
environmental regulations of the country of origin.

Printed and bound in Great Britain
by CPI Antony Rowe, Chippenham, Wiltshire

A lifelong history buff, **Georgie Lee** hasn't given up hope that she will one day inherit a title and a manor house. Until then she fulfils her dreams of lords, ladies and a Season in London through her stories. When not writing, she can be found reading non-fiction history or watching any film with a costume and an accent. Please visit georgie-lee.com to learn more about Georgie and her books.

Books by Georgie Lee

Mills & Boon Historical Romance

Scandal and Disgrace

Rescued from Ruin
Miss Marianne's Disgrace

The Business of Marriage

A Debt Paid in Marriage
A Too Convenient Marriage

Stand-Alone Novels

Engagement of Convenience
The Courtesan's Book of Secrets
The Captain's Frozen Dream

Visit the Author Profile page at
millsandboon.co.uk.

To all the writers who struggle through challenges
to achieve their goals.

Chapter One

England, September 1820

The crack of shattering porcelain cut through the quiet. Miss Marianne Domville whirled around to see Lady Ellington, Dowager Countess of Merrell, on the floor amid shards of a large *chinoiserie* bowl. Moments ago the bowl had been resting on the edge of a table while Lady Ellington had walked about the room, admiring the Italian landscapes adorning the panelling.

'Lady Ellington!' Marianne rushed to her companion. 'Are you all right?'

Mrs Stevens, their new friend, knelt on the Dowager's other side. Together, they helped Lady Ellington to sit up. Next to her lay a large sliver of the broken bowl, the razor-sharp edge rimmed with red from where it had sliced Lady Ellington's upper arm.

'I—I don't know,' Lady Ellington stammered. She clasped the wound as blood seeped through her fingers and ran down over the elbow to stain the top of her satin gloves. 'I tripped on something and somehow knocked the bowl to the floor when I fell.'

'Let me see.' Marianne tried to look at the injury, but Lady Ellington twisted away.

'You needn't fuss so much,' she chided in a shaky voice. 'It's just a scratch, nothing more.'

'Then allow us to examine it.' Mrs Stevens reached over and gently peeled Lady Ellington's fingers away from the wound. Her lips tightened as she studied the wide and bleeding cut.

'This needs immediate attention.' She pressed her handkerchief over it.

Lady Ellington winced and a fine perspiration spread out beneath the line of her light-blonde hair streaked with grey.

'Will she be all right?' Marianne asked as the embroidery on the linen blurred with red. One of her schoolmates at the Protestant School in France had cut herself this deeply. It had become inflamed and she'd gone from a lively child to resting in the churchyard in the space of two weeks. For all Marianne's misfortunes, none would equal losing Lady Ellington.

'Of course,' Mrs Stevens reassured in a motherly tone. 'But the wound must be closed. Fetch my son. He used to be a naval surgeon. He'll see to it.'

'But he wasn't at dinner.'

'He came in after we withdrew and is probably with the men. Go quickly. I'll stay with Lady Ellington.'

Marianne rose on shaky legs and walked in a fog of worry out of the study. She turned down one hall, then paused. The heavy sauce from the fish course twisted in her stomach. This wasn't the way. As she doubled back, the sweep of her footsteps on the carpet dulled the panicked thud of her pulse in her ears. She hadn't paid much attention when she'd followed the ladies to the study after leaving the sitting room. She'd been too busy fuming over Miss Cartwright's snide comments to concentrate on what turns they'd made to reach the distant room.

'Where's a footman when you need one?'

They'd been as thick as fleas along the wall at dinner and in the sitting room afterwards. Now there wasn't even a lowly maid scraping out ashes in any of the empty rooms flanking the hall. Lady Ellington might bleed to death before Marianne found her way back to the other guests.

No, she'll be fine. All I need to do is find Mr Stevens.

She turned a corner and the door to the wide front sitting room came into view. She exhaled with relief and rushed towards it, careful not to run. She didn't want to fly into a fit of worry, not with Lady Ellington relying on her to keep a level head. Hopefully, the men hadn't lingered in the dining room.

No such luck.

The women looked up from around the card table as Marianne stepped into the doorway. Their faces were no warmer or more welcoming then when she'd left them fifteen minutes ago.

'Can we help you, Miss Domville?' Lady Cartwright drawled, as if it hurt her to be polite.

'Lady Ellington has injured herself and is in need of help. I must find Mr Stevens.'

'*Sir Warren,*' Miss Cartwright corrected, her lips pulling back over one crooked front tooth as she laid a card on the pile in the centre, 'is in the dining room with the men.'

'I'll call a footman to summon him. After all, it can't be too serious,' Lady Cartwright sneered under her breath to Lady Astley and Lady Preston who sat with her at the card table.

'No, thank you, I'll fetch him myself.' Marianne made for the dining room, not about to lose time waiting for these hard women to decide whether it was more important to put Marianne in her place or to help Lady Ellington.

She didn't remember the hallway being so long when Lady Ellington had walked beside her, chatting gaily with Mrs Stevens about the new Italian landscape paintings they were about to view. Marianne quickened her pace, stumbling a little over a wrinkle in a rug before righting herself.

The deep laugh of men muffled by the double oak doors punctuated the growing whispers of the ladies congregating in the sitting-room doorway behind Marianne. They gasped in shock, practically sucking the air from the hallway as

Marianne pushed open the doors and stepped inside.

They weren't the only ones who were stunned. The footman jumped in front of her so fast, he almost lost his wig.

'Miss, you shouldn't be here.' He shifted back and forth to block her view, as if she'd walked in on the men dancing naked in front of the buffet.

'Move aside, I must see Sir Warren.' She slipped around the ridiculous footman and headed for the table.

The men were too lost in a weedy fog of tobacco and fine port to notice her. All the candles but those at the far end of the long table of Lady Cartwright's ridiculously long dining room had been extinguished, deepening the smoky shadows outside the circle of light.

'I tell you, Warren, it's an investment you can't miss.' Mr Hirst thumped the table in front of him. His words were thicker and more slurred than when he'd rattled on to her at dinner about his intention to import a new type of tobacco from North Carolina. He'd pleaded with her to speak to Lord Falconbridge about investing in his venture, addressing her breasts more than her during the discussion. *The noxious little man.* His lust was all she'd come to expect from most gentlemen. Carnal pleasure was the only thing the men who'd streamed through Madame de Badeau's entrance hall had ever wanted from her and they'd despised her for not giving it to them.

The men on either side of Mr Hirst nodded in agreement, except for Lord Cartwright who slumped forward on the high polished table, snoring beside an empty wine glass.

'You could make a fortune,' Mr Hirst insisted.

'Rupert, I've already made a fortune with my novels,' the man who must be Sir Warren replied. He sat with his back to Marianne, a glass of port held at a languid angle to his body.

'Sir Warren,' Marianne called out, interrupting his leisure.

Chairs scraped and men coughed and sputtered as they hurried to stand. Even Lord Cartwright was hauled to his feet by Lord Astley. Lord Cartwright's bleary eyes fixed on her.

'What in heaven's name are you doing in here?' he sputtered, wavering and nearly falling back into his seat before Lord Astley steadied him.

'I need Sir Warren. It's urgent.'

'I'm Sir Warren.' The man with his back to her set his drink on the table and turned.

She braced herself, ready to receive from him another chastising look like the others had flung at her, but it wasn't there. Instead, his deep-green eyes were wide with the same surprise filling her and it dissolved all of Marianne's sense of urgency. He was tall, with a broad chest she could lay her head on, if she was inclined to embrace people, which she wasn't. His long, sturdy arms ended in wide hands with slender fingers tinged a slight black at the tips. He was taller than the other gentlemen with long legs and narrow hips. The softness of the country hadn't set in about his flat stomach beneath his waistcoat or along the line of his jaw shadowed by the first hint of light stubble. He wore his blond hair a touch longer than the other men with a few strands falling forward over his forehead. There seemed something more professional man than gentleman in his bearing. Although his clothes were fine, they weren't as tidy or well pressed as the other gentlemen's and his cravat was tied, but the knot was loose.

Unlike his companions, he didn't appraise her

large breasts, which she did her best to hide beneath the chemisette and high bodice. Instead he waited patiently for her to explain herself, like Mr Nichols, the old vicar at the Protestant School in France used to do whenever he'd caught her being naughty. Where had this man been at dinner? With him by her side instead of old Lord Preston, she might have actually enjoyed the overcooked lamb.

The rest of the men weren't so kind, brushing her with their silent disapproval and more lurid thoughts.

'How can I be of assistance?' Sir Warren prodded, snapping her out of her surprise.

'You must come at once. Lady Ellington has cut herself badly and needs your help.' She reached out, ready to pull him along to the study before she dropped her hand. To touch a man, even innocently, was to encourage him and she needed his assistance, not his ardour.

His smile faded like the last flame licking at a coal in a fireplace. He slid a glance to Mr Hirst. It was a wary, troubled look like the ones Mr and Mrs Smith used to exchange during Marianne's first month at their house when they'd been forced to tell her Madame de Badeau still hadn't written.

Hollow disappointment crept into her already knotted stomach. Sir Warren wasn't going to help her. Like every other reputable gentleman, he'd swiftly but politely decline any involvement with her before rushing across the room to avoid the taint of her and her reputation.

How petty.

She opened her mouth to shout him down for not having the decency to rouse himself from propriety long enough to help an ailing woman, but he spoke first.

'I'll see to her at once.' Sir Warren motioned to the door. 'Please, lead the way.'

She clamped her mouth shut, near dizzy with relief as she hurried back across the dining room, keenly aware of his steady steps behind her.

'You there, lead us to the study.' She snapped her fingers at the footman, afraid she wouldn't remember the way and waste more time heading down pointless hallways.

The footman jumped at the command, walking briskly in front of them as Marianne and Sir Warren followed him out of the dining room.

'What happened?' Sir Warren asked in a voice as rich as the low A note held down on the pianoforte.

Marianne twisted her hands in front of her, noting the hard faces of the women watching them from the sitting-room doorway. 'She cut herself on a broken porcelain bowl.'

Sir Warren jerked to a halt in the hallway as if he were about to change his mind.

'Your mother said you could help,' Marianne encouraged, afraid to lose him now and in front of the sneering women.

'Yes, of course.' He lost his hesitation and they resumed their steady pace.

They approached the ladies clustered behind Lady Cartwright and her imperious scowl. Their whispers ceased as Marianne and Sir Warren passed, and Marianne could practically hear the scandal wicking through the countryside. She could stop and explain, but there was no point in wasting the breath or time. Some might understand and forgive her. The rest wouldn't be so charitable even if she were summoning help for the Archbishop of Canterbury.

'It's just the type of inappropriate behaviour

I'd expect from someone related to Madame de Badeau,' Lady Cartwright's barely concealed voice carried down the hall behind them.

'She should be ashamed of herself,' Lady Astley whispered.

Marianne winced, expecting their censure to make Sir Warren change his mind about assisting her. To her astonishment, he turned and strode back to their hostess.

'Lady Cartwright, would you be so kind as to fetch a sewing kit, a roll of linen, a few towels and vinegar and see them delivered to the study. Lady Ellington has been seriously injured and I need the items.'

Lady Cartwright's long face dropped as the crow finally grasped the urgency of the situation. 'Of course, I'll have the housekeeper see to it at once.'

She grabbed the skirt of her dress and fluttered off in the opposite direction, leaving her daughter and the rest of the ladies to huddle and whisper.

Sir Warren returned to Marianne. 'Shall we?'

'Yes, of course.' Marianne started off again, amazed at his command of Lady Cartwright and the alacrity with which he'd defended her. She wished she possessed the power to wipe the nasty sneers from the women's faces. After four years, most of the country families still believed she was as bad as the late Madame de Badeau. They couldn't see past all of the dead woman's scandals to realise Marianne, despite having the woman's blood in her veins, wasn't a brazen tart like her.

'Does Lady Ellington have a strong constitution?' Sir Warren asked as they turned the corner.

'The strongest.'

'You're sure? It'll matter a great deal to her recovery if the wound is deep.'

'I'm quite sure. I reside with her. She's my friend.' And almost the only person who'd accepted her once the scandal with Madame de Badeau had spread. Her support, and the influence of her nephew and his wife, the Marquess and Marchioness of Falconbridge, stood between Marianne and complete isolation from society.

As they continued on to the study, Sir Warren's presence played on her like a fine piano sonata. She'd never been so conscious of a man before, at least not one who wasn't ogling her from across a room. He didn't glance at her once as they crossed the hallway and he hadn't been inappropriate in his regard, not even when she'd first faced him in the dining room. She wondered at the strange awareness of him and if it meant the penchant for ruin did linger inside her, waiting for the right man to bring it out. After all, Madame de Badeau had been in control of herself for many years, until the thought of losing Lord Falconbridge had pushed her to near madness. If it did exist in Marianne, she'd stand strong against it, as she had all Madame de Badeau's wickedness, and make sure it never ruled her.

At last, the study door came into sight and she forgot Sir Warren as she focused on her friend.

'Stay here in case we need you,' Sir Warren instructed the footman and the man took up his place along the wall.

Marianne hurried forward, eager to know if Lady Ellington was any better or worse, but Sir Warren's hand on her upper arm brought her to a halt. He gripped her lightly, drawing her back to him. She whirled to face him, fingers curling into a fist, ready to strike him like she used to the lecherous men at Madame de Badeau's, but the melancholy shadow covering his expression made her hand relax.

'Miss?' he asked, the question as soft as his pulse flickering against her skin.

'Domville.' She braced herself, expecting recognition to ripple through his eyes and make him recoil from her.

It never came.

'Miss Domville, I'll do all I can for Lady Ellington, but you must understand how small an arsenal I possess against the chance of inflammation.'

Marianne began to tremble. 'Are you saying this to scare me? Because I assure you, I'm already frightened.'

He slid his thumb along her skin, the gesture subtle but comforting, soothing her in a way she'd craved so many times during her childhood at the Protestant School and in the face of Madame de Badeau's callousness. Deep in the back of her mind, the raspy voice of experience urged her to pull away. She'd learned years ago not to seek solace in others or to accept so familiar a touch from a man. Both were the quickest paths to disappointment. For the first time, for no logical reason she could discern, she ignored the voice and experience.

'I'm saying this because I have no desire to deceive you about the strength of my skills, or those of any man of my former profession,' he explained. 'We're helpless against everything but the most minor of ailments. Even those outdo us from time to time. It's a truth many medical men are loath to admit.'

There seemed more to his admission than a need to discredit himself. Something about his past in medicine drove him to speak when most physicians would be pushing expensive and useless treatments on her. She caught it in the tight lines around his mouth. Was it a failure or a lost patient? Whatever it was, the silent plea wasn't just for understanding, but for forgiveness. She covered his hand, her chest catching as he tightened his fingers around hers. Despite the inappropriateness of this exchange, she knew too much about pain to leave someone else to suffer.

'Sir Warren, Lady Ellington means more to me and has done more for me than anyone else and has never expected anything in return except my friendship. I understand the shortcomings of your profession and appreciate your honesty and willingness to help. Whatever happens, I won't blame you. I only ask you to do your best.'

He squeezed her hand. 'I will.'

Warren's palm went cold the instant he let go of Miss Domville. A trickle of perspiration slid down the arch of his back. He swiped at it, leaving his shirt sticking to his skin beneath his coat. If he didn't detest the feeling so much, he'd call it fear.

The candles in the candelabrum near the door wavered with the draught as he entered the study. Lady Ellington sat grimacing on the floor, pillows propped behind her. Faint streaks of drying blood ran the length of her arm beneath the soiled handkerchief. Darker drops littered the floor and stained her mauve skirt and the carpet.

Warren paused on the threshold, the brackish taste of mouldy cask water burning his tongue. He took a deep breath, coughing slightly as the scent of burning wood and gunpowder filled his nostrils.

His mother looked up, apology as heavy as concern for the patient in her expression. 'Warren, thank goodness you're here.'

Warren pushed forward, forcing his feet to move one in front of the other. He carefully brushed aside the broken porcelain pieces so he could kneel next to the regal lady and better view the laceration. He removed the blood-soaked handkerchief and steadied himself as he examined the gaping wound.

'How are you tonight, Lady Ellington?' He tried to sound cordial but the words came out tight.

'I've certainly been better.' She offered him a weak smile, her wide chest covered in diamonds struggling to reflect the low light.

'Miss Domville, please bring the candles closer.'

Miss Domville's dress fluttered behind her as she took the candelabrum from near the door and set it on the table above Lady Ellington. The memory of his assistant surgeon holding a candle over Warren's head while Warren dug splinters out of a seaman's neck flashed in the facets of Lady Ellington's diamonds. Some of the sailors had survived thanks to his skill. Many more hadn't, no matter how much he'd done for them.

Miss Domville knelt beside Warren. The whisper of silk and her fresh peony scent pushed back the old stench of seared flesh. He offered her an encouraging smile, wishing he could wallow in her faint answering one. He couldn't and focused on the patient.

'I'm sorry, Lady Ellington, but the cut is deep and will require sutures.'

Lady Ellington's pale face went almost transparent. 'It will hurt, won't it?'

'It will, but without them I can't stop the bleeding.'

'Don't worry, Lady Ellington, you've faced worse,' Miss Domville encouraged. The worry he'd caught in her voice in the hallway when he'd cautioned her about believing too much in medical men was masked by her reassuring words.

'You're quite right, my dear. We must soldier on tonight as we always do, mustn't we?' Lady Ellington reached out with her good arm and patted Miss Domville's knee. The young lady didn't stiffen beneath the older woman's touch as she had with Warren's, nor did the tenderness of her smile fade.

'Sir Warren, I brought the items you requested.' Lady Cartwright's voice ended the sweet comfort of the ladies' exchange.

At the door, Lady Cartwright covered her mouth in shock. Warren wasn't certain if it was for Lady Ellington or the now-stained carpet. He suspected the latter as he took the sewing box and bottle of vinegar from the stalwart housekeeper and set them next to him.

'Come away from there at once, Miss Domville.' Lady Cartwright flapped her hand at her guest. 'Next to a surgeon is no place for a young lady. You'll only get in Sir Warren's way.'

'No, I need her help and her friend needs her comfort,' Warren countered as he took up the needle and began to thread it with sturdy white silk. His hands were solid on the slender metal, but he felt the tremor rising up through his body. He was determined to finish the task before it swept over him and made him appear weak and incompetent. He took a deep breath, inhaling Miss Domville's sweet scent. It calmed him more than any drought of laudanum or dram of rum ever had.

When the needle was ready, he handed it to Miss Domville. 'Hold this, please.'

Their fingers met and she pulled away as if he'd pricked her, the tension he'd sensed when he'd touched in her in the hallway returning. He wished he could soothe whatever worries made her flinch, but it was the patient who needed him now.

He took up the bottle of vinegar, splashed some on to the clean cloth and pressed it to the wound. Lady Ellington winced.

'You might have warned me.' She scowled, a touch of humour behind the reprimand.

'It would have hurt more if I had,' Warren countered with a half-smile. He set the cloth and vinegar aside and took the needle from Miss Domville. He pinched the top of it, careful not to touch her this time. 'Put your hands on either side of the skin and push it closed.'

Without question or hesitation, Miss Domville did as she was told. A trickle of blood seeped over her long fingers, but she didn't flinch or blanch. He admired the girl's pluck. Most genteel young ladies would be swooning on the sofa by now.

Not to be outdone by a young woman, Warren drew in a bracing breath and set to work.

Lady Ellington whimpered with each pierce of the needle and draw of the thread, but she didn't scream or jerk away. Warren worked fast, eager to cause her as little pain as necessary.

Over his shoulders, an occasional whisper broke through his concentration. To Lady Cartwright's credit, she kept the other ladies from crowding into the room and interfering. To her detriment, she didn't staunch the steady stream of derision aimed at Miss Domville.

'She'll ruin her dress,' Lady Preston sneered.

'She's acting like a common camp follower,' Miss Cartwright hissed.

Warren made the final suture, tied it off with a neat knot and used the scissors in the sewing kit to snip the needle free of the thread. 'You'd make quite a surgeon's assistant, Miss Domville. You have the steady nerves for it.'

She frowned and glanced past him to the door. 'Not everyone agrees with you.'

'Ignore them.' He handed her a clean towel,

eager to see her lovely white fingers free of the red taint.

'I spend my days ignoring them.' She roughly scrubbed her skin.

He wondered what had happened to turn the others against her. Perhaps it was jealousy. She was sensuous like a Greek sculpture with shapely arms ending in elegant hands. When her fingers were clean and white again, she handed him the stained towel, avoiding his touch. Then she adjusted the lace chemisette covering her very generous décolletage. The brush of her fingertips across her breasts proved as teasing as it was modest. It made him forget the dirty linen in his palm as he watched her straighten a pin in her golden hair with its faint hints of amber circling her face. It was arranged in small twists which were drawn together at the back of her head, emphasising her curving neck and the small curls gracing it. While he watched her, he was no longer irritated at being drawn back to the sickroom he despised. If he'd known this beautiful woman was waiting in the sitting room for the men to finish their port, he'd have insisted they leave the dining room at once.

'Warren, perhaps you should see to the bandage,' his mother encouraged, interrupting his admiration of Miss Domville.

'Of course.' Warren took up the roll of linen and wound it over the wound, attempting to ignore the blood covering his fingers and to focus on Miss Domville's steady presence beside him. As he tied the bandage, a small spot of red darkened the centre, but it spread out only to the size of a thruppence before stopping. 'There now, Lady Ellington, all is well again.'

Lady Ellington looked at her arm and the dried streaks running down it. 'To imagine, all this trouble because I tripped.'

'It was no trouble at all. I'm glad you summoned me.' He patted her good shoulder, hoping his smile hid the lie. It didn't and his mother caught it, offering him a silent apology, but he ignored it. The old fear humbled him enough without anyone noticing it. 'Let's help her up to the sofa so she can rest.'

The moment Lady Ellington was settled against the cushions, the invisible dam holding the ladies back burst. They flooded into room, surrounding the Dowager Countess in a flurry of chirping and silk. Warren moved back, surprised to find Miss Domville next to him.

'She really will be all right, won't she?' she asked, her fear palpable. She wasn't the first person to seek his reassurance about a patient.

'There was no cloth pushed into the wound to fester and, given her robust health, I think she'll recover well.' It was the best he could offer.

Pink replaced the pale worry on the apples of her cheeks. He'd experienced the same reprieve the day he'd returned to Portsmouth and resigned his commission. He'd vowed that day never to climb aboard another Navy frigate again, and heaven help him, he wouldn't.

'I'll write out instructions for properly seeing to the wound while it heals and a recipe for a laudanum tonic to help ease any pain.' He walked to the escritoire, the activity relieving some of the tension of having attended to a patient for the first time since his sister's death over a year ago. He pulled out the chair, making it scrape against the wood floor, irked that a simple cut could affect him or dredge up so many awful memories. His reaction was as shocking as when he'd turned to find Miss Domville in the dining room asking him to help the same way his mother had asked him to intervene during Leticia's travails.

Seating himself, he selected a piece of paper from the stack on the blotter. He paused as he laid the clean sheet over the leather. Blood darkened the tips of his finger and the side of his hand. He rubbed at the stains with the linen towel, but the red clung to his skin as it used to during a battle. He tightened his hand into a fist, desperate for water and soap to rid himself of the filth.

He looked up, ready to bolt from the room in search of cleansing when his eyes caught Miss Domville's. She glanced at his clenched hands, then back to his face. It wasn't his mother's pity in the stunning blue depths of her eyes, but the same bracing strength she'd offered Lady Ellington before he'd begun his work.

He snatched up the pen, his fingertips pressing hard on the wood as he scratched out in shaky letters the directions for mixing the laudanum and alcohol. He pushed back the haunting memories of his cramped cabin below the waterline and focused on the proportions, determined not to get the dosage wrong and leave poor Miss Domville at fault for easing her friend's pain for good.

'My, it's cold in here,' Lady Astley's voice rang out above the noise.

A poker clanged in the grate and Warren flinched, running a streak of ink across the paper. The scrape of rods shoved down cannon barrels echoed in the sound, the balls buried deep inside and ready to wreak a destruction his surgical skills could never hope to undo.

'Ladies, I think Lady Ellington should be left alone to rest until the carriage is called.' Miss Domville's firm suggestion sounded above the clatter, silencing it.

Warren, pulled from the past by the steady voice, was surprised by the young lady's ability to remain composed in the face of so many hostile stares. She reminded him of a seasoned seaman calmly watching the coming battle while the new recruits wet themselves.

Lady Cartwright huffed up to Miss Domville, not content with a silent rebuke. 'I don't think *you* should instruct us on how to behave. You didn't even have the decency to tell us what was wrong, bursting in on the men and leaving us to think who knows what.'

'It was an emergency. There wasn't time for pleasantries.' The twitch of small muscles around the young woman's lips undermined her stoicism.

Lady Cartwright opened her mouth to unleash another blow.

'She was right to summon me as she did.' Warren rose to defend Miss Domville, tired of the imperious woman. Miss Domville had endured enough tonight worrying over her friend. She didn't need some puffed-up matron rattling the sabre of propriety over her blonde head. 'And she's correct. Lady Ellington needs space and rest. Lady Cartwright, would you call for her carriage? Mother, would you escort her and Miss Domville home? I'll send my carriage for you.'

'Of course.' His mother arched one interested eyebrow at Lady Ellington, who offered a similar look in return before her face scrunched up with a fresh wave of pain.

Lady Cartwright's nostrils flared with indignation, not nearly as amused as the two ladies on the sofa. 'I'll summon Lady Ellington's carriage. After all, we wouldn't want to detain Lady Ellington or *Miss Domville* any longer.'

She struck Miss Domville with a nasty look before striding off in a huff.

The long breath Miss Domville exhaled after Lady Cartwright left whispered of tired resignation. It was as if she'd waged too many similar battles, but had to keep fighting. He understood her weariness. Aboard ship, he'd faced approaching enemy vessels with the same reluctant acceptance.

Her gaze caught his and he dropped his to the paper as if he'd stumbled upon her at her bath, not in the middle of these chattering biddies. Unable to stand the noise any longer, Warren snatched up the instructions and quit the room. In the quiet of the hallway, he spat into his palm and rubbed the handkerchief hard against his skin. It smeared the red across his hand, dirtying the linen as it had stained the rags aboard ship. There'd never been enough buckets of seawater to clean the grime from beneath his fingernails.

He screwed his eyes shut.

This is nothing like then. Nothing like it. Those days are gone.

The war against Napoleon was over, his commission resigned. He was no longer Lieutenant Stevens, surgeon aboard HMS *Bastion*. He was Sir Warren Stevens, master of Priorton Abbey and a fêted novelist.

A fêted novelist who'd be destitute and a disappointment to his family like his father had been if he didn't finish writing his next book.

He opened his eyes and scrubbed harder until at last the red began to fade, cursing the troubles piling on him tonight.

'Sir Warren, are you all right?'

Miss Domville approached him, the flowing silk of her dress brushing against each slender leg. Beneath her high breasts, it draped her flat stomach and followed the curve of her hips. She stopped in front of him, her eyes as clear and patient as when they'd faced each other before.

Humiliation flooded through him. He wouldn't be brought low by memories. He clutched his lapels and jerked back his shoulders, fixing her with the same glib smile he flashed adoring readers whenever he signed their books. 'Yes, why shouldn't I be?'

'I don't know. You seem troubled.' She studied him the way his sister, Leticia, used to, head tilted to one side, her chestnut curls brushing her smooth cheeks. It had looked so dark, matted against her forehead with sweat, her hazel eyes clouding as the life had faded from them. Hopelessness hit him like a jab to the gut.

'I'm fine.' He handed her the now-wrinkled and sweat-dampened paper, ashamed by this bout of weakness. It had been a long time since the memories of his time at sea had overwhelmed him like this. He'd thought he'd overcome them in the ten years since he'd left the Navy. Apparently, he hadn't. 'Follow the directions precisely, otherwise you may do more harm than good.'

'I will, and thank you again for your help.' Miss Domville folded the paper, pausing to straighten out a crease in one corner as she glanced past him to the fluttering women. 'All of it.'

'It was the least I could do. Now, if you'll excuse me.' He turned and left, ignoring the confused crease of her smooth forehead as he all but sprinted away from her and the study. He regretted the abrupt departure, but he'd embarrassed himself enough in front of her already. Despite the draw of Miss Domville's presence, the faint desire to linger in her sweet smile and vivid blue eyes, he needed the solitude of home and his writing to calm the demons stirred up by tonight.

Chapter Two

'You entered the dining room where the gentlemen were?' Lady Ellington's cousin, Rosemary, Dowager Baroness of St Onge, gasped, clutching the long strand of pearls draped around her thin neck. 'By yourself?'

Marianne gritted her teeth as she poured Lady Ellington's tea. 'It was a matter of some urgency.'

'But, my dear, you'll be the talk of the countryside for being so bold.'

Marianne tipped a teaspoon of sugar in the cup. 'I'm already the talk of the countryside, whether I storm in on the men at their port or spend all my days practising the pianoforte.'

'But to interrupt gentlemen in the dining room.' Lady St Onge pushed herself to her feet. 'It just isn't how young ladies behave.'

'Now, now, Cousin Rosemary.' With a look of sympathy and a small measure of amusement, Lady Ellington took the tea from Marianne. The rings on every finger sparkled in the afternoon sunlight as she leaned back against her *chaise*. 'I'm sure everyone understands Marianne was acting on my behalf and not because she wanted to create a scandal.'

'You give them too much credit, Ella. I can almost hear the country ladies' tongues wagging from here.' Lady St Onge shuffled out of Lady Ellington's dressing room, a long string of muttered concerns trailing behind her.

Marianne frowned. 'Why can't she stay at your London town house while the roof of her dower house is being repaired? Why must she be here?'

'Patience, Marianne,' Lady Ellington urged, propping her injured arm up on the pillows beside her. After a restless night, Lady Ellington had regained her spirits, but not her usual vigour. 'You more than anyone know what it is to need a safe haven from the small troubles of life.'

'If only they were small.' She splashed tea into her cup and a hail of drops splattered over the edge and on to the saucer. Her undeserved reputation kept good men away while attracting scoundrels and gossip. Sir Warren had been proof of it last night. Despite his defending her against Lady Cartwright, he'd bolted from her the moment his services were no longer needed. Typical gentleman.

'Your problems aren't so very large they can't be overcome,' Lady Ellington insisted, ever the optimist.

Marianne peered out the window at the tall trees swaying over the front lawn. Welton Place, Lady Ellington's dowager house on the grounds of Falconbridge Manor, had proven a refuge for Marianne. However, the sturdy brick walls and Lady Ellington's solid reputation couldn't keep all the scandals and troubles from touching her. 'Lady St Onge is right, the gossips will talk. Even with your influence, they refuse to believe that I am nothing like Madame de Badeau.'

'They are stubborn in their views of you, which is surprising since Lady Preston has all but fallen on top of half the eligible gentlemen in the countryside and no one is cutting her. I think her old husband must not mind since it saves him the bother.'

Marianne laughed, nearly choking on her tea.

'Now there's a smile.' Lady Ellington offered her a napkin.

Marianne dabbed at the moisture on her chin.

'You're so pretty when you smile. You should do it more often.'

Marianne tossed the linen down beside the china. 'If I had more to smile about, I would.'

'Nonsense. You're too young to hold such a dim view of life.' She raised one ring-clad hand to stop Marianne from protesting. 'Yes, I know you've seen a greater share of trouble than most young ladies. But it does you no good to be morose. You'll only end up like poor Rosemary.'

'Now, that's unfair.'

'True, but we can't have you languishing here and becoming a spinster, not with your enviable figure and your money. We'll go to London next Season and find you someone.'

'No. I won't go back there.' She could manage the scrutiny of a few country families, but not the derision of all society. Besides, whatever hopes Lady Ellington harboured about Marianne's wealth and looks landing her a good husband, she didn't share them. Marianne brushed at the lace over her breasts, wishing she didn't possess so much figure, but it was what it was. As for the money, leaving her well settled had been the one and only thing the vile Madame de Badeau had ever done for her. Marianne shuddered to think how the woman must have earned it. 'The only gentleman attracted to me is the broke Lord Bolton. Hardly a suitable pool of suitors.'

'Then we'll increase it. After all you can't spend your entire life composing pianoforte pieces.'

What else is there for me to do?

The other young ladies in the country were planning amusements for the autumn while the experiences of their last Season in London were still fresh. Those not dreaming of winter balls and house parties were at home with the husbands they'd landed in the spring, or tending to their new babies. There was little for Marianne to look forward to, or to keep the days from passing, one dreary, empty one after another.

She dipped her teaspoon into her tea and listlessly swirled the dark brown water. She should be thankful for the tedium. She didn't want to flirt with temptation and discover she really was no better than the gossips believed.

'Speaking of things to do.' Lady Ellington took up a letter from the table beside her, eyeing Marianne with a whiff of mischief. 'Mrs Stevens sent a note asking after me. Tomorrow, we'll pay her a call and thank her and her son for their help.'

Marianne paused over her teacup, the steam rising to sweep her nose. 'So soon?'

'I'm not sick enough to lie about all week and I want to see how the repairs to Priorton Abbey are coming. Be a dear and bring me my writing box. I'll send a note to Mrs Stevens right away.'

With some reluctance, Marianne set down her cup and made for the writing desk. There was no good excuse she could contrive for why they shouldn't go. After all, they did owe them thanks for their help. She liked Mrs Stevens. She couldn't say the same about Sir Warren. Despite his assistance, in the end, his response to her had been no different from anyone else's outside the Falconbridge family. His all but running from her still grated. Who was he to cast judgement? He was no hereditary baronet, only a writer with the Prince Regent for an admirer.

Then again, who was she? The only relation of London's most notorious lady scoundrel.

She paused over the lacquer writing box, the Falconbridge family crest gold and red against a three-pointed shield. The loneliness which had haunted Marianne since childhood filled her again. It was the same aching pain she used to experience each Christmas at the Protestant School in France when all the other girls had received packages from their families while she'd received nothing. Madame de Badeau had never sent Marianne so much as a letter during all the time she'd spent at the school. The only thing she'd done was arrive on Marianne's tenth birthday and take her from the only family she'd ever known and carry her off to England before the Peace of Amiens had failed. On her way to London, Madame de Badeau had dumped her with the Smith family, all but forgetting about her for another six years until she'd thought it time for Marianne to marry. Then she'd dragged her to London to try and pawn her off on any dissolute lord who took an interest in her, no matter how old. Only Marianne's stubbornness had kept her from the altar.

A proud, wicked smile curled Marianne's lips. Madame de Badeau's face had practically turned purple when Marianne had tossed Lord Bolton's roses back at him when he'd knelt to propose. It had been worth the beating to defy the nasty woman.

Marianne's smile faded and with it her determined spirit. In the end, Madame de Badeau had got her revenge and ruined Marianne's life.

She grasped the cold metal handles on either side of the box. It didn't matter. There was nothing she could do except bear it as she had all the other disappointments and insults the woman had heaped on her. She started to heave the box from the table when the door swung open, stopping her.

'Lady Ellington, how are you?' Cecelia, Marchioness of Falconbridge, moved as fast as a lady so heavy with her second child could to hug Lady Ellington. Her husband, the Marquess of Falconbridge, followed behind. Lord Falconbridge was tall with a square jaw and straight nose, his blue eyes made more stunning by his dark hair. 'I was so worried when I heard about your accident.'

'You needn't fuss over a little scratch, not in your condition,' Lady Ellington chided. 'Randall, how could you let her scurry about the country when she should be at home resting?'

'I couldn't stop her.' Lord Falconbridge dropped a kiss on his aunt's cheek. 'Besides the two miles from Falconbridge Manor to Welton Place is hardly scurrying about the country.'

'It's the furthest I've been from the house in ages.' The Marchioness rubbed her round belly then shifted in the chair to turn her tender smile on Marianne. Her brown hair was rich in its arrangement of curls and her hazel eyes flecked with green glowed with her good mood. 'Thank you so much for looking after Lady Ellington. It means so much to us to have you here with her.'

With Lord Falconbridge's help, Lady Falconbridge struggled to her feet, then embraced Marianne. Marianne accepted the hug, her arms stiff at her sides. She should return the gesture like Theresa, her friend and Lady Falconbridge's cousin, always did, but she remained frozen. The Marchioness had always been kind to her, even before she'd risen from an unknown colonial widow to become Lady Falconbridge. It was the motherly tenderness in the touch Marianne found more unsettling than comforting. She wasn't used to it.

At last Lady Falconbridge released her and Marianne's tight arms loosened at her sides. Unruffled by Marianne's stiff greeting, the Marchioness stroked Marianne's cheek, offering a sympathetic smile before returning to the chair beside Lady Ellington.

Despite her discomfort, Marianne appreciated the gesture. The Smiths had been kind, but she'd never really been one of their family, as she'd discovered when the scandal of Madame de Badeau had broken. Afterwards, despite the years Marianne had spent with them, they'd been too afraid of her tainting their own daughters to welcome her back.

Marianne swallowed hard. Of all the past rejections, theirs had hurt the most.

'Oh, Cecelia, how you carry on.' Lady Ellington batted a glittery, dismissive hand at the Marchioness. 'You'd think I was some sort of invalid.'

'We know you're not, but we're grateful to

Miss Domville all the same.' Lord Falconbridge nodded to Marianne as he stood behind his wife, his hands on her shoulders. Four years ago, Marianne had discovered Madame de Badeau's letter detailing her revenge for Lord Falconbridge's rejection of her by seeing Lady Falconbridge assaulted by Lord Strathmore. Marianne had given him the letter from Madame de Badeau outlining her plans and with it the chance he needed to save Lady Falconbridge. The revealing of Madame de Badeau's plot had led to her ultimate disgrace and gained for Marianne the Falconbridge family's appreciation and undying dedication.

Marianne shifted on her feet. Lord Falconbridge's gratitude made her as uncomfortable as the hug. A notorious rake she'd once thought as hard as Madame de Badeau, love had changed Lord Falconbridge. What might it do for her? She wasn't likely to find out. No man worth his salt was going to push past the rumours and gossip to ever get to know her.

'Marianne, guess what? Theresa is expecting again. Some time in the spring,' Lady Falconbridge announced.

'How marvellous.' Despite Theresa being one of Marianne's only friends, the good news stung. It illustrated once again the love and happiness Marianne would never enjoy. 'I'll write to her at once with my congratulations.'

She fled the room before the envy and heartache found its way to the surface. She made for the sitting room downstairs near the back of the house, eager to reach the pianoforte and the smooth black-and-white keys. Once inside the room, the view of Lady Ellington's prized rose garden through the far window didn't calm her as it usually did. She withdrew a red-brocade composition book from the piano bench. The spine creaked when she opened it. She flipped through the pages and the notes bounced up and down on the staffs, punctuated every few lines by a smudge of ink or her fingerprint. It was her music. It had comforted her during the long, lonely hours at Madame de Badeau's, and afterwards, before her life had settled into the even cadence of Lady Ellington's dower house.

Selecting her most recent composition, she propped the book up on the music stand and lifted the cover over the keys. Wiggling her fingers, she rested them on the ivory until it warmed. Then she pressed down and began the first chords, wincing at each wrong note until she settled into the sweet and mournful piece. Through the adagio, she concentrated on the shift of the foot pedal and the strength with which she struck each key and how long she held it until sweeping on to the next. The black notes tripped along in her mind, memorised from hours of practice.

Finally, the piece reached its slow, wailing end and she raised her hands. The last notes vibrated along the wires until they faded away. Blinking through wet lashes, her cheeks and neck cold with moisture, she studied her hands. They were smooth and limber now, but some day they'd be wrinkled and stiff and here she'd be, with any luck, living under the protection of the Falconbridge family, the scandals as forgotten as she.

She wiped the tears from beneath her chin and turned the page to one of her slightly less sombre compositions. Crying wouldn't do any good. If Lady Ellington didn't think it was hopeless, then perhaps it wasn't. If nothing else, there was always Lord Bolton.

* * *

'There's a fortune to be made here, Warren, can't you see it?' Rupert Hirst, Warren's brother-in-law, paced back and forth across the rug in front of Warren's desk. A little wrinkle rose up in the patterned carpet where his heel dug in to make the turn.

Warren frowned. If Rupert paced long enough, he'd wear a hole in the thing and then it would be another repair for Warren to pay for. The workers were behind enough already, despite the rush to finish before the good weather ended, and the costs were increasing by the day. If Warren didn't write this book and get it to William Berkshire, his publisher, and collect the remainder of his advance, there'd still be holes in the roof come the first snow.

Lancelot, Warren's red Irish setter who chased sleep more than he did birds, watched from where he lay on the hearthrug, not bothering to rise.

'I can see the potential. I can also see myself losing a great deal of money if your optimism proves unfounded.' *Which wouldn't be the first time.* Despite his brother-in-law's best efforts,

Rupert hadn't made a go of his last venture and it had faltered. Even his love for Leticia had proved destructive in the end.

Warren twirled his pen in his fingers. It wasn't fair to blame Rupert. He'd loved Warren's sister. If only Mother Nature had been so enamoured. The cruel witch had turned her back on Leticia and her poor little babe, failing to answer even Warren's entreaties for help as he'd struggled to save them both.

'I'm committing most of my small inheritance to hiring the best captains and ships to import the tobacco, and securing the crops of numerous farmers, so it can't fail. I won't let it,' Rupert protested, frustration and desperation giving his voice an unappealing lilt. 'I need your backing, not just financially, but your name. It will attract others and once they've invested or become buyers, the risk to you will be minimal.'

'But not non-existent.' Warren gathered up a small stack of books from the corner of the desk and carried them to the dark wood bookshelves lining the lower floor of the study. He examined the spines in the bright daylight filling the room from the row of leaded glass windows behind his desk. At least the sun saved him the expense of lighting candles. 'The repairs to Priorton are proving expensive. I can't afford to risk money on a business venture.'

Warren climbed the curving staircase to the balcony and opened a glass case and deposited a thick medieval text inside. If he could write the next damned book he might be able to take a chance. The manuscript was already months overdue. Mr Berkshire was a friend and a patient man, willing to wait for the next great sensation from Sir Warren Stevens, but he wouldn't wait for ever. Neither would Warren's readers. They'd move on to another emerging novelist if he didn't produce something soon.

'If my plan to import the new tobacco succeeds, you'll have plenty of money,' Rupert persisted.

'And if it doesn't, it will ruin my financial standing and my reputation.' Warren looked over the polished wood banister at Rupert. His company was tolerable enough and his vices nonexistent, but there was nothing special about him. He still couldn't understand what Leticia had seen in him. 'I have no wish to go from celebrated author to hated hawker of bad investments.'

'But I need your support. I think it's the least you can do, considering.' The words came out low with the edge of a growl. Even Lancelot raised his head at the sound.

'Careful, Rupert.' Warren gripped the banister, setting hard on his arms as he leaned forward, staring the man down. 'She was as much my sister as she was your wife.'

'I'm sorry. I didn't mean to imply anything or to sound desperate, but some days I feel so lost without her.' He hung his head, raking one hand through his thinning dark hair, the simple gold wedding band glowing on his finger. 'If she were here, I'd have her support and it would make it easier to deal with the setbacks and disappointments.'

Warren eased his grip on the banister at the anguish in Rupert's words. Warren had lost his greatest supporter, too, when Leticia had died. She'd edited and read all of his manuscripts, telling him where they were best and what could be improved, and she'd believed in them, and him, even when he hadn't. Not even Mr Berkshire had matched her enthusiasm for his work and now she was gone.

He slid his hand over the banister, then took the spiral staircase step by slow step. He could almost hear Leticia begging him to help Rupert. She'd begged Warren to invest in Rupert's first business after they were engaged so he could make enough to allow them to marry. Warren had been as wary of that venture as he was this one, but Leticia had stood in front of his desk, like Rupert did now, pleading with him to change his mind, to help Rupert and to make her happy.

He approached his brother-in-law, the differences in their height making Warren look down on the slender man. Whatever Rupert's shortcomings, Warren had taken him on when he'd given his consent for the marriage. If Rupert did manage to make a go of things, Warren could make a great deal. He'd need it, especially if he failed to deliver this next book or it didn't sell as well as the previous one. Without Leticia here to edit it, it might not. Since her death, his stories had all but deserted him.

'All right, tell me how much you need and I'll

discuss it with my man of affairs. I can't give you everything you're asking for, but perhaps I can do something.' The key was not to risk too much.

Rupert snatched up Warren's hand and shook it. 'Thank you, Warren, you don't know how much this means to me.'

He did. Mr Berkshire had taken a chance on Warren's first manuscript ten years ago, paving the way to Priorton and Warren's title. He hoped Rupert enjoyed the same success. If not, it would be the last time Warren helped him.

'Warren?' His mother appeared at the door, a letter in her hand. Lancelot roused himself and trotted to her, his jingling collar joining the faint echo of hammers and saws trickling down from the upper floors. 'Lady Ellington and Miss Domville are coming to tea tomorrow. I'd like you to join us.'

Miss Domville.

Warren undid his loose cravat and twisted the ends back into an uncooperative knot. To say he was startled when he'd turned to find her in the dining room last night was putting it mildly. He couldn't have been more stunned if she'd marched in claiming he'd fathered a child. Since then, to his ire, he'd thought more about her than the heroine of his latest manuscript. Her sharp cheeks highlighted by the fair hair pulled into tight ringlets at the back of her head, the blush of youth across the sweep of her skin and the azure eyes watching him with suspicion, had proved fascinating. She'd dressed modestly, with a higher bodice than even a vicar's daughter, but the raw appeal of her curving body had been jarring—just like her request for his help.

Shame made his cravat tighter and he pulled loose the knot again. Not even the other gentlemen's disapproving and less polite scrutiny had been enough to shake her determination, but his near refusal had. When he'd hesitated, it had sent a whisper of fear through her clear blue eyes before her determination had overcome it. She'd been like the most stalwart of captains, unwilling to let anything stop her from achieving her goal, not even a ridiculous sense of propriety. If only all people possessed the same judgement and resilience. The Admiralty certainly didn't, heaping pay and praise on physicians who did nothing but hide from illness onshore while the underpaid surgeons choked below deck treating the wounded men.

Warren gave up on the cravat and allowed the loose linen to dangle around his neck. He shouldn't have been so quick to leave Miss Domville last night. She'd caught his struggle with the past and despite her own concerns she'd reached out to him. Instead of thanking her for her sympathy, one people rarely offered him, he'd shoved her away. Despite his misstep, it was probably for the best given his inability to stop thinking about her. He didn't have the time or money for anything as expensive as a wife and family, even if the woman possessed means. He wasn't about to make his fortune by marrying it. He'd earn it as he always had, and as a man should, through his own industry.

'Warren, you can't be rude to Lady Ellington.' His mother shook her head at him, her lace cap fluttering over her dark hair which was more grey than chestnut now. 'Her nephew is a marquess who could do a great a deal for you and your career.'

'I have the Prince for a patron. I hardly need a lowly peer,' he teased with a grin she matched with a slightly more serious one as she patted Lancelot on the head. 'I have too much work to do. I'll rely on you to speak glowingly of me and cultivate her support.'

'So you won't come for Lady Ellington, I understand. But I thought for sure you'd want to see Miss Domville.' His mother was far more tenacious than Rupert, who'd watched the conversation with interest, but her company much more pleasurable

'Not if you want to maintain your good reputation,' Rupert snorted now.

'She's a very charming young lady,' Warren's mother corrected, silencing Rupert's chortles.

He didn't respond and Warren didn't press for the story behind his snide remark. Gossip didn't interest him and he hated encouraging the spread of it by asking for whatever tale Rupert had heard.

'Now, if you'll both excuse me, I have chapters to write.' He opened his arms and caught his mother by the shoulders and gently guided her to the hallway. He waved Rupert over and Rupert jogged forward to join them like a summoned spaniel.

'Perhaps you could discuss my business venture with Lady Ellington,' Rupert near panted. 'If she or the Marquess could be convinced to invest—'

'One thing at a time, Rupert.' He clapped him on the back, unwilling to solicit the county on his behalf, not when he could devote the same time and energy to selling his next book. Assuming he could write it.

'Come, Rupert, I'll show you the new plasterwork in the sitting room before you return to London.' His mother took Rupert's arm and led him into the hallway as Warren slid the study door closed.

He sagged against the heavy oak. Lancelot's eyebrows shifted as he watched his master.

Chapters. Warren had barely written a page today, much a less a whole chapter. It wasn't for lack of trying. His desk and the floor around it were littered with discarded papers full of useless words for pointless stories of boring characters that went nowhere and would make him no money.

Warren dropped into his chair and stared at the silent and cold collection of books and medieval manuscripts surrounding him. In the midst of it all, he felt as lonely and isolated as he had aboard ship when no one had understood his struggles or his dreams for a different future, except Leticia. And then he'd killed her.

He snatched up his pen and held it over the paper, determined, as then, to forge on. He wouldn't allow his doubts or guilt to hinder him, not with so much depending on his continued success and the money it would make him. The half-filled page taunted him from the blotter, along with the incessant banging of hammers from somewhere overhead. Pressing the nib to the paper, he wrote one word, then another, determined to push through. He had no choice, there was no one else who could do it or save him.

Chapter Three

Sir Warren still hadn't made an appearance by the time the butler removed the tea service. Mrs Stevens said he was busy at work and couldn't be disturbed. More than likely he was avoiding Marianne and her damaged reputation like every other gentleman of quality. The same couldn't be said of the large portrait of him hanging over the fireplace. It was of Sir Warren at his desk, an open book balanced on his knee, the pen in his hand poised over what must be his next great creation. Mr Smith used to devour Sir Warren's novels of medieval knights and ladies. Once, during a snow storm, when the family had been stuck inside for three days, he'd read a novel aloud. Marianne had only half-listened. Historical novels were not to her taste.

It wasn't the open book balanced on his knee or the manuscript which kept bringing her back to the portrait. It was Sir Warren's posture, the subtle way his body turned, his attention focused on the distance instead of the viewer. His brow shaded his green eyes, stealing their light. The haunted expression hinted at some threat just beyond the frame, something only he could see, like whatever it was that had troubled him at Lady Cartwright's. It undermined the confidence in his firm grip on the book and reminded her of his pained expression when he'd written out the laudanum recipe after helping Lady Ellington, before he'd darted away from her.

Irritation more than the warm autumn day made her tug at her high collar.

'How we must be boring you with all our talk of Italian landscapes,' Mrs Stevens apologised from across the round tea table.

Marianne jerked her attention to Mrs Stevens's kind round eyes, her son's eyes, and shook her head. 'No, not at all.'

'Liar,' Mrs Stevens teased. 'When I was young I used to hate sitting with old ladies and listening to them talk. Lady Ellington tells me you play the pianoforte. We have a lovely Érard in the music room. The man who sold us the house said it was once in the Palace of Versailles, but I'm not sure I believe him.'

'A French-made Érard!' Excitement filled Marianne more than when the carriage had approached the house, before it had become obvious Sir Warren had no intention of joining them. 'I used to play one at the Protestant School in France. Do you play?'

'Oh, heavens, no.' She laid a thin hand on her chest. 'I hate to think of a fine instrument going to waste. If you'd like to try it, you may. It's just down the hall in the music room. Third door on the left.'

'May I?' Marianne asked Lady Ellington, as eager to see the instrument as to escape the staring portrait.

Lady Ellington slid a sly glance at Mrs Stevens whose eyebrow arched a touch. 'I don't see why not.'

Marianne threw her companion a questioning look, wondering what she was up to. Lady Ellington ignored it in favour of adjusting the clasp on her diamond bracelet. The ladies must be eager to discuss something more salacious than Italian landscapes out of her hearing. Whatever it was, Lady Ellington would tell her about it later. Her companion didn't see the need to shield her from reality, not after Marianne had learned so much at Madame de Badeau's.

Marianne rose and shook out the skirt of her dress. 'Then I'd be delighted to play.'

'Wonderful.' Mrs Stevens beamed as Marianne made for the hallway. 'Leave the door open so we may hear your beautiful playing.'

Marianne stepped into the long main hall running the length of the front of the house. The faint dragging of a saw across wood and the thud of hammers carried down from somewhere upstairs. She headed left, past the large marble fireplace situated across from the main door, a medieval relic left over from the house's days as a priory. Mrs Stevens had told them something of the house's history over tea. Old swords and helmets dotted the panelled walls, creating a more menacing than welcoming effect in the low-ceilinged entrance hall with its thick exposed beams.

She followed the neat line of black-marble diamonds inlaid in the slightly uneven floor, counting the solidly spaced doors with their rounded tops and thick iron handles.

When she reached the third door on the left, she slid one of the wide panels aside, stopping as Sir Warren's eyes snapped up from his desk to hers. The troubled eyes from the portrait. They widened with shock before crinkling with annoyance, then embarrassment. In front for him were books arranged in an elaborate set of triangles and balanced against one another like a house of cards.

'You should have knocked.' Sir Warren jumped to his feet and rounded the desk. The large red dog sitting beside him raised its hindquarters in a stretch before trotting past his owner and up to Marianne. 'I was working.'

'Yes, it's quite a labour.' She leaned to one side to peer around his solid chest at his creation, ignoring the flutter in her stomach at this unexpected meeting and the cutting realisation he had been avoiding her. 'Is it a castle or a barn? I can't tell.'

'It's a castle.' Amusement replaced the flush

of anger. 'I'll have you know, half of all writing is procrastination.'

'Then it appears you're making great progress.' Marianne tapped the dog lightly on the head with her fingers, then waved him away. He obliged, wandering over to the hearth rug and settling down on the spiral weave.

'If only I were.' He dismantled his castle and stacked the books in two neat piles. Then he faced her, leaning back against the desk and admiring her with more amusement than censure. His coat was missing and the wide sleeves of his shirt were flecked with small dots of ink. Dull black boots that wouldn't pass muster in London covered his calves and feet, and around his neck his cravat sat loose and crooked. 'Rather bold for a young lady to be wandering alone in a gentleman's house.'

'It isn't the first time I've been bold in the presence of a gentleman.' She approached him, determined to appear confident and collected and reveal nothing of the thrill racing through her at his unguarded humour. It would end soon when he decided it was best to not be alone with her and bolt off to see to some other matter in another part of the house.

'Nor do I suspect it will be the last.' Not a speck of derision marred his smile as he stroked his strong jaw. The play of his fingers along his chiselled chin, his sure stance and the curious way he regarded her proved as captivating as the time she'd watched the workers in the Falconbridge Manor fields in the evening, their shirts discarded as they'd swung their scythes. She could picture him among them, the gold sun across his back, his thick arms swinging the blade, the honey skin glistening in the low light. Marianne adjusted her collar, stunned by her suddenly lurid imagination. This wasn't the way she normally regarded men. It was dangerous.

'I'll have you know I wasn't wandering, but searching for the Érard. Mrs Stevens told me it was in the music room, the third door on the left.' She couldn't have counted wrong. Three was not a difficult number.

'The music room is the second door on the left.' He cocked his thumb at the wall and the arched door set snug between two bookcases. 'There's another entrance through there, if you'd like.'

'My apologies then. I'll leave you to your work.' And make sure it was she and not he who did the quick leave taking this time.

'No, please, stay.' He moved to place himself between her and the library door. The dry tang of dusting powder clung to him, punctuated by the faint richness of cedar. It struck her as strongly as his state of undress. It was too intimate for a woman of Marianne's undeserved reputation.

'No, I must go.' She tried to step around him, but he moved first, agile for a man of his robust build. The dog watched them as though he were bored.

'Please, I'd like it if you'd stay.'

'Why?' He wasn't the first gentleman to try and corner her alone in a room. If he dared to touch her, he also wouldn't be the first to feel her knee hitting his unmentionables. She'd learned fast how to defend herself against the lecherous gentlemen who used to haunt Madame de Badeau's. She'd had no choice. The awful woman hadn't lifted a finger to protect her.

'I wish to apologise for leaving you so abruptly at Lady Cartwright's. You were concerned about me and instead of thanking you, I was rude. Please, forgive me?'

She blinked, stunned. No one, not even Madame de Badeau when she'd been dying of fever in Italy, had ever asked for Marianne's forgiveness. To Hades with his state of undress, she'd stay for this and savour the moment. It would probably be the last time she'd receive an apology from anyone outside Lady Ellington's house.

'It's been quite some time since I've attended to a patient,' he continued in the face of her silence, something of the shadow from the portrait darkening his expression. 'It brought back a number of painful memories and made me forget my manners.'

'What memories?' She didn't usually pry. People were all too eager to tell her their business and everyone else's without any entreaty, but she couldn't stop herself from asking. He hadn't rushed to condemn or insult her like so many others did. It made her curious and less wary about him than she should have been.

The bang of a dropped board echoed on the floor above them. She thought he wouldn't answer, but to her surprise, he did.

'During my time as a surgeon in the Navy, I saw horrors so awful, if I wrote them into my novels, readers would think I'd exaggerated for titillating effect.' He snapped his fingers and the dog strolled to his side. He dropped his hand on the dog's head and ruffled the silky fur. 'For a year or two after I left the Navy, the memories used to trouble me. Usually it would happen at night, but once in a while a familiar smell or something equally trivial would bring them back during the day. Eventually, it stopped and I thought myself past such episodes, but it happened again when I attended to your friend. It's why I left so quickly. I didn't wish to explain it to you, or anyone else. It's not something people outside my family are aware of, or something I'm proud of.'

'Then why tell me about it?' It was insults people usually heaped on her, not confidences.

'You remind me of my sister, someone who might understand and not mock me for it.'

The faint connection they'd shared outside the study at Lady Cartwright's whispered between them once more. Sir Warren was offering her honesty and respect, treating her like a real person, not a tart to be pawed or derided. It was how she'd always longed to be viewed by strangers, especially gentlemen.

'No, I couldn't.' She fingered a small embroidered flower on her dress. 'It makes me a little ashamed of how much I pore over my own troubles. They're nothing compared to yours.'

'What troubles you, Miss Domville?' His voice was low and strong, like a physician trying to sooth an anxious patient.

'Don't tell me you haven't heard about me?' She flicked her hand at the study. 'I'm sure the neighbours rushed over to tell your mother the stories the moment the removers left.'

'We weren't here when the removers left and they didn't remove much. I bought the property lock, stock and barrel.'

'And no one informed you at Lady Cartwright's?' At times, it seemed as if the only topic anyone could discuss.

'I was delayed and missed the dinner. I left the party as soon as I finished with Lady Ellington. Why don't you tell me the real story, then I'll know the truth when Lady Cartwright gives me the exaggerated version.'

Honesty. He was holding it out to her again except this time it would be her sharing instead of him. She shouldn't, but she was tired of dragging the past and the secret of her lineage around like a heavy chain. Perhaps with this gentleman who treated her like an old friend instead of a pariah, his concern for her as genuine as Lady Ellington's, she could take the first step to being free of it. 'You've heard of Madame de Badeau?'

'She was the French courtesan who tried to ruin the Marquess of Falconbridge.'

She nodded as she twisted the slender gold band encircling her little finger. She should leave him as ignorant as everyone else of the truth about her relationship to the woman. She didn't know him, or have any reason to trust him, except for the strange calm his presence created in her. It reminded her of the first day she'd arrived at Lady Ellington's after Lord Falconbridge had stumbled on her trying to run away from Madame de Badeau's. The gracious woman had taken Marianne in her arms as if she were a long-lost daughter. Not even Mrs Nichols or Mrs Smith had ever hugged her so close. Marianne had earned Lady Ellington's affection by helping her nephew and his wife avoid ruin. Sir Warren owed Marianne nothing, yet he still looked at her as Lady Ellington had that first morning, as if she was as deserving of care and respect as anyone else. She should stay silent, but under the influence of his sincerity, she couldn't hold back the story any more than she could have held back the tears of relief in Lady Ellington's embrace.

'All my life, I and everyone else thought she was my sister. What few people really know is she was my mother. She had me long after her husband, the Chevalier de Badeau, died. She passed me off as her sister to hide her shame. I don't even know which of her many lovers was my father.' Her stomach clenched and she thought Mrs Steven's lemon cakes might come up. She shouldn't have told him. No one outside the Falconbridge family knew and there was no reason to expect his discretion. If he repeated the story, then the faint acceptance Lady Ellington provided would disappear as everyone recoiled further from the illegitimate daughter of a whore.

She waited for his reaction, expecting him to curl his lip at her in disgust or march into the sitting room and demand his mother have no further dealings with her. Instead, he nodded sagely as if she'd told him her throat hurt, not the secret which had gnawed at her since she'd riffled through Madame de Badeau's desk four years ago and found the letter revealing the truth.

'Your mother isn't the first woman to pass her child off as her sibling,' he replied at last.

'You're not stunned?' She was.

'No.' He turned back to his desk and slid a book off of the top of the stack, an ancient tome with a cracked leather cover and yellowed pages.

His movement left the path to the music room clear. Marianne could bolt out the door, leave him and her foolishness behind, but she held her ground. She wouldn't act like a coward in front of a man who'd been to war.

He flipped through the book, then held out the open page to her. 'Lady Matilda of Triano did the same thing in 1152.'

Marianne slid her hands beneath the book, running them over the uneven leather to grasp it when her fingers brushed his. She pulled back, and the tome wobbled on her forearms before she steadied it. It wasn't fear which made her recoil from him as she used to the men at Madame de Badeau's. It was the spark his touch had sent racing across her skin. She'd never experienced a reaction like this to a gentleman before.

She stepped back and fixed her attention on the beautiful drawing of a wan woman holding a rose, her blue and red gown a part of the curving and gilded initial, trying not to entertain her shocking response to Sir Warren's touch. She stole a glimpse at his hands, wondering what they'd feel like against her bare skin. She jerked her attention back to the open book, wondering what she was going on about. She'd spent too many years dodging the wandering hands of Madame de Badeau's lovers to search out any man's touch now.

'She hid her son to keep her brother-in-law from murdering the child when he seized the Duchy of Triano,' Sir Warren explained, his voice soothing her like a warm bath. 'The truth came out ten years later when the uncle lay dying and Lady Matilda revealed her son's identity to secure his rightful inheritance.'

She returned the book to him, careful to keep

her fingers away from his. 'A lovely story, but my mother's motives weren't so noble.'

'You're not to blame for what your mother did.' He set down the open book on the desk.

'You're the first stranger to think so. Lady Cartwright and the others are determined to believe I'm just as wanton and wicked as Madame de Badeau and they only think she's my sister. I'm not like her. I never have been.' It was a declaration she wished she could make in front of every family in the country and London, one she wished deep down even she believed. She was Madame de Badeau's daughter, it was possible her mother's sins were ingrained in Marianne and nothing would stop them from eventually coming out.

'I can see you're not like her. Not like most women. I recognised it the moment you insisted I help Lady Ellington and then refused to leave her side.'

'What I did was nothing,' she whispered, as unused to compliments as she was to embraces.

'It was everything. I've seen men sacrifice themselves for their fellow sailors, hold down their best friends while I sawed off a mangled limb. I've also watched cowards leave their comrades to suffer while they steal provisions, or hide in the darkness of the surgeon's deck with a minor wound to avoid fighting. I doubt Lady Cartwright or any of her other guests would have done half as much as you did for your friend.'

She stared at him, amazed by this near stranger's faith in her and how freely he offered it to her. It frightened her more than her belief in her own weakness. If it was easily given, it might easily be revoked. She eyed the door to the music room, wanting to be through it and at the keys of the piano and away from this uncertain familiarity. She'd revealed too much already, foolishly making herself vulnerable. 'If you don't mind, I'd like to play now.'

'Of course.' He pulled open the door, revealing the stately black instrument dominating the area in front of the large, bowed window at the far end of the room.

She strode to it, relief washing through her. Music was her one constant and comfort, though even this had threatened to leave her once. 'It's beautiful.'

She slid on to the bench and raised the cover

on the keys. Flexing her fingers over the brilliant white ivory, she began the first chord. The piano-forte was as well tuned as it was grand and each note rang true and deep. They vibrated through her and with each stanza she played, her past, her concerns, Sir Warren and everything faded away until there was nothing but the notes. In them the only true happiness she'd ever known.

Warren didn't follow her into the room. He leaned against the door jamb and watched as she drew from the long-silent instrument beauti-ful music laced with a strange, almost efferves-cent melancholy. Lancelot came to his side and leaned against Warren's leg as Warren scratched behind the dog's ears.

The pianoforte faced the window overlooking the garden. She sat with her back to him so he couldn't see her face, but the languid way she moved in front of the keys, her arms losing their stiffness for the first time since she'd happened into his study, didn't escape his notice. The in-tensity of her focus and the graceful sway of her body in time to the music told him she was no longer here, but carried off by the piece to the same place he drifted to whenever a story fully gripped him. He was glad. She was too young to frown so much or to take in the world, or his compliments, with such distrustful eyes. He wished he could have brought her as much peace as her playing but, like him, her past still troubled her and she had yet to conquer it.

It wasn't the past facing him today, but the future. No matter how much he wanted to stand here and listen to her, he had to return to work. He needed the money. He left the door open to allow the notes to fill the study. As Warren settled in at his desk, Lancelot stretched out on the hearthrug and returned to his nap. Warren picked up his pen, dipped the nib in the inkwell and settled it over the last word, ready to write, to create, to weave his tale.

Nothing.

The deep notes of the piano boomed before sliding up the scale into the softer, higher octaves.

He read the last paragraph, hoping to regain the thread of the story. It wasn't so much a thread as a jumble of sentences as dull as the minutes of Parliament.

The higher notes wavered, then settled into the smooth mid-tones like water in the bottom of a bowl.

He dropped his head in his hands and rubbed his temples. Today wasn't going any better than yesterday, or last week or the past year.

He glanced over the top of the pages to where the medieval book lay open. Lady Matilda's sad yet determined stare met his from the vellum. He reached out and ran one finger over the black lines of her face and eyes. The pensive notes of the pianoforte slid beneath the image, the despair in the lower octaves contradicted by the hope ringing in the brief tinkle of the higher ones.

He chewed the end of his pen as he listened to Miss Domville playing, his teeth finding the familiar grooves as a new story began to separate itself in his mind from his worries and frustration. He took a deep breath and closed his eyes. The image of a regal lady wearing a fine blue kirtle over a red-velvet dress slid through the mist blanketing a thick forest. Lady Matilda, one slender hand on a damp and knotted oak, paused as if finally ready to reveal what she'd been keeping from him. He rolled the scarred wood of his pen between his thumb and forefinger as he watched the elusive lady threatening to vanish into the mist-covered trees.

'Come on, out with it,' he growled, frustrated by her coquetry. He needed her to guide him and help release the steady stream of ideas being held back by this interminable block.

Behind the teasing curve of Lady Matilda's smile, the melody of Miss Domville's playing curled like smoke around him and the woman. In the vibrating notes, Lady Matilda's tale suddenly revealed itself.

He opened his eyes, slid a clean sheet of paper on to the blotter and began to write. The words flowed as fast as the notes of first one piece and then another as page after page took shape beneath his pen. He was so engrossed in the story, an hour later he failed to notice when the music faded into nothingness, the cover pulled down over the keys and soft footsteps left the music room.

The only things which remained were his story and the faint scent of peonies.

Chapter Four

Marianne played the section again and frowned. The last note wasn't right. She tried the C instead of the D, then nodded. Taking up her pen, she dipped the nib in the inkwell next to the stand and drew a quarter note on the staff. She played the section again, smiling as the stanza fell into place, the first half of her composition nearly complete. Reaching the end of it, she held her foot down on the pedal, allowing the chords to resonate off into the air.

Lady Ellington's Broadwood was a gorgeous instrument, but not as grand as Sir Warren's Érard. She wondered how rich and full the piece would sound on his instrument.

Excellent, I'm sure. She picked up the pen and changed the half note at the end to a whole one. She wasn't likely to play at Priorton Abbey again. Her skin prickled beneath the netting of the fichu covering her chest as the memory of Sir Warren listening to her story about Madame de Badeau came rushing back. She shouldn't have confided in him. She'd been in a panic for days over her mistake, waiting for any hint of the truth of her parentage to make the rounds. There'd been nothing but silence on the matter. The only gossip she'd heard had concerned Lord Malvern's near indiscretion with a maid at Lord Cartwright's hunting party.

She replayed the stanza, holding the end longer to reflect her correction, contemplating Sir Warren's silence more than her music. With no word from anyone at Priorton since their visit, it was plain the incidents from two weeks ago had been forgotten. It irritated her as much as a missed note, even though she should be glad. She'd allowed his kindness to trick her into revealing her ugly secret. Heaven knew what other mistakes, or deeper weakness, might have been revealed if she'd had the chance to know Sir Warren better.

'Beautiful, as always, my dear.' Lady Ellington applauded as Marianne ended the piece. The pianoforte didn't face the window at Welton Place as it did at Priorton Abbey, preventing the blooming roses in the garden from distracting Marianne while she worked. 'It's a shame I'm the only one who ever gets to hear it.'

Marianne closed the red composition book, leaving it on the stand. 'You're not the only one. Lady St Onge used to listen to me play before she decided to return to London for the winter.'

'You know what I mean.' She sat down on the bench beside her. 'A letter from Theresa arrived for you.'

Marianne took the missive and flicked the edge with her fingernail, in no mood to read about her friend's happiness. It only made her lack of it more obvious. Theresa was at Hallington Hall, the estate on the other side of Falconbridge Manor, with her young son, husband and his family. It wasn't far to travel yet Marianne had barely seen her this summer. She shouldn't have stayed away. As much as she loved Lady Ellington's she'd been restless lately for no good reason. The shortening days and cooler weather and the isolation of Welton Place added to her disquiet.

'This also came for you.' Lady Ellington handed her a package wrapped in brown paper. A prong holding a diamond in place on one of her rings snagged the securing twine before she freed it. 'It's from Priorton Abbey.'

Marianne gripped the package tight, crinkling the smooth paper. *He hasn't forgotten about me.* She eased her hold on the slender package, refusing to get her hopes up about Sir Warren's interest in her or to pine after a man. Her mother had obsessed about Lord Falconbridge and look how that had ended. 'It must be from Mrs Stevens. Sir Warren wouldn't send me anything.'

'Perhaps you charmed him with your playing.'

'It would be a change from what my presence usually inspires in people.' The knot came loose and she tugged off the twine.

'Don't be so hard on yourself. You inspire more than gossip in many people.' She squeezed Marianne's arm. 'Now open it. I want to see what it is.'

Marianne tore off the paper to reveal the back of a journal. She turned it over and read the handwritten title on the white cover plate. '*Lady Matilda's Trials*, by Sir Warren Stevens.'

She opened the front cover and a note slipped out from between the pages. She plucked it off the rug then unfolded the card and read aloud the words printed on the thick paper.

Dear Miss Domville,
Enclosed is a copy of my latest manuscript. Your lovely piano-playing was invaluable to the creation of this story. I hope it's to your liking and I would very much appreciate your thoughts on it before I send it to my publisher.
Your faithful scribe,
Sir Warren

'My goodness.' Lady Ellington laid one sparkling hand on her ample bosom, rainbows from her diamonds spraying out over her dark blue dress. 'I didn't think the two of you were so well acquainted.'

'We aren't. I spent more time with his Érard than I did with him when we visited.' The spine cracked as she opened the journal. She tapped her toes against the floor, as puzzled as she was flattered by his gift.

Lady Ellington rose. 'Hurry and read it so you can give him your thoughts on it when we visit them tomorrow.'

Marianne brought her toes down hard against the parquet, leery of another meeting with him. 'Can't I simply send him a note?'

'Not for something like this.' A wicked twinkle lit up her pale blue eyes before she strode to the door. 'You'll have to play for him again and see what else you might inspire.'

Marianne frowned, not quite as amused by the situation as Lady Ellington, but certainly intrigued. She ran her finger over the title on the front of the journal, the one written by Sir Warren. He was asking her, a person he barely knew, to critique his work. It would be like her giving him one of her compositions to play. For all the flowers and stupid poems Lord Bolton had sent her, none had touched her as much as Sir Warren's simple request.

Leaving the pianoforte, Marianne wandered through the double French doors overlooking the garden, past where the aged gardener, Walker, knelt in front of the rose beds. The heady scent of the summer blooms no longer hung in the air. It had been replaced by the crisp chill of autumn and wet dirt. She strolled along the gravel path, passing the fountain in the middle of Zeus and a nymph in an evocative embrace.

Too evocative. The same could be said about most of the statues scattered throughout the garden. Marianne passed by them without a second look. The peculiarities of Lady Ellington's brother, the prior Marquess of Falconbridge, and his taste in statuary, didn't interest her. Instead, with the journal clutched to her chest, she wondered if maybe Lady Ellington was right and it was time to stop hiding away from the world at Welton Place. If a famous man like Sir Warren could see the value in an acquaintance with her, perhaps some other gentlemen who weren't Lord Bolton might do the same. It was almost enough to convince her to accept Lady Ellington's offer of a Season in London, but not quite.

She reached the far side of the garden and followed the path winding up through the copse of trees to the brick orangery hidden among the oaks. Arched and latticed windows marked the front-left side while those to the right had been bricked in. She stepped through the double doors and into the comfortably furnished garden building. Sets of *bergère* chairs with generous cushions all done in the Louis XV style dominated the window side of the room. A tall screen embroidered with a mythic scene of Apollo seducing Calliope, as shocking in its depiction of love as the garden statuary, shielded a wide sofa situated in the darker half. The gaudy gilding reminded Marianne more of her mother's boudoir than it did an outbuilding. Like the garden, the orangery owed its decorations to the old Marquess, a bachelor rake she'd heard so much about from Madame de Badeau she'd often wondered if the woman hadn't bedded him too.

The orangery, despite its gaudy and erotic decorations, was, for Marianne, a small retreat from the dower house and a good place to be alone. She'd come here after more than one afternoon party to fume over the whisperings of Miss Cartwright or Lady Astley.

She chose a comfortable chair near a window and settled in to read Sir Warren's note again. His handwriting was bold, each letter crafted from slashing lines and thick strokes. It was a stark contrast to the small flourishes and graceful twirls which filled her composition book.

She read it a third time, but nothing about the words changed. Like the Smiths' daughter, who used to pore over each 'good morning' from the farmer's son hoping there was more to the salutation, Marianne was looking for a deeper meaning which wasn't there. It was silly of her to do so. She'd learned long ago at Madame de Badeau's that when a man said something it was what he meant and little more. If Sir Warren was thanking her for inspiration, then he was thanking her. It didn't mean she'd sent him into raptures. She stuffed the note in the back cover, glad not to arouse a grand passion in a man. Other people's passions had already caused her no end of troubles.

She set to reading, focusing on Sir Warren's work instead of him, determined to be worthy of his faith in her. However, with each turn of the page, each paragraph outlining Lady Matilda's story, disbelief and dismay began to undermine the peace of the orangery. By the time she reached the end of the manuscript, Marianne wanted to toss the journal in the fountain at the bottom of the hill and watch the thing turn soggy and sink. She couldn't. It was too good a story. Too bad it was hers.

'I didn't work so hard to gain Priorton to sell it off piece by piece the moment things get difficult,' Warren insisted, his boots coming down hard on the stone of the cloistered walk in the garden. Lancelot trotted beside him, panting lightly. The garden ran wild in the current fashion, leading from the back of Priorton to the tree line beyond. In the centre of it, weathered stone statues lounged between the beds of dying summer plants and wildflowers.

'Then you must let some of the field labourers go,' Mr Reed, Warren's bespectacled man of affairs warned, on Warren's heels as they returned to the house after surveying the fields. The harvest had been good this year, but not nearly as profitable as either of them had hoped, or counted on.

'No, not with winter coming. I won't see families suffer because of my mistakes.' He, his mother and Leticia had suffered because of his father's financial mistakes. His father had been a good man, but he'd been careless in the management of his school, never charging enough or collecting what was due and leaving his family near destitute when he died. After refusing to apply for relief in the very parish where his father had preached, they'd been forced to rely on Warren's reluctant bachelor uncle for support. It had been his uncle's brilliant idea for Warren to enlist and save the time and money required by a lengthy apprenticeship. At sixteen, the clean, comfortable life Warren had known had been ripped from him and replaced with gore and filth, and the need to support his sister and mother. He still hated the old salt for forcing Warren into it and resented his father for failing to leave his family with means. He wouldn't visit the same misery on other families, especially those under his care.

'The second half of the payment for your next book will cover current repairs, but after they're complete, you must stop for a while,' Mr Reed instructed.

Warren slapped some dirt off of his breeches. The payment wasn't coming any time soon. He didn't tell Mr Reed, not wanting to send the little man into an apoplectic fit. The costs of the house were forcing him to live from one payment to the next as he'd done in the Navy. This time the sums were more considerable and the chance of ruin, starving and having nowhere to live much greater. The risks would soon be eased by the publication of *Lady Matilda's Trials* and the payment of the second half of his advance. The money would help, but it wasn't enough. Even if he received Miss Domville's thoughts on the story today, it would be some weeks before the novel's release, and more after that before money from the sales began to arrive.

Warren's feet came down hard on the stone walk as he and Mr Reed approached the house. He'd taken a chance sending Miss Domville his manuscript and asking for her opinion, but he suspected she'd be blunt in her assessment it. He hoped she was. With his mounting doubts, and Leticia no longer here to read his work, it was growing more difficult for him to judge if his tales were accomplished or piles of rubbish. He wasn't about to send Mr Berkshire a second-rate novel.

How the devil did I get myself into this predicament?

Through the arched sides of the cloister separating the garden from the wild field, he admired the peaked and turreted roofline of Priorton and the hazy sky behind it. This was everything he'd ever wanted, his dream and his sister's too, the one they'd shared in childhood. He'd achieved it for both of them, but at times it seemed more crippling than magical. For all the money he spent on Priorton, he didn't enjoy it as he should. In the spring he went to London. The rest of the year was consumed with stories, bills and repairs. It was difficult to spend an hour wandering in the garden when he must toil to pay for it all. During the long, dark hours on the orlop deck, this was what he'd imagined, what he'd strived for and now he stretched to achieve it. He hoped it didn't break him, the way his father's dream of running a vicarage school had broken him.

'You could seek a loan,' Mr Reed suggested as Warren held open the back door and waved Mr Reed inside. 'To tide you over until you receive your advance.'

'No, I've never taken money from anyone before, I won't start now. We can sell off some of the sheep.'

'With wool prices falling, it won't gain us much.'

'At least we won't have to spend money to feed them.'

They strode down the long front hallway. Through the diamond-leaded front windows Warren caught sight of Lady Ellington's carriage in the drive. He tugged open his slack cravat, then struggled to retie it, wondering if Miss Domville was with the Dowager. Last night, the memory of her flowery scent and the gentle tone of her voice had disturbed his sleep more than new story ideas.

They entered his study and Warren settled himself at his desk while Mr Reed stood before it outlining expenditures. As soon as he was finished with Mr Reed, he'd join the ladies and discover what Miss Domville thought of his manuscript. Perhaps he could convince her to play for him again and inspire another story. He needed more inspiration, especially with Mr Reed rattling on about expenses.

'You can't afford to invest any additional money in Mr Hirst, beyond what you recently advanced him,' Mr Reed cautioned. 'We've yet to see any profit from his ventures or even documents outlining your shares.'

Warren organised a stack of papers on his desk. 'I don't intend to give him any more.'

'Then you'd better tell him. I heard from one my associates in London he's using your name to push his current venture. You must distance yourself from it in case it fails. You don't want to be blamed.'

'I'll write to him at once and make it clear he's not to use me as an endorsement.' The bumbling fool. It seemed Rupert's current scheme was already faltering, and taking Warren's money with it. He should have known better and not allowed emotion to play any part in his business dealings. It wouldn't happen again.

Mr Reed opened his thin lips to say something else when the study door slid open with a bang.

Warren peered around the slender man of affairs to find Boudicca herself standing beneath the lintel in the very appealing figure of Miss

Domville. So much for avoiding her until his interview with Mr Reed was complete.

'If you'll excuse us, Mr Reed,' Warren asked.

Mr Reed flipped closed his ledger and tucked it under his arm, needing no explanation for why he should go. It was clear in the storm in Miss Domville's eyes. 'Yes, of course.'

He slipped from the room, leaving Warren alone to face the fury.

'Good day, Miss Domville, it's a pleasure to see you.' Almost too pleasurable. She marched up to him, her breasts covered by a sheer chemisette and the thin silk of her gown. It was all Warren could do to rise from his chair like a gentleman and keep his eyes fixed above her chin. Damn, she was beautiful, earthy and angry. 'I'd hoped to see you today.'

'Good, because we must discuss this.' She slammed his journal on the desk, making a stack of papers curl up, then settle back down. 'How could you use my story?'

He stared at the slightly rumpled pages. 'You didn't like it?'

'No, it's a wonderful story, quite enthralling.' She leaned forward on her palms. He riveted his eyes to hers to keep his attention from sliding down and increasing the fury reddening her cheeks. 'Except you took what I told you about my mother and twisted it into a tale to amuse dairy maids and hack drivers.'

'I took something you've been ashamed of and made it into something you could be proud of. I thought you'd be pleased.'

'You were wrong.' She glowered at him like a schoolmarm ready to switch a naughty student, except she was the kind of woman who filled a young man's fantasies, not his nightmares.

'No one will see you in Lady Matilda, or think her story has anything to do with yours. I hid it too well.'

'Of course they will, especially when they realise we're acquainted with one another.' She whirled around, her blue dress fluttering about the curve of her hips as she marched to the door.

'Miss Domville, wait.' She didn't stop, but took hold of the wrought-iron handle. He couldn't let her go. 'I won't publish the story if it troubles you so much.'

She released the handle. It dropped against the door with a thud as she turned to him, as astonished by his offer as he was. 'You won't publish it?'

'I won't make money off your unease.' Even if he lost everything else, his word and his honour would still be his, he'd make sure of it. 'In fact, you may keep this copy of the manuscript.'

He held out the journal to her, his grip tight on the paper as the full weight of what he'd volunteered to do settled over him.

She returned to him and took the story out of his outstretched hand. 'And your original copy? How do I know you won't send it to your publisher after I leave?'

'I'll burn it, now, so you can be sure.'

'You'd do such a thing, for me?' She clasped the journal to her chest and for a moment he was jealous of the book resting against her soft curves.

'Yes.' He picked up the stack of loose pages and tapped them twice against his palm, hesitating before he tossed them into the grate beside him. The gesture burned him as much as the flames did the parchment. Lady Matilda's story had been a godsend after months of nothing. Now he was no better off than before. 'It was never my intention to betray your trust.'

She watched with him while his words turned to ashes. 'Then why did you write it?'

'Because, until the day you came here, I hadn't been able to write a single useful word for months. With the exception of Lady Matilda's story, I still can't.' He looked at her, noting how the light from the rising flames consuming the manuscript reflected in her clear eyes. He'd hidden his failing from everyone, from his mother to Mr Berkshire. It was a relief to finally admit it someone.

'I'm sorry, I didn't realise.' Nor did she offer to let him publish her copy of the work. He wouldn't ask her either. He'd made a pledge to her, and he would keep it, as he had all the others he'd made to himself, his mother and to Leticia's memory, no matter how much it hurt.

'It's all right. I'll write something else.'

She flicked a glance at the wads of papers scattered around his chair. 'How?'

That's what I'd like to know.

Warren watched the flames die down, their new fuel spent. Miss Domville's playing had bolstered him like Leticia's encouraging letters used to do when he'd written in the semi-darkness of the ship. The influence Miss Domville's playing had exerted over his creativity had left with her. In the last few days, since finishing Lady Matilda, he'd tried everything he could think of to reclaim it, even hiring a young man from the village church to play while he'd worked, but it hadn't been the same. There'd been something about her presence, as at Lady Cartwright's, which had soothed and encouraged him and he wanted more of it.

He tugged on his loose cravat as an idea as unbelievable as it was tempting began to come to him. If Miss Domville could help him overcome his block once, she could do it again. No, it was foolish to draw her into his struggles, or to tempt himself with her company. She wasn't one of the London widows eager to discreetly amuse him, but a young lady fighting for respectability. For him to suggest any relationship with her outside of a betrothal and marriage was to risk her reputation further and he shouldn't even consider it, except he needed her. With his talent failing him, he might lose everything he'd achieved and find himself as destitute as his father had been at his death. He wouldn't allow it, or be forced by weakness back to the Navy to make his living. With blank pages and bills facing him, he couldn't allow his muse to escape.

'If you agree to come here and play the piano for me, I can create another story.' He smiled with all the charisma he employed to woo patrons in London, hoping she didn't dismiss the idea outright. He didn't doubt, given her fierce entry into his study, she'd shrink from turning him down.

She laced her arms beneath her breasts and stepped back, the cynical schoolmarm returning. 'And what instrument do you hope I'll play afterwards? I'm not Madame de Badeau, a woman to be hired as a mistress.'

He didn't blame her for being cautious. Once he'd achieved fame, the number of people he could trust had shrunk significantly.

'I don't want a mistress, but a muse.' It was difficult to look at her and not think of twining his hands in her golden hair, tasting her pink lips as they parted beneath his and freeing those glorious breasts from their prim confines. He'd better not concentrate on them if he wanted to win her co-operation and keep himself free from distraction, and bankruptcy. 'I need you.'

'No one needs me.' The same worthlessness which had torn him apart the morning Leticia had died hung in Miss Domville's words. He gripped his hands hard behind his back, silently raging at himself and the world. A woman of Miss Domville's loveliness and innocence didn't deserve to feel the way he had that awful morning.

'I do. I realise it's a ridiculous request, but if I don't have something to turn into my publisher soon, I could lose everything.' Lancelot trotted to his side and sat down next to him. Warren dropped his hand on the dog's head and stroked it, the simple motion easing the anxiety of waiting for Miss Domville's answer.

'Maybe what you need isn't a new novel, but a rich wife.' She slid him a brazen glance from beneath her long eyelashes, inviting him to come closer like a siren eager to dash him against the rocks. If she wrecked him, it would be no one's fault but his own. He only hoped the destruction waited until he was done with his next novel.

'I'm not so mercenary about marriage and not about to live off a wife, especially not after everything I've done to achieve what I have.' He opened his hands to the room and the very house around them. 'My request is nothing more than a business arrangement, not a ridiculous courting ruse.'

'Good, because I have no interest in a husband.' At least they held similar views on matrimony, though it saddened more than heartened him. She was alone and isolating herself further from the world. It wasn't right. 'I also have no desire to become the talk of the countryside because of this proposed arrangement and the attention my connection to a famous author might bring.'

'Then we won't tell anyone about it, beyond those who must absolutely know. My mother will act as chaperon.'

'Even if we tried to keep it a secret, people will find out, they always do. Then what'll happen? Lady Ellington has spent a great deal of time and effort trying to rebuild my reputation. She won't throw it away by consenting to something as ridiculous as this.'

* * *

'I think it's a lovely idea.' Lady Ellington clapped her hands together, making her many gold bracelets jingle on her arm.

'I do too,' Mrs Steven concurred, exchanging a happy smile with her guest.

Marianne gaped at them. *They've all gone mad.*

'I don't think you understand what he's asking for?' Marianne stuttered, still not sure what he'd requested. He wanted her to play for him on his marvellous Érard while he worked in the next room, to inspire him. It seemed simple, but it wasn't and she was the only one who appeared to see it.

'It would be lovely to have your music filling this dreary house,' Mrs Stevens added. 'All the dark wood and wrought iron is rather oppressive.'

'Mother,' Sir Warren groaned. He stood beside Marianne, Lancelot at his side.

'It's true. Miss Domville's playing would cheer it up and give me something besides the workmen to listen to all day.'

Sir Warren levelled his hand at his mother

while pleading with Marianne, 'See, I'm not the only one who needs your talent.'

'I didn't say I'd stay all day, or at all,' Marianne reminded him, tripping over the word 'need'. It was the second time he'd said it, but it didn't make it any less awkward to hear than mangled French. People scorned her, they rarely needed her.

'Nonsense, you spend hours at my pianoforte at home. Why not do it here?' Lady Ellington steepled her fingers and touched them to her lips in amused scrutiny. 'Say you will, my dear. I'd so love to have your beautiful compositions heard by others.'

Marianne shook her head at Lady Ellington, warning her off further mention of the compositions. If she decided to play for Sir Warren, she certainly wouldn't bring those. She refused to stumble through wrong notes and odd stanzas or reveal her failings, and a good measure of herself through her music while he sat in the next room. No, she wouldn't come here and all she had to do was say so and it would end the matter, but the words wouldn't come out. She'd stood firm against Madame de Badeau's selection of suitors and the woman's more demeaning demands. Why couldn't she simply say 'no' to this?

Because of Sir Warren. She studied him from the corner of her eye, hesitant to face him straight on. He stroked the top of the dog's head, his ink-stained fingers ruffling the red fur. The relaxed gesture didn't hide his eagerness for her answer or settle the anxiousness in his green eyes. His talent was his sanctuary, just like hers, and he was afraid of losing it. She understood. The summer Madame de Badeau had plucked her from the Smiths' house and dropped her unprepared in London, Marianne's fingers had grown stiff, the keys awkward beneath her hands. The beautiful notes which had always comforted her had faded under the pressure of Madame de Badeau's screeching insults and the lecherous leers of her male visitors. The temporary loss of her talent had been more terrifying than when she'd left France with Madame de Badeau, then a stranger to her, or during her first few days with the Smiths. Without it, she was nothing.

'Well, Miss Domville, what do you say?' Sir Warren pressed, ending the long silence punctuated by the rough laughter of workmen overhead.

Marianne turned the gold ring on her small finger. He didn't need her. In time, his talent would return just like hers had when she and Madame de Badeau had settled into a tolerable hatred of one another. She should stop making herself so available or vulnerable to Sir Warren. It had already caused enough trouble and this was inviting more. She'd seen too much of gentlemen and their appetites at Madame de Badeau's to trust Sir Warren's motives to be purely innocent. However, he was offering her more than a tryst, fine dresses and a house in Mayfair, but a sense of purpose. To play for him was to use her music for something other than escaping the loneliness which swathed her, but to inspire a story, maybe even one better than Lady Matilda's.

It was dangerous and wrong to agree to this, but she'd caught the torment of his past in Lady Matilda's tale, the one he'd been willing to put aside to protect her. Sir Warren wasn't just overcoming his time in the Navy, but trying to excise it from his life. He couldn't do it without his work and she couldn't leave him to suffer without the thing which had sustained him through all his difficulties. It would make her as cruel and unfeeling as her mother and she'd vowed never to be like that witch.

Lady Ellington's carriage pulled away from Priorton Abbey, leaving Sir Warren and Mrs Stevens standing in the drive. Marianne crossed her ankles beneath her dress, refusing to peer out of the back window at the man.

What in heaven's name did I just agree to?

'I don't know how this won't result in a scandal.'

'What if it does? We've weathered them before, we'll weather them again.' Her companion rarely fretted about stories, but she'd never been this cavalier either. It, and Lady Ellington smiling from across the carriage as if she'd just purchased a new diamond ring, made Marianne suspicious.

'What are you about?' Marianne demanded, not sure what to be more irked about, her inability to refuse Sir Warren's request or Lady Ellington's encouragement of it.

'Nothing.' Lady Ellington snapped open her fan and waved it in front of her face. The warm October day was a surprise after the previous cooler ones. 'Except, I've always said your music shouldn't be hidden away.'

'Priorton Abbey isn't a concert hall.'

'But from here who knows where you may go? Perhaps to Paris now all this business with Napoleon is at an end, or even Vienna.'

'Are you eager to be rid of me?' Everyone else, especially the Smiths, had been quick to distance themselves from her when the scandal with Madame de Badeau had broken. At some point Lady Ellington and the Falconbridges would grow tired of shielding her too, especially if gossip about this silly arrangement between her and Sir Warren lit up the countryside.

'Of course not, my dear. I adore you, but you need a life of your own, to have friends your age.'

'Theresa is my age,' though in reality she hadn't seen her in quite some time. Theresa's contentment made Marianne's lack of it more stark and it was hard for her to be near her friend.

'And I adore her, but she's a wife and mother

now. You need to be around other young people who wish to enjoy their time before those sorts of responsibilities come about, friends who will help you be frivolous once in a while instead of so serious. It won't happen in my sitting room.'

'But you think it'll happen at Priorton, with Sir Warren?' With the medieval swords and armour hanging on the walls, frivolous was not a word she would use to describe the old priory.

'No, he's a touch too serious. I've read his books and some of his battle scenes are quite dreadful, but at thirty he is closer to your age than I am.'

Marianne leaned back against the squabs and peered out of the carriage window. On a rise in the distance stood Falconbridge Manor. The light stone of its columns was stately against the forest of red-and-orange leaves behind it. This summer, Marianne had been more agitated than a sparrow hopping around a garden, bored with the endless quiet days. Lady Ellington was right, Welton Place was no longer enough. It didn't mean Sir Warren was the answer to her dilemma, or she the answer to his, no matter what he might claim. The man was famous and the attention paid to him would magnify her notoriety when all she sought was to disappear into obscurity. A connection to her would also taint him.

'Why would a man like Sir Warren, whose livelihood depends on the good opinion of everyone, want to entangle himself in all my scandals?'

'Because he's taken an interest in you.'

Marianne fingered the manuscript resting in her lap, refusing to entertain the hope Lady Ellington's observation sparked inside her. The day she decided she wanted a man it would be for a sensible reason like companionship or a travelling partner, not for something as foolhardy as desire. 'Because he thinks I can benefit him, or he wants my money like Lord Bolton and all the rest. It's the only reason any man would risk tying himself to me.'

'My dear, you think you're an expert on gentlemen from your time in London, but I assure you, you've learned all the wrong things from all the wrong sorts.'

She wondered what sort Sir Warren was. He'd been no different in admiring her breasts than any other man, simply more discreet about it. She adjusted the fine silk covering her generous cleavage, for the first time thankful she wasn't one of those flat-chested women she saw near the walls at dances. When his eyes had flicked down, she'd wanted to remove the chemisette and not smack him for his insolence. It wasn't her usual reaction.

'Even if I go there every day, what you're hoping for won't happen. He made sure to tell me he isn't interested in marrying.' His announcement had bothered her as much as her inability to refuse his request. Was it marriage he was against, or just marriage to her?

'You can't believe everything a man says,' Lady Ellington dismissed with a wave of her bejewelled hand. 'Randall was quite adamant about never marrying and now he and Cecelia are happily wed.'

Lord and Lady Falconbridge had fallen in love in their youth. Despite a separation of ten years and the entire Atlantic ocean, they'd found one another again, thanks, in no small part, to Lady Ellington's involvement. Now, it appeared the Dowager Countess was attempting to throw

Marianne and Sir Warren together. If so, she was wasting her time. Marianne didn't share her companion's faith in love. For all the poets' writings about motherly love, Madame de Badeau hadn't been able to conjure up enough concern to even admit to being Marianne's mother, much less care for her. She doubted any sweeping ardour would change Sir Warren's stance on matrimony, not while he was struggling to save his house and his career, unless landing a rich wife was his intention, but she was sure it wasn't. Despite the outrageousness of his suggestion, nothing he'd told her today had been false, unlike all the 'confidences' Lord Bolton had tried to share with her, most of which had been in his breeches.

'Sir Warren may not be interested in marriage, but he must know a number of young gentlemen who are. It is to your benefit to become better acquainted with him.'

Marianne wasn't so convinced, but if Lady Ellington saw an advantage to this arrangement, then perhaps Marianne should too. This could be her chance to at last capture something of the normal life every other young lady in the county enjoyed, assuming their time together didn't create more problems for them both. It might, depending on whose notoriety more powerfully influenced whose.

She opened and closed her gloved fingers, wishing she were home and at the keyboard. She needed the calm of the ivory to better view this situation clearly. Sir Warren had cajoled her into this arrangement with flattery and a small measure of guilt. It didn't mean she'd allow herself to believe there was anything more to the arrangement than his need to write another book. She'd play for him, uphold her end of the agreement and nothing more. After all, once he realised she was a liability rather than an asset, he'd drop her like a hot stone. His loss of interest would sting less if she maintained her distance.

Chapter Five

Marianne finished the Mozart and began a Haydn. She glanced over her shoulder at the open door between the music room and Sir Warren's study, wondering if he was listening. No one else was. As fast as Mrs Stevens had ushered Marianne in to the Érard this morning, she'd rushed out, pleading all sorts of responsibilities while assuring Marianne she'd be down the hall listening.

Shirking her chaperon duties is more like it.

Marianne brought her fingers down hard on the low notes. She hardly needed anyone hovering over her since Sir Warren had yet to make his appearance. If it wasn't for the jingle of Lancelot's collar whenever the dog scratched himself she wouldn't even know Sir Warren was in the next room, much less the house.

She slid her fingers along the keys and into the treble clef.

Good. I'm here for us to work, not to converse.

Except he was the only one working. She was playing pieces she could perform in her sleep while her own compositions remained neglected at home. For all the effort Sir Warren was making to find inspiration, she hoped he was getting it. She still wasn't certain what she was gaining from the bargain other than a reason to leave Welton Place every day.

Playing two higher notes, she leaned back on the bench again, trying once more to see around the corner into the other room. All she caught was the wall of bookcases and the spiral staircase leading up to the balcony.

'Are you looking for me?'

Years of practice kept her from missing the next succession of notes. She turned the other way to catch Sir Warren striding in through the main door, the dog trotting beside him, smacking his jaws as if just roused from sleep.

She trilled the keys faster before forcing herself to slow down, but she couldn't stop watching his approach. He moved with the erect discipline of an officer, his gait steady and smooth. He was without his coat again and a glimpse of his smooth chest was just visible beneath the open V of his shirt under his loose cravat. She peered at it, trying to see if his chest held the same hint of a seaman's tan which graced his face and the backs of his hands. She wondered what his darker skin would look like against the lighter skin of her thighs or her stomach.

'Why did you sneak up on me?' she retorted, playing the bass notes hard, as rattled by her lurid turn of thoughts as his unannounced arrival.

'I didn't sneak up. I walked in.' He stood beside the piano and rested his elbow on the corner near the stand. She wrinkled her nose at how the weight of his body changed the tone of the piece. It made it deeper when it was supposed to be much lighter. He straightened off the instrument. 'You don't want me to listen?'

She shrugged, never losing the pace of the concerto. 'You may if you like.'

'Good.' He leaned on the case again and she frowned. She'd have to stand over him the next time he wrote and see how he liked it. She would if it didn't mean inhaling the thick, woody scent clinging to him and the linen sleeves of his shirt.

She glanced at his ink-smudged hands lying on the Erard, thinking she should be scandalised by his lack of proper dress, but she wasn't. She wondered if this was some inward failing, or simply having spent too much time at Madame de Badeau's where the gentlemen hadn't held back from making themselves comfortable and asking her to do the same.

The dog left his master's side and trotted forward to sit beside her and rest his head on her leg, weighing it down as she worked the pedals. She jiggled her knee, trying to dislodge him but he wouldn't move.

'I'm glad you didn't change your mind.' Sir Warren's full lips curled up a touch with amusement as he watched her struggle with the dog. He snapped his fingers and pointed at the floor. The dog's eyebrows shifted as it looked from him to her and ignored his owner. 'I was afraid you would.'

'I tried to, but Lady Ellington hustled me into the carriage with so much chatter I could barely get a word in edgewise.' She finished her piece and pushed against the dog, trying to make it shoo, but it leaned harder against her. The animal's stubbornness frustrated her as much as Sir Warren standing so close and the way her heart raced because of it. If her being here bothered Sir Warren, it didn't show. He was calm and relaxed in his stance and it helped soothe the unease she usually experienced around anyone outside the Falconbridge family. She gave up struggling with the dog and stroked its head, making it close its eyes. She was here to make friends with Sir Warren. It did her no good to be cross with his pet, or him. 'Have you made progress with your novel today?'

'Not as much as I would have liked. You will come back tomorrow, won't you?'

She was as shocked by Sir Warren's desire to be near her as Lancelot's. He was a famous writer, an accomplished man who'd built himself up from a common surgeon to baronet through his own hard work. There was no reason for him to be so concerned about her, yet he was. It flattered and terrified her all at once. It was time to place some distance between them. 'I will return. Not for you, but for the Érard.'

* * *

Warren pressed his fingertips into the hard piano case as Miss Domville stretched out one slender arm and stroked the top of the lustrous instrument. The gesture was reverent and suggestive and almost knocked him over. She wore a pale yellow gown with a contrasting blue cord tucked beneath her magnificent breasts. What he wouldn't give to see her creamy skin against the dark wood and to elicit from her as much passion as she drew from the now-silent strings.

'Care to join me for a walk?' he asked, distracting himself from his wandering imagination yet again. This morning, after he'd heard her arrive, he hadn't been able to focus on the new story until she'd finished a very long polonaise and one nocturne. Even then, it had taken all his effort not to wander to the door to watch her or to interrupt her playing with conversation until he'd completed at least one chapter.

'I'm not sure your dog will let me go outside.' She pulled one foot out from beneath the lounging canine and rolled her ankle. The hint of the slim calf clad in a semi-sheer stocking just above the top of her half boot made Warren's need to move more pressing.

'Lancelot likes you.'

'It seems he isn't the only one.' Her flush of mirthful confidence was as teasing as it was meant to be off putting, especially when she rose and stepped over the dog, the hint of *derrière* beneath her dress drawing him along after her.

Warren hurried past her to pull open the arched door leading outside. The scent of warm earth combined with her peony perfume enveloped him as she slid past him into the daylight. The sun brightened the satin ribbons trimming her dress and made her hair glow like a halo around her face.

In two steps he was beside her while Lancelot trotted off to follow a scent. He shouldn't be up from his desk, but taking advantage of their short time together to make progress. He'd found the inspiration for a new tale in one of his medieval manuscripts last night and, although it didn't enthral him like Lady Matilda's had, it offered the hope of his finishing something within a few weeks. He still had at least two more chapters to complete before his dinner at

Lord Preston's tonight. However, every flick of Miss Domville's skirts above the toes of her boots, each subtle breath which met their exercise eroded his desire to go back inside.

'Where's your mother?' she asked as she raised her hand to her forehead to shield her eyes from the sun. As she admired the stone house with its numerous jutting corners and stepped peeks, her fingers rested in a graceful arch above her brow, as enticing as when they'd stroked the Érard.

'Sewing in her room.' He pointed to a bay of windows on the second floor. 'She can see us from there. I assure you it's all very respectable.'

She tilted her head at him and pulled her lips into a disbelieving smile. 'Nothing about this arrangement is respectable.'

'But it is interesting,' he prodded, the hint of red the chill brought to her full cheeks entrancing him.

'That remains to be seen.' She strolled off down the walk, as natural among the wildflowers as at the piano. The sun caressed her pale skin while her curls danced with each of her elegant steps. This was how he'd imagined her when he'd written his novel. Except then he'd met her stride, turned her to face him and tasted her full lips.

Stop it, he commanded himself. She was here to assist him, not to tempt him, but a man would have to be dead to avoid the allure of her stunning body.

Warren hurried to join her and, as they wandered around to the back of the house, he pointed out the repairs he'd made to the windows and plasterwork, trying not to think about the cost and how much was still to be done.

'I'm glad you've left it as it is instead of knocking it down,' she remarked as they reached the centre of the garden. She rolled her shoulders and the motion raised and lowered her chest, almost to the detriment of his rational mind.

'I didn't think you liked history,' he answered with a grin to mask the more heady response coming from further down his torso.

Her blue eyes widened. 'Who told you that?'

'My mother. She said you told her you don't care for historical novels.'

'I don't, especially after the last one I read.' She shot him a teasing smile, then circled the stone sundial in the centre of the path.

'Hopefully, my next one will change your mind.' He plucked a stick off of the ground and flung it away for Lancelot to chase.

She ran one graceful finger up the edge of the sundial's gnomon. 'We'll see.'

She turned and walked off down the path.

Warren rocked back on his heels before stepping forward to follow her. He thought he couldn't work without her here. He was beginning to wonder if he could work with her here. He wasn't writing now and another day was slipping away from him. Strangely enough, the lost time didn't panic him as it had yesterday, or the many long days before. She fascinated him, as much as one of his characters, and as with them, he wanted to learn more about her.

'Lady Ellington said you wrote compositions.' He motioned her towards the cloister walk separating the somewhat orderly garden from the wild field beyond. Lancelot bolted off into the high grass, scaring up birds. 'You should work on them while you're here. This time is as much for you as it is for me.'

'I'd rather not.' She stopped and picked at a loose stone in one of the pillars. The sunlight cutting through the arches slid across the nape of her neck while the shadows caressed her straight nose and the downturned curve of her mouth. The wounded young lady beneath the confident woman revealed herself. She wasn't as worldly as all her smiles and artifices tried to make him believe and he was glad. He'd seen enough worldliness during his time in the Navy. 'Besides, they're only silly little pieces, hardly worth anyone listening to.'

'Don't demean or dismiss your talent, but hold your head up high and speak with confidence,' Warren encouraged, the way Leticia used to do with him. It disturbed him to see her think so little of herself as much as it had disturbed him to interrupt her playing.

'You don't understand.'

He leaned against one arched opening. 'You think I don't know how difficult it is to show your work to the world, to risk them laughing at it or telling you it isn't good enough?'

'You're wrong, Sir Warren. I've spent a large portion of my life listening to people tell me I'm not good enough. Criticism of my compositions would pale in comparison.'

He pushed up from the wall to stand over her. The wind caught the curls dangling by her cheeks and made them tease the unblemished skin. He kept his arms by his side despite wanting to wrap her in them and ease the tension in her lips with his. With her brows knitted together, she barely resembled the woman who'd played the pianoforte with passion. 'Don't let them trouble you, Miss Domville.'

Her eyes met his and hope rippled through them like the cool breeze between the arches. Then it vanished and she took a large step away from him. 'Why does it matter to you what bothers me and what doesn't?'

'Because you're my friend and I hope to be yours.'

'Friend? Is that what they call it?' The teasing vixen he'd glimpsed from across the sundial appeared again. There was something false about it, as when his sister used to try on his mother's dresses as a budding young lady and the gowns hadn't fitted. This wasn't the real Miss Domville, but the one meant to keep him at a distance.

'You think you're the only one who suffers alone, the only one afraid of being ridiculed?'

She raised her chin in defiance. 'What do you know of ridicule? All of England adores you.'

'And not one of them was there when I was simply Lieutenant Stevens and not Sir Warren,' he said sharply, irked by her dismissal of his struggles. 'Nor were they there after my first battle as a surgeon's assistant when I staggered up to the empty forecastle to retch overboard, afraid the grizzled old surgeon would catch me and have me drummed out for being so weak. I needed my naval surgical training to establish a practice once I was demobbed and I counted on my pay to keep my mother and sister from starving. My father hadn't had the sense to pay off his debts or save enough to keep us, leaving it to me to do. There were no fans adoring me when I used to write every night, determined to make a living without cutting into men, even while the officers laughed at me and told me I'd never succeed. The only people who were there for me were my mother and sister and my own belief in my ability to pull myself out of hell.'

'I—I'm sorry, I didn't realise,' she stammered, as stunned by his forceful words as he was. 'I thought with your fame your troubles were behind you.'

'They aren't and in some ways they've increased.' He pressed his fists against his hips and stared at the large scuff on the toe of his boot, working to rein in his irritation. It wasn't her fault she didn't know the challenges he'd faced in achieving his goals. He'd rarely discussed them with anyone, so why the hell had he told her? He looked up at her. She stood as serene as a painting, except for her eyes. Uncertainty sharpened their blue and increased the guilt building inside him. He'd told her because, deep down, he sensed she'd understand and he wanted it as much as he did her inspiration. Her not walking away told him she did. 'The problem with penning great novels is more are expected. My most ardent admirers, even my publisher, will abandon me if I don't give them what they want.'

'Then you should return to your study.' A cloud passed over the sun, covering the garden in shadows followed by a chill breeze. She clasped her arms across her chest, bracing herself against a shiver. 'Besides. I don't play well when my fingers are numb.'

She hurried back to the house, stiffness marring the elegance of her gait as she retreated inside. He wanted to call her back, to resume their walk and the quiet conversation they'd enjoyed before his outburst, but he didn't.

He strode across the cloister and swept a pile of leaves off the corner of an arch before turning and marching back to the other side. He should be glad she was pushing him away. She wasn't here for him to pour out his old sorrows to like some heroine in one of his novels, but to help him work. Except he wasn't at his desk, but pacing like a nervous animal.

He let off a sharp whistle to call Lancelot. The dog bounded up to him and the two of them made for inside. He didn't need this distraction, or to have emotion drag him into yet another risk as Leticia's memory had entangled him with Rupert. Steady industry, determination and perseverance were what he needed and nothing else, no matter how much Miss Domville irritated or captivated him.

Marianne closed the cover over the keys. Turner, the butler, had come in a few moments before to announce the arrival of Lady Ellington's carriage. She hadn't noticed how late it was until she'd looked up and seen the deepening shadows beneath the trees outside. She'd been hesitant to come here this morning. Now, she was reluctant to leave. She ran her fingers over the smooth case of the Érard. It was the piano she didn't want to leave, or so she told herself.

After the walk in the garden, she'd rushed back here to her music, eager to lose herself in the peace of the instrument. Everything Sir Warren had said had struck a chord deep inside her, one she feared. In a much more forceful way than Lady Ellington, he'd urged her to not worry about the opinions of others and live her life as she wished. It was a wonderful idea and impractical. She'd defied everyone at Lady Cartwright's to help Lady Ellington. Despite her noble motives, all it had done was garner more derision. She could well imagine how everyone would react if she suddenly decided to throw off all concerns for propriety and do as she pleased. They'd say she had at last proven she was no better than her mother.

From the adjoining room, she could hear the

faint scratch of a pen nib across paper, the crackle of the fire and the even snoring of Lancelot. As she peered through the open door at the books lining the far wall, she wondered why everyone was suddenly so concerned with her being out in the world when all she wanted was to be left alone, except she was tired of being alone.

She slid off the bench and gathered up her reticule and made for the study. Even though she'd all but sneered at his past difficulties in the garden, the least she could do was bid him goodnight and thank him for a mostly pleasant day. She wasn't likely to be welcomed back tomorrow. She should be glad—it would end the risk of them becoming the subject of country gossip—but she wasn't. She wanted the chance to make amends for her misstep in the garden, even if she didn't know how.

Lancelot rose from the hearthrug and trotted over to her when she entered the study. She stroked the dog lightly on the head as she cautiously approached the desk. 'Goodnight, Sir Warren.'

He didn't look up from where he sat hunched over his paper, but waved his left hand over his head. He continued writing with his right, his pen flowing over the paper except when he dipped it with flicking jabs in the inkwell. 'Goodnight.'

Her chest tightened and she tried to tell herself his dismissal didn't matter. People did it quite regularly and she didn't care. She cared tonight because she deserved it. For all the times she'd wished for someone to see her as more than rumours, he had and she'd insulted him, then fled like a scared rabbit. No wonder he wasn't eager to engage in more confidences or conversation.

'Come, Miss Domville, I'll see you out.' Mrs Stevens startled Marianne with the stealth of her approach.

The defences she'd lowered to approach him were jerked up again. 'Apparently, I'm no longer needed here.'

She followed Mrs Stevens out of the room and through the dimly lit front hall to the arched front door, trying not to regret leaving, or today.

'Don't be too hard on him. Warren gets in a mood when he's in the midst of one of his stories. As rude as he might be, I'm glad he's hard at work. It's been too long since I last saw him so engrossed, not since before his sister—' Her voice faded away, sadness draping her like it used to Mrs Nichols whenever a student succumbed to fever. Then it was gone, replaced by her always charming smile. 'Well, it doesn't matter. He doesn't mean any insult by it.'

'I'm not insulted at all.' She wanted to believe it was him and not her, but it was hard. He'd treated her with kindness and respect and she hadn't extended him the same courtesy. Maybe she was as unworthy of it as so many believed. 'I too dislike being interrupted when I'm composing.'

They left the warmth of the entrance hall and stepped out on to the chilly drive. The sun was low in the west and the shadow of the house fell hard over Lady Ellington's maroon-lacquered coach waiting to take Marianne home.

'I'm glad you understand. Thank you again for coming. Your help means a great deal to Warren and me.'

Mrs Stevens gave Marianne's arm a motherly squeeze and Marianne forced herself not to pull back. Relief filled her when Mrs Stevens let go.

Marianne climbed inside the carriage and settled into the seat as it pulled away. So many times, being alone in the vehicle after a trying encounter had been a relief, but not today. Her reaction to the kind woman's touch shamed her as much as her behaviour with Sir Warren. In the garden, when Sir Warren had spoken to her of his past and his pain, it was as if he'd seen inside her to the doubts she tried to hide. It unsettled her how quickly he could sympathise with her. This, as much as him standing over her in the cloister, his green eyes as dark as fine velvet, his chest so close to hers she could have laid her cheek on it, had sent her running back to the pianoforte.

No, he doesn't want my affection, but to be my friend.

He'd said as much and proven it with his willingness to confide in her once again. Instead of accepting it, she'd scoffed at it and pushed him away. It was difficult not to. She'd been betrayed too many times by people who should have cared for her to give her faith so easily.

It had been a mistake to let people's past failings influence her now. Lady Ellington was right, she needed more acquaintances her age.

It would only happen if she worked to overcome her reservations to cultivate friends, instead of hiding away from them, as she'd begun to do with Theresa. Sir Warren might not be the answer to all her troubles, but he might be the beginning of the change she'd desperately sought for years. He could lead her to other people who didn't judge her and a life different from the lonely one encompassing her. Like his mother, he'd reached out to her. It was time for her to accept it and his friendship. If she dared to venture back here tomorrow, if he still wanted her to, she would.

The gentlemen and ladies gathered in Lord Preston's sitting room applauded as Warren finished reading the first chapter from his last book aloud. He bowed under their admiration, thinking he looked more like the trained elephant he'd seen in India than an accomplished writer. He craved the quiet of Priorton, but soirées like this were part of his fame and crucial to garnering more readers who could influence society in his favour. These people purchased his stories, promoted his work and some day, when he at last had enough money to think of a family, their children would be his children's companions.

'Well done, Sir Warren,' Lord Preston commended as he shook Warren's hand with his palsied one. 'I've often thought of writing. Perhaps I could give you my story and you could write it for me.'

'I couldn't do it justice, Lord Preston,' Warren answered through a stiff smile, holding back a groan. For all his fame, lands and new title, the difference between Warren and his aristocratic patrons was notable. They admired his novels, but couldn't fathom the hard work it took to write them and achieve everything they possessed by luck of birth.

'You were magnificent, Sir Warren.' The young Lady Preston, with her dark hair and conniving eyes, stood at her elderly husband's elbow, practically licking her wide lips in anticipation of devouring Warren. He knew what she was after and it wasn't his literary flourish. 'Sir Warren, you must be thirsty after so much reading.'

She snatched Warren away from her husband and escorted him to the refreshment table at the back of the room, throwing her watching friends a haughty smile of triumph. Warren struggled to maintain his cheerful and deferential mood. This wasn't the first time a bored wife had tried to snare him and notoriety among her friends. Warren wasn't interested in becoming her prized catch.

'Try one of these, they're heavenly.' With slender fingers she plucked a pink pastry from a silver tray and held it up to Warren. 'Should you wish to savour one of my delicacies, it's easy to arrange. I could do a great deal for your career, especially among the ladies of London.'

Warren avoided her attempts to slide the treat into his mouth by taking it from her. 'I'm flattered, Lady Preston, but I don't sail my host's schooner, if you take my meaning.'

Lady Preston stared at him as if she couldn't decide whether to be angry or embarrassed. It didn't matter. Warren nodded to her, then strode away, leaving the woman to return to her friends without her conquest. He'd never seduced a woman as a means to increase his fame or profits and he wouldn't do so now, no matter how much he needed money. Lord Byron he was not, as Miss Domville was not Lady Preston.

He flicked a glance at Lady Preston who stood clucking with her friends, her eyes as sharp as broken glass as she viewed him with the hate of disappointed plans. Miss Domville had been torn apart too many times by women like Lady Preston to be like them. Instead she was original and innocent despite all her worldly experience. She didn't blatantly flaunt her more sensual charms as Lady Preston did, but kept them reserved. It was her opinions she needed to keep to herself.

Warren returned to the men and their discussion of hunting. He struggled to focus on where the best shooting was to be found because all he could think about was his conversation in the garden with Miss Domville. While other ladies drooled over him, she was at times contemptuous. He was Sir Warren to her and nothing more, as she'd proved today when she'd walked away from him. After the return to the house, he'd considered ending the arrangement, more vexed than inspired by their encounter, until she'd started to play. For the first time in too long, the words hadn't just come to him while he'd listened, but the depth of feeling for his characters, the passion which used to grip him in the centre of each story, had returned. He'd run mad with it, as he and the other sailors used to do in port cities when they went ashore. Even while the ground had still rocked beneath their feet they'd praised and revelled in the solid land. He'd done the same with his novel. As much as Miss Domville had irritated him, she'd also inspired him once again.

'Gathering wool, Sir Warren?' Lord Preston chuckled. 'Which would be well advised considering Priorton isn't earning as it should, or so I understand.'

'The previous owner didn't manage it well which is why he was forced to sell it. I assure you, it will be one of the finest estates in the county under my management,' Warren boasted, throwing out his chest to match the surety of any titled man, refusing to allow them to belittle him or the property he'd worked so hard to acquire.

'Not too fine for a purchased estate, I hope,'

the rotund Lord Astley drawled in his none-too-subtle reference to Warren's humble background.

Warren riveted his superior with a look as sharp as a scalpel. 'The finest.'

He was sure of it. With Miss Domville playing for him, he'd continue to write like he had today and soon there'd be another great sensation from Sir Warren Stevens, and all Lord Preston's and Lord Astley's doubts about him would be conquered, as well as his own.

Assuming Miss Domville returned to Priorton tomorrow.

Warren plucked a glass of port off the tray of a passing footman and took a deep drink. He'd been heavy handed in his insistence she stand up to the bullies in society and he couldn't blame her for snapping back at him. She probably resented his prodding as he did all the story ideas he received from well-meaning readers. He hoped it hadn't cost him their arrangement. He needed her as much as he'd needed Leticia in the days before his first book had been published. He'd been as certain it would be a flop as Miss Domville was convinced she'd always be a social outcast. Leticia, through her letters, had helped Warren to see he was wrong. He wanted to do the same for Miss Domville and he would if she gave him another chance.

Chapter Six

Marianne brought the *étude* to a thundering close, holding down the Érard's ivory keys until the ringing notes faded away.

'Is that one of your compositions?' Sir Warren applauded as he approached. The fall of his feet on the wooden floor was as melodious as a well-played drum and the sound of it tripped through her as powerfully as his voice.

His welcome eased the tension which had marred her playing since her arrival. This morning, when no note had come to Welton Place cancelling their engagement, she'd set out for Priorton wondering what she'd find. She was glad to see him smile at her as if their tiff in the garden had never happened. Without thinking, she returned it.

'No, Sir Warren, it's Schubert.' She'd considered bringing the composition book as a kind of peace offering, but at the last minute she'd changed her mind. Every heartbreak, fear and sense of loss echoed in each note in the book. She wasn't about to allow him to hear it. Despite what she'd told him about Madame de Badeau, there were limits to how many confidences she intended to share with him.

'Please, call me Warren.' He sat down on the bench beside her, his nearness more unsettling than an out-of-tune instrument.

She shifted her hips, ready to slide away before she stopped herself. He was tempting her into confidences again and she was wary of intimacy. She'd allowed herself to grow close to the Smiths and they'd made her regret it. It remained to be seen if Warren would do the same, but there was no way to find out without keeping her promise to accept his friendship and take the risk. 'And you must call me Marianne.'

'A very pretty name.'

'A common one in France.' She shrugged, trying to shake off the delight of his compliment, but he wouldn't allow it.

'It's still pretty.'

She started another tune, a soft one which allowed her to focus on the keys and the pedal instead of him watching her. She expected him to return to his writing, but he remained beside her, listening. She glanced up at him. He offered her a pleasant smile which made her duck back into the music, afraid to stumble through the notes.

'Who taught you to play?' he asked in a soft voice which mingled with the melody more than it interrupted it.

'Piano lessons were required at the Protestant School in France where I was raised, but once Mrs Nichols, the headmistress, noticed I had a gift for it, she spent more time with me.' For all Marianne's happy memories of the hours at the keyboard with Mrs Nichols, she couldn't forget the long nights in the dormitory. The girls used to taunt her about her lack of a mother. They'd been jealous of the extra time Mrs Nichols had spent with her, unable to see how blessed they were to have parents who cared about them. Back then they'd merely thought of Madame de Badeau as her scandalous and distant sister. They would have crucified her if they'd learned the truth. 'Once we had a recital for the parents. I was seven and I played the most important piece.' She played a few notes. The pride of having performed it for the crowd of gentlemen and ladies filling her before it faded. 'I was the only girl who had no family in attendance.'

She slid her hands off the keys, wondering why she'd told him such a thing. He didn't need to know.

'I'm sorry.' His condolence wasn't flippant but heartfelt and the tenderness of it wrapped around her like a warm pelisse. The old memory didn't seem so cold in his presence.

'It doesn't matter, I've all but forgotten it,' she lied.

He scrutinised her as though he didn't believe her, but didn't debate the matter. Instead, he spread out his fingers over the keys and began an old tune she remembered from France.

'You play?' she asked, astonished.

'No, my sister made me learn this duet a long time ago so we could perform it together.' He continued to struggle through the tune, his ink-stained fingers awkward on the keys. 'It's the only one I know. As you can see, I'm not very good at it.'

'You're doing quite well.' She joined in, taking the high octaves while he did the low ones. 'It's been years since I've played this.'

After she'd left France she'd stopped learning duets. There'd been no one to play them with.

Warren focused on the keys as he played, some of them still warm from Marianne's touch. He missed more notes than he struck and she slowed her playing to give him time to draw out the old tune from his memory. All the while he was aware of Marianne next to him, her hands coming close to his as the music drew them together.

From the corner of his eye he caught her watching him. She wore a pale pink gown, the neck high as always, but it wasn't her figure which captured him, but the lightness in her blue eyes. While they played the suspicious, wary young lady vanished, replaced by a vibrant, excited one.

'I spent hours practising this with Leticia,' he explained, 'the whole time wanting to be outside running with the boys from my father's vicarage school. It was his dream, a chance to make something of himself, though he never managed to make much of the school.'

'How very unfortunate,' she sympathised, her playing and compassion effortless.

'For all of us. The debt from it sunk us after he died. It's why I work so hard. I won't ever be in so precarious a situation again.' Warren plucked at the keys, irritation making his fingers jerky before he settled it. He intended to enjoy this time with her, not wail about the past or be pulled down by his current troubles. He'd made some mistakes this year with Priorton and it had been compounded by his inability to write, but the risk to his solvency would soon pass. With Marianne here he was already creating and would soon be as productive as before.

They continued the piece, their pace increasing as the old motions came back to him. During one lively section, her arm brushed against his and he missed the next note, then stumbled over a few more before regaining his rhythm. She didn't wince or bang the keys in frustration, demanding they start again like Leticia used to do. Instead she waited for him to catch up to her.

'Does your sister still play?' Miss Domville

asked, the innocent question tearing him like splinters from a shattered mast.

'No, she died over a year ago.' He choked down the hopelessness which had filled him when he'd left his sister's room, forced to admit his defeat.

'I'm sorry.' She stopped playing to lay one hand over his, the touch as light as sea spray but much warmer.

He stilled beneath her and stared at her pale skin against his. The same calm she'd inspired in him at Lady Cartwright's filled him again. It, and her fresh peony scent, stretched out to envelop him and drive away the cold memories like the sun does the clouds after a storm. No woman had ever had such a powerful effect on him and it troubled him. Things were complicated enough at present without throwing a woman into it, but he couldn't push her or her soothing presence away.

He slid his hand out from under hers and rested it on his thigh. The awkwardness of their nearness which had dissolved during the duet returned. He should let it be, encourage it and the aloofness which was a basic tenet of their agreement, but it ate at him as much as his old troubles. She'd comforted him and he wished he could give her the same relief from her troubles, help her as she was helping him. Beneath his hand, the ivory keys spread out in either direction and gave him an idea. 'Have you ever considered performing your compositions for others?'

She began to play a quiet piece, her lips curling up in a sarcastic grimace. 'I can see the advert now. The notorious sister of Madame de Badeau plays the pianoforte. It'll draw a larger crowd than the Elgin Marbles.'

'What about simply publishing them? You could become a famous author, like me.' He winked at her.

'Maybe then I can carouse with the Prince and gain a baronetcy too.'

He trilled his fingers on his leg, wanting to shoot back and tell her it was hard work which had earned him his title and nothing else, but the sideways smile she pinned him with silenced him. She was teasing him, not insulting him, and he enjoyed it as much as the sparkle of her eyes beneath her long lashes.

'If the Prince handed out titles solely based

on men carousing with him, the House of Lords would be overflowing with newly ennobled men.'

'And their wives and lovers too.' She laughed, the sound as beautiful as her playing. For the second time today she'd surrendered to emotion instead of trying to hide it behind her wary distrust of everyone and everything. He wanted to see more of this impetuous woman, but as fast as she'd allowed the slip, she covered it again. 'It's a generous offer, Warren, but I've found the less notoriety, the better. While you may crave fame, I want nothing but to be ignored.'

It wasn't true and they both knew it, but he said nothing. It was her scandals she wanted ignored. She craved attention from people who would treat her well, the way he wished to treat her. 'You could write under a pseudonym. It's done all the time.'

'No. Despite what anyone thinks of the work, if they happen to learn it's by me, they'll shun it.'

'The world is much bigger than London. I assure you, there are musicians in Vienna who care nothing about the *ton's* gossip, and people in England who have more to consider than your past.'

'You haven't even heard my pieces. They could be awful.'

'Coming from someone with such a genuine love of music, I doubt it. Of course, you could always play them for me so I could be certain.'

She didn't answer, but stopped playing and went silent as though he'd asked her to reveal her darkest secrets, which in a way he had. He silently urged her to overcome her hesitation as she had at the Cartwrights' when she'd refused to allow the ladies' insults to deter her from helping her friend. He didn't want those same women hindering her dream, or her faith in herself like all the laughing sailors and officers had tried to do with him.

'Let's assume your compositions are magnificent,' he continued as her silence stretched out. She hadn't refused him, but she hadn't agreed either. 'I can show them to my publisher and convince him to print them. I'll lend you the strength of my name, which is something I haven't done for even my brother-in-law.'

'Why?' She eyed him like an apple on a cart,

wondering if there were worms beneath the red flesh. This wasn't how he wanted her to regard him and some day he would see to it she didn't.

'Because ten years ago Mr Berkshire took a chance on me and it made all the difference. I want to do the same for you. You don't have to decide anything today, but please consider it.' Warren didn't want to press her as he had yesterday and send her fleeing, or rejecting his offer outright. 'Publishing would give you something more to do than locking yourself away at Lady Ellington's. A real purpose.'

She opened her full lips, ready to answer when a voice from the door silenced her.

'There you two are,' Warren's mother observed as she bustled into the room.

Marianne moved away from Warren as if he was an uncoiling anchor rope about to catch her leg and drag her down. He wasn't so fast to pull away. 'Miss Domville, Lady Ellington sent the carriage early for you today.'

'The Girls' School meeting. I almost forgot.' Marianne bounded from the bench and gathered up her reticule and pelisse like a pupil late for class. The quickness of her movements gave her a youthfulness Warren admired. It was so different from the cautious seriousness which usually stalked her.

'When I didn't hear music, I thought you'd gone to the garden,' his mother mentioned as she and Warren led Marianne to the waiting carriage.

'Doesn't your room have a view of it?' Marianne asked, casting suspicious eyes on Warren.

'Yes, but it isn't a very good one,' Warren's mother answered, not a party to Warren's small lie from yesterday.

The truth exposed, he ignored the chiding glance from his muse.

They reached the carriage where the footman held open the door. Warren followed Marianne forward to the vehicle while his mother remained behind.

'Think about what I offered.' Warren held out his hand to Marianne, ready to help her into the carriage. She stared at it, not as quick to take it as she'd been to comfort him inside. He was about to withdraw his and allow the footman to assist her when she reached out and laid her palm against his. The pressure was light and heady and he curled his fingers to capture hers. Beneath the whinny of the horse, he heard her subtle intake of breath as he bowed over the delicate skin, noting a small freckle near her thumb, tempted to press his lips to it, but he couldn't, not with his mother watching. He straightened to find her staring at him as though he'd suggested he climb in the conveyance with her. He would have if she'd invited him.

She let go and dipped inside. The footman closed the door, then took his place on the back. Warren waited for Marianne to appear at the window, but she remained hidden by the shiny side of the carriage as it set off down the drive, kicking up a small cloud of dust behind it.

'You interrupted us,' Warren muttered to his mother, more irritated than grateful as she stepped forward to join him.

'I wouldn't be a very good chaperon if I hadn't.'

Warren studied his unapologetic mother. She was enjoying this, though which aspect of this, the interrupting or Warren not being thrilled about it, he wasn't sure. 'I was telling her about Leticia and how much she used to like to play.'

His mother's smile vanished. 'Please, Warren, don't remind me.'

He didn't say more. They rarely spoke of Leticia and sometimes he wondered if his mother blamed him for what had happened, like Rupert did. If she did, she'd never say so. His mother possessed a generous heart. He hoped it was charitable enough for her to forgive her son. He still hadn't forgiven himself.

'Why do you stand by Miss Domville instead of joining with Lady Cartwright and the others?' he asked, needing to discuss something else.

His mother clasped her hands in front of her stomach as she used to do when explaining the rules to a new pupil at his father's school. 'In all my years at the vicarage, more than one young lady in a difficult circumstance came to me for advice. When I used to listen to their stories, I could always tell which ones had eagerly gone to the man and which ones had genuinely been led astray. The ruined young ladies, despite their unfortunate experience, lacked a worldliness which the eager ones couldn't hide. Miss Domville has the same innocence as those misled young ladies. Whatever she'd been accused of, she hasn't done it. I'm as sure of it as you and the Falcon-bridges.' His mother turned to him, as serious as the day she'd sat him down in the vicarage garden when he was fourteen to tell him of the weakness invading his father's lungs. 'Be very clear about what it is you want from her. If you break her heart, she won't recover like one of your London widows.'

Warren blanched. 'What London widows?'

She wagged one finger at him. 'Don't think I don't know what you get up to when we're in town.'

He crossed his arms over his chest, refusing to discuss his non-writing activities with his mother. 'I want nothing more from Miss Domville than her inspiration. She's well aware of it and expects nothing more from me. Maybe in a few years I'll consider taking a wife, but I won't ask a young lady to wait on my whims to see herself settled.'

His mother shook her head in disappointment. 'You're work isn't everything, Warren.'

The muscles in his neck tightened as the peace of Marianne's presence faded. With her, for a short while, he'd been able to forget all the demands pressing down on him. They returned now with as much potency as the afternoon sun on the lawn. 'It's everything we have to live on.'

He left the tranquillity of the front garden and went back inside, passing the dull armour and swords adorning the hall as he returned to his desk. He'd vowed long ago to work hard and make enough so he and those he loved would never be in poverty, or forced to endure the same horrors he had as a young man. He couldn't allow a pretty face or some misguided need for sympathy to deter him from his goals. Even if the lady had money, if he didn't, it meant nothing. He wouldn't depend on others. He'd discovered what a mistake it was to do so during the year they'd lived with his uncle.

He entered his study and stepped over Lancelot where he lay in the centre of the room. Seating himself at his desk, Warren took up his pen. He'd had been distracted enough by Marianne already. It was time to write, even if it took him a full hour to stop tilting his head to listen for Marianne's playing. The lingering scent of her perfume kept convincing him she was mere feet away.

* * *

'We've been invited to Lady Astley's musical evening next week,' Lady Ellington announced as the carriage carried them to the Girls' School on the far side of the village.

'Must we go?' Marianne sighed. 'It's bad enough I have to face her this afternoon as a school patroness, but at her house? The woman isn't much better than Lady Cartwright. Why must she and the others always be so rude to me?'

'Lady Cartwright is one of those unhappy people who, instead of looking for ways to build herself up, rips others down. All is not well between Lady Astley and her husband and I believe Lady Preston is ashamed of her past. She might be a baroness, but I don't think she's ever been comfortable with the change from merchant's daughter to titled lady. It's difficult enough at times for those of us born to it. I can only imagine what it must be like for her, and Sir Warren.'

'He seems to have taken to it well enough.' With the exception of the Falconbridges, it was yet another argument for ignoring the society of toffs, of which Sir Warren was a part, though not really. He'd raised himself up from humble beginnings and filled his coffers every day through his work. She admired him for his accomplishments. It was more than most men she'd encountered were willing to do.

'He's sure to be at the musical evening which is a good reason for you to attend.'

'Is it?' She wasn't so certain, especially not after their time alone together today.

'Or as a reason to purchase a new dress, something to play up your less musical talents.' Lady Ellington circled her hand at Marianne's abundant chest hidden beneath her fichu and the restraining influence of her stays. 'I saw the most beautiful pattern for a blue ball gown in my lady's magazine. It would bring out your eyes.'

Her eyes weren't the only thing a more revealing dress would bring out. In the past, the few men who'd seen her wear the single gown she owned which accentuated her décolletage had lost their ability to speak. Unfortunately, they had retained excellent control of their pawing hands. Yet it wasn't so much them she imagined seeing her in the dress as Warren. It was almost enough to make her agree to having it done up.

'I can't. If I wear anything too revealing, everyone will call me a tart.'

They called her one anyway, even while she dressed like a nun. Warren didn't. When he'd stood over her in the cloister and today when he'd held her hand in the drive, he'd viewed her as if she were the most magnificent thing he'd ever seen. Marianne rubbed the palm of her hand, the pressure of Warren's skin against hers still vivid. She'd arrived at Priorton this morning determined to be friendly with him, but during their time together, something more than comfort or companionship had curled between them. It was something she was hesitant to consider. He was no more interested in courting than she was, and if she allowed her emotions to run away with her, who knew what mistakes it might lead to, or what weaknesses in her it might reveal.

'We're here,' Lady Ellington announced as the carriage rocked to a stop in front of a modest two-storey brick house.

With a sigh, Marianne followed the Dowager out of the carriage, wishing she could forgo this meeting, but she couldn't. To do so would mean giving the other patronesses complete control of the school and she didn't trust them to be generous to the orphan girls being trained for service. She and Lady Ellington had helped refound the school last year after it had almost faltered due to a lack of funds. In doing so, they'd been forced to take on other patronesses such as Lady Preston and Lady Astley who were as free with their censure as their financial help. At least with Lady Ellington involved, the other ladies were forced to maintain a touch of decorum where Marianne was concerned.

Marianne followed Lady Ellington into the school, nodding and smiling to the little girls lined up on either side of the front walk to greet them.

'Welcome, Lady Ellington and Miss Domville,' Miss Speith, the slender assistant headmistress, sang out as they stepped inside. Beside her stood Mary, the oldest girl of ten with wildly curly hair.

'Good day, Mary. Here's the sheet music I promised you.' Marianne handed her the new sheet music recently arrived from London.

'Thank you, Miss Domville.' Mary clasped the

music to her chest as if it were a gold sovereign. The reaction warmed and saddened Marianne. Like her, Marianne had fed off small kindnesses as a child too. There'd been few people to offer them to her. Not even Mrs Nichols, who'd had so many girls to take care of at the Protestant School, had been attentive enough.

Marianne and Lady Ellington proceeded into the dining room in the centre of the house. Like every other room it was sparse, decorated for purpose rather than pleasure. With books needing to be purchased along with food and material for clothes, there wasn't much reason to spend money on pictures. Some day, when the school was financially secure, Marianne would see it more cheerily done up.

'Good afternoon, ladies,' Mrs Croft, the long-faced headmistress with pince-nez glasses on the bridge of her nose, greeted. Marianne and Lady Ellington took their seat at the table across from Lady Menton, Lady Preston and Lady Astley.

Once everyone was settled, Mrs Croft picked up the pen beside her and looked over the list of topics in the journal before her. 'The first item to discuss is—'

As Mrs Croft led the meeting, Marianne braced herself against the other women's narrow-eyed stares, doing her best to ignore them. She'd heard enough rumours from the servants, especially about Lady Preston, to know they were no saints and yet they dared to sneer at her. If only she had the fortitude to meet their derision by calling out their sins directly to their faces. She'd catch hell for being so bold, but it might be worth it to see Lady Preston go pale beneath her overly red hair.

'Miss Domville, if you're to be a part of these meetings we need your full attention,' Mrs Croft chided as though Marianne was one of her students.

She sat up straighter in her chair, refusing to be rebuked. 'I'm part of these meetings because my money helps fund this school.'

'And we thank you for your generosity,' Mrs Croft mumbled before returning to her list. 'As I was saying, I think it best to forgo the Christmas boxes this year.'

'No, we can't do away with them,' Marianne protested. 'Not every girl has a family to send her presents.' If it hadn't been for Mrs Nichols giving her the gold pinky ring the Christmas she'd turned ten, Marianne never would have received one yuletide gift during all her years at the Protestant School.

'I realise it will be a disappointment…' Mrs Croft peered over her pince-nez '…but our duty is to prepare these girls for their futures. For most of them, life won't be pretty boxes of sweets at Christmas.'

Marianne gripped the arms of her chair as she struggled to remain polite. 'Some of these girls have suffered enough hardships without being denied a little treat at a festive time of year. I'll pay for the boxes myself to ensure they have them.'

'That's very generous of you, Miss Domville, but I think—'

'It's a wonderful idea,' Lady Ellington cut off Mrs Croft. 'Don't you agree, Lady Menton?'

Lady Menton paled, but was prudent enough to agree, especially with Lord Falconbridge backing her son, and Theresa's husband, for MP. 'I do.'

'I do, too,' Lady Astley mumbled, following Lady Ellington's none-too-subtle hint. The Baron's wife didn't possess so pressing a reason to align herself with Lady Ellington except the pleasure of having more illustrious guests than the local farmers and tradesmen at her musical evening. Lady Preston nodded as if it physically hurt her to agree, too awed by the Dowager's lineage to openly defy her.

'Then it's settled. Mrs Croft, you may continue with the meeting,' Lady Ellington instructed.

The headmistress scratched the item off her list with a flick of her bony wrist. 'The next issue concerns the reading-book selection.'

While she spoke, Marianne silently seethed. Despite all Marianne's hard work on behalf of the school, if Lady Ellington weren't involved, Marianne would be driven away, her money and help rejected because of rumours and suspicions. It didn't matter what good deeds she did, all of these people were determined to tear her down, except Mrs Stevens and Warren. She wished she could face her critics and prove to them once and for all she was more than the wicked woman they believed her to be.

You could publish your works.

Warren's suggestion came rushing back to her

as she plucked a piece of Lancelot's red hair off her dress and dropped it on the floor.

She might have scoffed at his idea, but there'd been no deriding the sincerity behind his offer or his desire to encourage her like Lady Ellington always did. She wished it didn't mean playing her pieces for him. It was one thing to distribute music to anonymous people. Everyone played the way they wished, despite all the allegros and fortissimos written in the staff. It was quite another thing for an artist to perform their own composition exactly as it was meant to be done. It revealed the true intention behind each note, the real feeling underlining every stanza. However, he must hear them if he was to judge the quality of her work and whether it was worthy of his endorsement.

She caught Lady Preston staring at her and met her hard eyes until the woman looked away first. If everyone was so determined to condemn her no matter what she did, then she might as well do what she wanted. Warren believed she should and she was sure Lady Ellington did too. Her success would defy these women's low expectations of her and prove to them she was more than a whore's relation.

Fear slipped in to undermine her determination. For them to know she would have to publish under her real name and risk society's reaction. If Lady Preston and her surreptitious glares were any indication, it wouldn't be good, but Warren was right, London was not the centre of the world. Her success as a composer was in the future. This was now and he was giving her an opportunity she might never have again. She knew how quickly everything which she believed was sure and good and constant could change. Anyone or anything might swoop in to snatch Warren and his offer away from her. Until then, she'd seize this moment and take full advantage of it. Tomorrow she'd take her composition book to Priorton Abbey.

Chapter Seven

Warren listened to the notes drifting through the open library door. The tone of Marianne's playing was different today. It wasn't continuous, but paused here and there before starting back a few stanzas and beginning again.

She's playing her own composition.

He set his pen in the stand and grasped the arms of his chair, ready to rise before he stopped. She was working with a focus he recognised. To disturb her would mean upsetting her progress as she tried one note and then another until the succession seemed right. He settled back in his seat and struggled to follow the rhythm and predict where it might go. Then, when she played it all together, it flowed like the thread in one of his stories.

He returned to his work, his progress matching hers with words coming rapidly and filling page after page. He was so engrossed, he didn't notice the music had stopped until a voice startled him.

'Warren?' His name on her lips was even prettier than her playing.

He stood as she approached his desk, moving like a dream in the cream-coloured dress. The sleeves were sheer, revealing the curve of her arms. The high neckline covered her chest, but didn't rise to her neck, leaving a hint of her glorious cleavage visible above the gold trim of the bodice. Its colour matched the tone of her hair and the small gold bracelet encircling her wrist.

She stopped in front of his desk. Lancelot stretched and trotted over to her. She scratched behind his ears, making the dog tilt his head in delight. While her fingers mussed his hair, she peered at the book lying open on Warren's desk. 'Am I disturbing you?'

'Not at all. I heard you composing.'

'Piano concertos. They're my speciality, but difficult to write when one forgets to bring enough ink.'

So it wasn't curiosity which had drawn her in here. He was a touch disappointed as he opened a desk drawer and took out a fresh bottle. 'Lucky for you I keep a great deal on hand.'

He held out the glass jar and she reached for it, her fingers curling over his. She didn't jerk away at the meeting of their skin, but allowed the tips of her fingers to caress the back of his as she slid the bottle from his grasp. Red spread along the arches of her cheeks and a faint surprise flicked through her blue eyes. They stayed as they were for a few moments, the crackle of the fire in the grate punctuating the heavy silence.

He waited for her to make an excuse and slip away from him like his stories sometimes did if he didn't write them down fast enough. She didn't and he was the one who drew back first, fingering the edge of the top book in the stack next to him. His mother's warning to be cautious with her rang in his ears. He should take up his pen and send her into the other room. This was a distraction, a very lovely one, but he didn't need it.

He was about to suggest they both return to their work when she leaned forward and peered at the half-filled paper on his desk. 'What are you writing?'

'My version of a Robin Hood story.'

'You enjoy the myths about him?'

'Not as much as Leticia used to.' He touched the yellowed pages of the book on castles lying open on the desk. The place was well marked from all the times Leticia had studied the illustration of the Locksley keep as a girl. It had been one of her favourites. 'She shared my love of medieval stories. When we were children, we used to dream of living in a castle some day. At least one of us achieved it.'

She rested her hand on Lancelot's head. 'How did she die?'

He patted his thigh and Lancelot left Marianne to lean against Warren's leg. He stroked the dog, not wanting to relive the morning. He already did every time he thought of his sister. Maybe silence wasn't what he needed, but to talk about it the way he used to discuss the Navy with Mr Berkshire or some of his old seamen friends. They'd listened to him and recognised what it was like to be in the midst of battle, scared for your life but still doing your duty. Yet when it had come to losing Leticia, they hadn't been as sympathetic about the trials of childbed and what it had been like for Warren to lose the most important patient he'd ever cared for. He took a deep breath, drawing on his courage the way he used to before battle. Under Marianne's gentle gaze, he couldn't hold back. 'She and my poor little niece did not survive her confinement.'

'And there was nothing you could do for them.' It wasn't an accusation, but a statement of support and tenderness which almost crushed him. He didn't deserve her or anyone else's pity for what he'd failed to do.

'No. I'd stitched captains back together, saved unconscious seamen from being pitched overboard by proving they were still alive, but there'd been nothing I could do for my sister or her poor babe.'

'It's not your fault they died,' she offered as if hearing all the regrets and second guesses which continued to torture him.

He'd spent too many nights contemplating if he should have done something different, tried some procedure he'd read about. He still wondered if he could have saved one or the other, or both of their lives if he'd been less cautious in his treatment. 'I'm not so sure. Neither is Rupert and sometimes, I suspect, my mother.'

'Not her. She's too kind.'

He closed the book on castles and the gilded title caught the sunlight from the window behind him. 'She never talks about Leticia.'

'Most mothers do so love their daughters. It must be difficult to realise she's gone.'

'It is, for both of us. Leticia was my greatest supporter. She was the one who first found Mr Berkshire. She pursued him for weeks, begging him to read my manuscripts, the ones she used to critique and edit. He finally gave in to her just so she'd stop pestering him.' He smiled at the memory of Mr Berkshire blustering on in faux outrage during their first meeting while Warren had been on leave. Leticia had beamed at the publisher's compliments about her tenaciousness and Warren's gratitude for it. The humour in the memory left him and he pressed his fingertips into the top of the desk, bracing himself against defeat. 'She believed in me when I needed it the most. Then, when she needed me, I failed her.'

'You told me the night you helped Lady Ellington there's very little medical men can do except patch people up and hope they survive.'

'Most of the time they don't.'

'But sometimes they do. I'm sure there are many sailors who are still alive because of what you did for them.' Marianne studied him like the apparition he'd once seen aboard ship in the middle of a fever—an angel of strength with a hint of vulnerability beneath her gossamer silk. A vision like Miss Domville was the reason why men believed in mermaids. They were peace.

'Yes, there are.' The faces of seamen who'd left his sick bay to return to their lives or their stations trickled through his thoughts. He had made a difference to some men, and in the end, through his hard work, to his and his mother's lives. He smiled at Marianne, amazed at how, when he'd been so determined to help her, she was the one helping him. Whatever man she decided to finally reveal her full self to would be lucky. Despite all his protestations about avoiding distraction, at this moment he very much wished to be the one she chose.

'Enough of my tales of woe.' He shoved his experiences into the dark hold in his mind and beamed at her like he did his admiring readers, refusing to ruin their time together with all his misery. 'It's your beautiful music I want to hear today.'

She cocked her head at him as if to say she wouldn't forget what he'd told her, or allow him to evade revealing more of himself in the future. 'Weren't you listening to me play while you wrote? Isn't it the whole reason I'm here?'

No, not the whole reason.

It was becoming more difficult to lie to her and himself. 'May I see your composition book?'

She clutched the ink tighter, as if he'd asked to peek under her petticoat. 'Why?'

'I'm curious. I've been listening to you all morning. I want to see what you've accomplished.'

'What have you accomplished?'

He picked up his manuscript and held it out to her. 'Five chapters. Not an entire novel, but it soon will be. I'll let you read it when it's done if you'll let me see your composition book.'

She waved away his manuscript and with an 'as you wish' shrug made for the music room, making it clear he was to follow. He didn't mind.

From behind, he caught the faint outline of her figure from the light coming in the window filtering through her dress. It emphasised the tempting curve of her hips and the slenderness of her waist. She approached the Érard, set the ink next to the composition book on the stand and sat at the keyboard.

He stopped in the middle of the room. Lancelot rested at his feet while Marianne posed one foot over the pedal. Her bearing was as alluring as the arch of her neck beneath the loose blonde curls brushing the nape. He trilled his fingers on his arms where he crossed them, wanting to sweep her skin with his lips and savour the sweet melody of her sighs.

Unaware of the desire for her more than her talent making him shift on his feet, she spread out her long fingers over the keys. Her hands slid across the black and white, drawing from the instrument something of her soul. The beauty of it drowned out everything—his story, his grief, even his desire for her. Her music was no longer something to fill the background while he worked. It was everything and each note wrapped around him like he wished her shapely arms would do.

The complexity of the composition reminded him of her experiences with the world. She'd suffered more of its ugliness than she deserved, just as he had in the Navy. Her loneliness rang in the mournful bass beneath the treble. It reminded him of the creaking timbers and snapping sails during the dark nights when he used to stand at the balustrade staring out at the darkness. The overwhelming solitude of the sea crept into a man's soul like the damp did everything aboard ship. Even now, late at night when he rose to stare out at the dark gardens or stood in the midst of a London crowd, he sometimes shivered with the memory of it.

She hadn't shaken her isolation either. She knew what it was like to be alone among many, to carry sadness like buckets of seawater, never able to scrub away the past. Someone so young and innocent didn't deserve to suffer the way he had during his first days in the Navy. He would make her happy, see her smile not with stoic reserve but the unrestrained joy of a young lady. In freeing her from her past, he might forget his too.

* * *

Marianne never once turned to look at Warren, confident he was there. She couldn't tell him how difficult it had been to be torn from the Protestant School and Mrs Nichols. She couldn't express how much it seared her heart when the letter from the Smiths had arrived after Madame de Badeau's scandal. If it hadn't been for Lady Ellington holding her while she'd cried, the piece she played would be darker and uglier.

Marianne moved into a more chilling stanza, her fear even this great lady would eventually leave her echoing down the length of the piano wires. There was nothing binding Lady Ellington to her any more than there had been the Smiths or the Nichols. Unlike them, Lady Ellington wasn't paid to care for her, she just did. Marianne feared Lady Ellington's regard would one day turn to disgust and she'd be as alone and wretched as she had been in Madame de Badeau's house. Lady Ellington was the one bright light in her life, until she'd met Warren.

Moving to a softer portion of the piece, she threw a subtle glance over her shoulder. She could see nothing more than the silhouette of

Warren near the windows at the edge of her vision. He listened in respectful silence, not interrupting or intruding into the undefined space which enveloped her while she played. Even without seeing his expression, she knew he didn't listen with leering amusement as though she were an overly adorned Cyprian, but because he wanted to hear what she couldn't express in words.

She almost snatched her hands off the keyboard and ceased to play. Even without seeing his expression, she knew he heard the deeper meaning beneath each carefully chosen note just as she'd empathised with his pain over his sister and all he'd endured in the Royal Navy. She might not have witnessed the smoke and bloodshed of battle, but she'd fought her own war against the vile men and women who'd demeaned her for years. Like him, she'd experienced the grief of being ripped away from someone who'd cared for her. Mrs Nichols hadn't died like Leticia, but after the Peace of Amiens had failed and the blockade had ended all correspondence with France, it was as if she had passed away.

Marianne played for his anguish and hers, but

with a hope they could overcome it. She drew strength from his presence and touched each key with passion, putting all of herself into the music until at last she reached the end and the final note vibrated into nothing.

He didn't clap or compliment her, but came to sit beside her on the bench. Lancelot remained where he was on the rug. The cold tones of her piece faded under the heat of Warren's arm next to hers. She turned to him and admired the serenity which softened the lines at the corner of his mouth. They didn't speak, as raw and open to one another as if they were naked. The vulnerability didn't frighten Marianne or make her raise her defences like some kind of drawbridge to shut him out. He laid his hand over hers where it rested between them on the bench. His pulse beat a steady tune against her skin, drawing her to him like the Érard did every day.

She turned her hand over and curled her fingers around his. The peace and safety which filled her at Lady Ellington's swept through her. There was no reason to fear Warren, not with her person or her heart. With him, she wouldn't be alone. It was as terrifying as it was exhilarating, like his leaning towards her. She titled her face up to his and closed her eyes.

The meeting of their lips struck her as hard as the first time she'd heard an accomplished organist perform Beethoven's *Fifth Symphony*. She'd never willingly surrendered to a man's affection, determined to remain in control of her urges and her body in a manner Madame de Badeau had failed to master. Today, she tossed it all aside as Warren slid his hand along her jaw. She shifted closer to him, raising her arm so his free one could wrap around her waist and pull her tighter against him. The press of his chest against hers and the weight of his breath across her cheeks was as glorious as the fine silk of a new dress.

She rested her hand on his arm, marvelling at the hardness of his muscle beneath the linen. It wasn't the strength of a Navy surgeon who could wield a saw, but the writer who spent every day dedicated to his craft. He didn't work for only fame and notoriety, but for the safety of his family and a home no one could take from him. She wanted to slip into the circle of his comfort and protection, forget everything he'd told her in the other room and all she'd conveyed in her music. None of it mattered except him and the peace of his embrace.

It didn't last.

'Warren, are you in here? Your mother said you were working.' A man's voice broke the quiet. Marianne stiffened beneath Warren as the sound of boots on the adjoining study floor banged through the stillness. 'Where are you?'

'Damn it,' Warren cursed as he jumped to his feet and hurried to the far side of the instrument. He placed as much distance as he could between them before Rupert strolled in as though he owned the house.

'What are you doing here?' Rupert took in the room with amazement. 'I don't think I've ever seen you in here.'

His curious gaze fell on Marianne. Her once-languid spine had gone stiff beneath Rupert's interested gleam. There was nothing else about her, not a touch of colour in her face or the nervous casting down of her eyes to suggest there'd been anything more going on than her playing for Warren. It still wasn't enough to put Rupert off.

'Good afternoon.' Rupert bowed to her, his greeting more salacious than salutary.

'What are you doing here?' Warren demanded. No introduction was necessary. They'd met at Lady Cartwright's.

'Now there's a warm reception,' Rupert complained before he focused again on Marianne, or more correctly, her chest. 'Miss Domville, it's a pleasure to see you again. I hadn't expected it to be at Priorton.'

'Where did you expect it to be?' Her question was as sharp as it was challenging, but it failed to knock the cocky arrogance out of Rupert.

'Not with Warren.'

'Miss Domville is an accomplished pianist. Mother invited her to play the Érard.' The excuse for her being here sounded about as convincing as the ones the schoolboys used to tell his father after arriving late to lessons.

'You should come and play for me some time. I'd very much like to enjoy your well-developed talent too,' Rupert sniggered.

'Shut your mouth, Rupert.' Warren rounded the curved back of the piano and placed himself between Marianne and his brother-in-law.

'When you're in my house you'll act like a gentleman to all my guests or I'll demand the return of my funding for your venture. Do you understand?'

'I do,' he stuttered, stunned out of his smarmy regard.

'Then apologise to the lady.' He stepped aside and motioned to Marianne.

With the petulance of a schoolboy, Rupert bowed to her. 'My apologies, Miss Domville.'

She said nothing. Warren didn't blame her for not offering her acceptance. Rupert's apology wasn't heartfelt.

'Where's your mother?' Rupert glanced around, making the lack of a chaperon apparent. Warren wondered the same thing. She'd sent Rupert here, why hadn't she followed? He'd promised Marianne there'd be no scandal and he'd keep his word.

Marianne rose from the piano and collected her composition book without any stumbling rush of excuses as to why she'd been caught alone with a gentleman. Her expression was as solemn as an angel's on a gravestone. It would be Warren's headstone she'd erect for this near miss. Thankfully, his mother appeared, out of breath as though she were in a hurry.

'Here I am. The cook waylaid me with some silly thing about dinner. Rupert, you were supposed to wait for me,' she chided, adding more credence to there being nothing out of the ordinary taking place in the music room. 'Miss Domville, thank you so much for allowing me to listen to your wonderful playing. Lady Ellington's coach is waiting for you. I'll walk you to it.'

'Good day, Sir Warren.' Marianne dipped a curtsy to him, her eyes revealing little of her thoughts until she flicked a hard glance at Rupert. Without another word, she followed Warren's mother out of the room.

Once she was gone, Warren headed for his study, doing his best to act as uninterested in her departure as she did. He wasn't sure her lack of regret was an act or a real desire to be as far away from him and his reprehensible brother-in-law as possible. He didn't know when he'd find out either. After this mishap, she wasn't likely to return. Panic reared inside him, but he quickly brought it under control. He'd been in worse fixes and overcome them. He'd deal with this as well.

Rupert followed him into his office, his steps tight.

'What are you doing here?' Warren asked again. 'You weren't supposed to come until next month', with plenty of time for Warren to arrange for Marianne to not be here and to avoid a potential scandal. His promise to her was at risk of being undermined and he wanted to pound his brother-in-law into the floor. Everything he'd gained with Marianne had been stomped on by this clod who wasn't likely to keep his mouth shut about what he'd seen. Curse the fool and himself for being so careless with Marianne.

'I have some things to discuss with you in regards to the business and they couldn't wait. I'd like to stay here for the next few days while I visit some potential investors.' He glanced back and forth between Warren and the study door. 'I thought you were worried about your reputation. Isn't it why you were hesitant to invest in me?'

'It is and it was.'

'Then what are you doing entertaining a woman like Miss Domville?'

'You mean a woman with the ear of Lord Falconbridge, the protection of his aunt, the Dowager Countess of Merrell. What should I do? Call her a harlot to her face like you did? How many copies of my book do you think the Marquess and his friends will buy then? After your insult, you can kiss any hope of patronage from that corner goodbye.'

Rupert ran his hand through his thinning hair, realising too late his mistake. 'There must be a better way to curry Lord Falconbridge's favour than entertaining a woman of her reputation.'

'Neither of us will have to worry about her reputation or ours if you don't tell anyone you saw her here.' His stomach tightened with the whiff of deceit behind the comment, but he didn't want Rupert to mention Marianne's presence to the wrong person. If Rupert had a stake in keeping her visit a secret, he was more likely to watch his stupid tongue.

'Of course I won't say anything. I don't want our venture tarnished any more than you do.'

'It's not *our* venture. It's *your* venture.' Warren rubbed his hand over Lancelot's head as the dog came to sit beside him. It didn't calm him like it usually did. 'You're to stop using my name to promote it.'

'Yes, yes, I got your letter. I need you to sign the investment papers for *my* venture,' Rupert testily clarified. 'I also need the other half of the money you promised.'

'I never promised it. The amount I already gave you will have to do.'

'Damn it, Warren, I was counting on more.' Desperation replaced the spite in his brown eyes. 'I've already spent the funds from the other investors.'

'On what?'

'Necessary expenses,' Rupert mumbled.

Warren stared at the man, disgusted. 'You squandered it, didn't you?'

'There was a ship and a captain to hire and investors to woo.'

'How many fancy dinners and bottles of wine fed your cravings instead of wooing investors or paying for crews?'

He had the gall to appear insulted. 'You're using these unfounded accusations to renege on your promise.'

'Then show me your ledgers. Bring them here

and outline each expense and how it was used to further your business. I'll have Mr Reed go through it and we'll see how unfounded my accusations are.'

Rupert's jaw ground as he worked to concoct another lie, another excuse to explain his dishonesty.

'Don't bother telling me anything else,' Warren warned.

'What am I going to do without your support?'

'You have your small inheritance, which is more than I had when I first started out. Use it to save yourself or did you squander it too?'

The angry pursing of Rupert's lips told him he had. 'You have tons of money, but you deny me even the smallest help.'

'You had the chance to take my assistance, and that of everyone who believed in your venture, and do something with it. Instead you wasted it. From here on out, whether you succeed or fail is according to your own effort and will, which, from what I've seen, is sorely lacking.'

Rupert swallowed hard, staring at the floor as if Lancelot might rise up to help him win the argument. 'You wouldn't have behaved like this if Leticia were still alive.'

For the first time, Rupert's reminder didn't fill Warren with guilt. 'You're right, but she isn't.'

'And whose fault is that?' Rupert hissed.

Warren slammed his fist on the desk, making the ink jars rattle in their holders. 'Get out and don't ever step foot in this house again. You don't deserve my help.'

Rupert flung one last look of hate at Warren before turning on his heel and storming out of the room. It was then Warren noticed his mother hovering in the doorway.

Warren righted the ink jar, trying to calm the tremors of rage filling him. Even when Rupert's whole world was crumbling in on him, he still tried to blame Warren for both his failures and Leticia's death. For too long he'd allowed him to use her memory against him, to ignore the worm of a man in front of him as though she were still alive. He wouldn't allow it any longer. 'How much did you hear?'

'Enough to confirm something I've been considering for a long time.'

Warren rubbed the side of his stinging hand.

'I held on to him because he reminded me of Leticia.'

'We both did.' She came up to Warren and laid a comforting hand on his arm. 'I know I don't talk about her much and have often discouraged you from speaking of her as well. I worried about you when you went into the Navy, frightened each time the post came I'd learn you'd been killed. I didn't want to lose you. I didn't think she'd be the one to die young.'

Warren stared down at his mother, stunned. It was the first time she hadn't shied away from discussing Leticia. His openness had increased hers and it never would have happened if he hadn't told Marianne. Once again, when he'd wanted to help her, she'd been the one who'd helped him. 'I didn't know.'

'We're too much alike, not admitting to others how we really feel. Your father used to complain about it.' She offered him a light smile which quickly faded. 'You blame yourself for what happened, but I don't blame you. You did everything you could.'

Warren sighed, weary of it all. 'It wasn't enough.'

'Sometimes nothing is. I saw so much of it in

all the parishes I was in with your father.' His mother touched the book on castles. 'I don't say this lightly because like you, I miss her every day, but it's time for us to recall other, better memories.'

He didn't know how to move past his sister's death any more than he knew how to rid himself of the horrors of the Navy. Leaving Leticia to the past felt too much like a betrayal of her memory and everything she'd ever done for him, yet clinging to his grief had not brought her back. He looked at the ink jar, thinking of Marianne as she'd stood here listening to him. In her quiet voice, she'd told him Leticia's death wasn't his fault and for the first time, he'd believed it. Maybe she was the one who could lead him out of this grief stealing his voice and threatening to ruin his entire life.

Lancelot's collar jingled as he scratched himself with his back paw.

'What'll you do about Miss Domville? She was very hesitant when I asked if she'd return tomorrow,' his mother asked.

Warren pinched the bridge of his nose, the promise of Marianne decreasing as the troubles of the last half-hour increased. There was nothing stopping Rupert from telling anyone his suspicions about Warren and Marianne, and Warren wouldn't put it past the weasel to say something simply out of spite. Despite the risk, Warren wouldn't pay Rupert to keep silent or allow his brother-in-law to influence him ever again. He'd find another way to protect Marianne and uphold his promise to not allow their arrangement to result in a scandal. If it did, she would need him and he would stand by her, not because he was the cause of it but because he cared for her. She had fast become more than his muse.

Marianne crept closer to the downstairs sitting room, not wanting to announce her presence to Lady Ellington and Lord Falconbridge. They must not have heard the carriage return from Priorton Abbey, but she'd seen his horse in the stable and knew he was here. Marianne leaned against the wall beside the open door to listen, the composition book clutched in her hand. She hadn't done this since she'd lived with Madame de Badeau. Back then, she used to listen at keyholes all the time. She couldn't help it this afternoon.

'I have my reservations about this arrangement.' Lord Falconbridge's deep voice carried out from the room. 'You remember how it was with you and Uncle Edgar and how he almost dragged you down with his appalling behaviour.'

'Edgar also taught me to live my life as I please and not to allow others' opinions to influence me. I want Marianne to learn the same lesson,' Lady Ellington insisted.

'And you think Sir Warren is the one to teach it to her?'

'Yes. He's a single gentleman of good reputation and means with an interest in her. Granted, he's come up with a very complicated way of going about things, but there's a man for you,' came Lady Ellington's cheerful if not practical response. 'Look at how difficult you made things with Cecelia.'

The rumble of Lord Falconbridge's laugh filled the hallway before he sobered. 'But this arrangement could do her more harm than good. Miss Domville doesn't have our stamina for weathering storms.'

'If you hadn't created so many tempests in your youth, neither would you.' The clink of the crystal stopper in Lady Ellington's plum wine decanter drifted out of the room.

'What if you're wrong about him and he doesn't pursue her?' Lord Falconbridge pressed.

Marianne clutched the composition book against her chest, the worry she'd carried home from Priorton intensifying. Lord Falconbridge's fears weren't unfounded. Warren had said he wasn't interested in marriage and she'd still flung herself at him moments before his snake of a brother-in-law had walked in. If he hadn't called out and alerted them, who knew what he might have seen.

'I'm not wrong,' Lady Ellington insisted.

'For Miss Domville's sake, and her future here in the country, I hope so.'

Panic made it impossible for Marianne to stand here without revealing herself. She hurried away, tiptoeing up the main staircase, past Lady Ellington's impressive collection of Italian landscapes covering the stairway wall.

Once inside her room, she closed and locked the door, then slumped into the chair in front of the writing table. Yet another letter from Theresa waited for her on the blotter. She covered it with her composition book, not possessing the fortitude to open the missive and read about her friend's happiness, not when her present situation was so precarious. Beneath them lay the journal with *Lady Matilda's Trials*, another glaring example of the mistakes she was making with Warren.

She rose to pace across the room. Her lack of discretion and judgement with him was putting her place with the Falconbridges in jeopardy and there was more than her reputation at stake. For all Lord Falconbridge's and Lady Ellington's support, it had only ever been against invented and imagined scandals. Whether they'd continue to stand with her in the face of a real one of her own making, she wasn't sure. She'd been acquainted with Lord Falconbridge through her mother in the days before he'd married Cecilia. Back then, he'd been hailed as one of the most formidable rakes in London. He'd abandoned his old life and reputation when he'd married the Marchioness. He wouldn't appreciate it being revived because of Marianne's wanton behaviour, especially with his children to consider. If Marianne crossed the line of decency, he might insist the family abandon her, just like Mr Smith had.

I should have been more careful with Warren. I never should have kissed him.

She'd resisted the lechers without money and the lechers with it to rise above the filth Madame de Badeau had tried to mire her in. The kiss proved she couldn't resist Warren or his continued eroding of the distance she needed to maintain between them. Except she didn't want to stay away.

She slipped *Lady Matilda's Trials* out from beneath the letter and composition book and flipped through the pages, admiring Warren's fine handwriting filling every line. Marianne traced the large M in Lady Matilda's name, the memory of Warren's light hair curling over his proud forehead, his striking green eyes and the firmness of his body against hers stirring something inside. Their kiss today hadn't been about lust or loss of control, but compassion. She'd offered him a glimpse of her soul and instead of turning away he'd embraced her. If she pushed him out of her life, she might never discover where her heart and his might lead them, assuming he did want to pursue her. Lord Falconbridge was right. Warren might not crave anything more from her than a dalliance. She didn't want to be punished for wanting love or affection, but she feared losing Lady Ellington over something as thin as possibility. She hoped Warren didn't make her regret being so free with him today.

She flicked the book shut. What had hope ever garnered her except more heartache? At the Protestant School, she'd hoped every Christmas for a real family, and then her real mother had snatched her away. In London, she'd hoped to return to the Smiths, but they hadn't wanted her. She pulled opened the desk drawer and shoved the journal inside then slapped it shut. Her agreement with Warren was over. She wouldn't return to Priorton Abbey or perform her compositions for anyone outside this house. She wouldn't risk losing the safety of Lady Ellington's care for the uncertainty of Warren's promises. No matter what came of today, her behaviour from this moment forward must be beyond reproach. It was the safest course, and the most disheartening.

'Lord Cartwright, thank you for meeting with me on such short notice about the business.' Rupert all but grovelled beside the Baron, who accepted a loaded gun from his footman.

'Yes, yes, of course,' the haughty man mumbled as he raised his gun and let off a shot, bringing down a pheasant. His dog took off in search of the carcase. 'I understand from my man in London Sir Warren is backing this venture of yours?'

'He believes in it so much, he's—'

'Wait a moment.' Lord Cartwright raised his gun and let off an ear-piercing shot at another pheasant flying up out of the grass. He missed. 'Damn it, Alton, something is wrong with this gun.'

'Yes, sir.' The footman exchanged the empty gun for another and laid the offending piece aside.

'What were you saying about Sir Warren?' Lord Cartwright lowered his barrel to the ground, keeping an eye on the grey sky as he listened to Rupert.

'Sir Warren has placed Priorton Abbey up for collateral against any debts the company incurs. Even if things go wrong, you can't lose your investment.' Warren might not know it, but he'd help Rupert one way or another. 'If a man like him has faith in me, surely you can. He also has the backing of the Marquess of Falconbridge through his connection with Miss Domville.'

'What's he doing associating with her?' Lord Cartwright raised his gun and fired. This time he hit his mark and another dog went running into the field.

'Sir Warren and Miss Domville are quite *intimately* acquainted.' Rupert took Lord Cartwright's empty gun and handed it to the footman before taking the loaded one and offering it to the Baron. How he hated these grand men and all their privileges. Warren thought he was one of them and better than Rupert. Rupert would show him and make him pay for insisting he beg before him like one of the serfs in his novels.

'Really?' Lord Cartwright appeared more interested in the gossip than all Rupert's talk of investments and collateral.

'I expect the Marquess to invest heavily in the business because of it. You could make a great deal of money, enough to finance your daughter's second Season.' Rupert had heard the rumours of Lord Cartwright's mounting gambling debts and his displeasure at his daughter's failure to make a lucrative match last Season.

Lord Cartwright rubbed his thumb over the shiny brass work on his gun, allowing a few pheasants scared up by the beaters to fly away as he considered Rupert's suggestion. 'You're sure it's secure?'

Rupert tried not to scream in frustration. What did this man care if it was secure or not? With his lands and money he could stand to part with a few pounds. Even if he couldn't, with his heritage he'd be shielded from his debts in a way Rupert hadn't been when his last venture had collapsed. Even then Warren had lectured him like a child about the need for responsibility. Rupert would teach him a lesson about where his responsibilities really lay. 'Sir Warren's name and fame is a guarantee against loss.'

'All right,' Lord Cartwright said at last, handing the gun to the footman. 'I'll write to my man to deposit double the amount we discussed in your account.'

'You're too gracious, my lord.' Rupert kept the smile on his face, despite his disgust. This man had nothing but assets and lands and Rupert was forced to cajole and wheedle to get a few pounds out of him. The man should give it willingly and more, he owed it to people like Rupert, just like Warren did. Rupert would see to it they both felt the sting of being selfish, especially Warren who'd regret treating Rupert with so much disdain.

Chapter Eight

Marianne sat at the pianoforte at Welton Place, trying to reclaim the flow of the music, to allow it to carry her away like it usually did, but she couldn't. It had been a full day since Warren's brother-in-law had stumbled in on her and Warren at the Érard. Every time she passed a clutch of whispering maids, she wondered if they were talking about her. She was sure any moment now the rumours about her and Warren would begin, followed by Lord Falconbridge demanding an explanation.

She glanced at the garden where Walker was raking leaves, considering a walk, anything to settle the nervousness making her tap her foot against the floor. Potential gossip wasn't the only thing making her want to stride out of the French doors. She'd sent a note to Warren first thing this morning to tell him she wouldn't come today. She hadn't gone as far as to end their arrangement, nor had she offered a reason for her absence. After yesterday, she hardly thought one was necessary.

She'd heard nothing from Warren in response. He hadn't sent her a note, come to call or, at the very least, sent his mother for tea. Maybe he'd at last decided she was more of a detriment to him than an asset and it was best to distance himself from her. After all, he had a reputation to protect too. Her chest constricted at the thought, making her fingers clumsy on the keys when she attempted to play again. He was going to turn his back on her like everyone else. She'd been a fool to grow close to him, to reveal so much and to believe it would make a difference.

'Are you still here, my dear?' Lady Ellington strolled through the room on her way out to the garden to oversee the pruning of her roses. 'Isn't Sir Warren expecting you?'

'I don't feel like going to Priorton today.'

'Did something happen when you were last

there?' Lady Ellington perched her elbow on the edge of the pianoforte.

'No.' She couldn't tell Lady Ellington about the kiss, not because the woman would dance with glee, but because she feared a completely different reaction.

'Marianne?' Lady Ellington pressed, increasing Marianne's guilt over her lack of faith in her friend. Lady Ellington had always believed in her, she shouldn't doubt her faith now.

Marianne stopped playing and picked at a small imperfection in one of the white keys 'Yes, something did happen.'

Lady Ellington stood over Marianne and listened as she told her about the brother-in-law and his coming in on them alone together and insulting her. Marianne omitted the kiss, but given the scrutinising tilt of Lady Ellington's head, it was clear she suspected something more than the two of them performing a duet. If she minded or was disappointed in Marianne for having been so weak with Warren, it was difficult to discern.

'He stood up for you against a man related to him by marriage. It says a great deal about Sir

Warren's regard for you,' Lady Ellington observed.

Marianne had a better inkling of his regard for her than Lady Ellington realised, but she didn't dare say so. 'He was being polite and if Mr Hirst is still there, I don't want to place Wa— I mean Sir Warren in another difficult situation.'

Lady Ellington worked to hide her smile at Marianne's near slip. 'Sir Warren is a grown man and more than capable of deciding which situations he wants to be in and which he does not.'

'If he wanted me to come back, I'm sure he would have said something by now, but he hasn't.' Nor had she ventured from Welton Place. She wouldn't run after Warren, but deport herself with dignity.

Darby, Lady Ellington's stone-faced butler, appeared in the doorway. 'Sir Warren to see Miss Domville.'

Marianne's eyes snapped to Lady Ellington's. He was here. He'd come to see her.

Lady Ellington clapped her hands together in delight. 'One day without you and he's already sprinting over here to visit you.'

'It took him quite a few hours to sprint,' Marianne grumbled, wishing she'd gone for a walk in the garden. It would take crossing all of the Falconbridge lands to calm her now since she couldn't very well pace a hole in the floorboards.

'You'll learn, my dear, it takes men a little longer to come around to things. Darby, show Sir Warren in at once.'

The butler left before Marianne could stop him.

'What if he isn't here to see me, but to end things?' This was what she'd wanted when she'd drafted the letter ending the agreement, the one sitting unsealed on her writing table in her room. She should have sent it and made things clear before he could come over here and clarify them for her. It would hurt less if she was to break with him instead of him breaking with her.

'If he wanted to end things he'd send a note, not come here in person.'

She hoped Lady Ellington was right. She didn't want to endure another rejection like the one the Smiths had sent her four years ago.

Marianne dropped her hands in her lap and twisted around to face the sitting-room door. She attempted to affect her usual air of indifference, but it wasn't easy. Whatever he said, she would disregard it as she did Lady Cartwright's snide remarks. She could cry over it later.

No, I won't cry.

Warren entered the room and Marianne willed the creeping smile from her lips. He wore a dark blue coat as wrinkled as his untidy cravat. His hair was combed smooth over the back of his head, but the ends possessed a wildness which matched his attire. A generous smile lightened the dark circles beneath his eyes and increased the faint flutter in her stomach. No one smiled so wide before they ended an affair as she'd seen more than once at Madame de Badeau's.

He bowed to them, clutching a notebook and writing case in his left hand. 'Good morning, Lady Ellington, Miss Domville. I'm very sorry Miss Domville was unable to come to Priorton today. I hope it isn't too presumptuous of me to ask if I may work here instead.'

He wants to be with me, to keep our arrangement.

It thrilled her as much as when new sheet music arrived from London. Dread quickly squashed it.

She still had no idea what was happening with Mr Hirst and what, if anything, had come of his visit. She wanted to ask Warren about it, but with Lady Ellington present she couldn't. Whatever had taken place between them after she'd left it must not have been too awful if he was here.

'What a lovely idea,' Lady Ellington answered while Marianne remained too lost in her thoughts to speak. The Dowager guided him to the escritoire to the left of the pianoforte. It sat against the window so anyone working there could see the garden with their back to the instrument. 'I've missed having music in the house these last few days. Are you sure you can work here?'

He leaned one hand on the rounded chair back, his other hand perched on his hip and drawing his coat back to reveal his solid middle. The sensation of his body against hers, his wide hand on her neck, his flat chest firm against hers made her skin flush at the memory.

'I used to write aboard ship, in the middle of storms. A foreign desk and some lovely playing won't distract me.' His eyes met Marianne's. She kept her outward stature as impassive as possible while inside she was running in circles.

He hadn't left her, but had sought her out as though she were more important than rumours or brothers-in-law or anything else. However, it had taken him a day to do so. Had he wavered during their time apart or considered not coming here? If he held any doubts they were not in his soft eyes or the sureness of his stance. 'I won't disturb you, will I?'

'Of course not.' She flicked through the pages of her composition book, searching for something to play as if he were not here. For all her excitement at his arrival, the old caution refused to release its hold on her. She'd been careless with him yesterday and she wouldn't allow it to happen again.

The shift of his shoulders while he arranged his things on the desk undermined her determination. She studied the width of his back, noting how the wool wrinkled and flattened with each movement, sliding up over the curve of his buttocks as he leaned forward to set out his ink. She gripped the book tight, wrinkling a whole note near the edge of one page. She wanted to wrap her arms around his waist, lay her head on his shoulder and breathe him in like the mist in the morning.

Don't be silly.

She smoothed the wrinkled edge of her music and set the book on the stand. Her mother had thrown herself at any man with a title and money. Marianne had never behaved so basely. Her experience with Warren was an exception, not a habit, and she wouldn't allow it to continue. She'd find out more about Mr Hirst later, then make it clear to Warren their behaviour from the other day was not to be repeated. He wanted a muse and she'd be one. He could find more physical inspiration elsewhere.

As Marianne played, Lady Ellington waved her fingers in time to the music, her smile so wide one would think she'd arranged this. She probably had. Marianne should be annoyed by her friend's meddling, but she wasn't. At least the Dowager was more conscientious in her chaperon duties than Mrs Stevens.

Marianne paused to scratch a few notes in the composition book when Lady Ellington interrupted. 'If you'll excuse me, Walker is waiting for me in the garden.'

And there went the chaperon. Marianne frowned as the breeze fluttered the hem of Lady Ellington's grey pelisse as she hurried out of the French doors to where Walker waited with his pruning shears to trim the roses.

Warren turned in his chair, about to speak, but Marianne resumed her playing, not wanting to talk. It had already landed them both in too much trouble. He didn't interrupt her as he returned to his writing.

Under the influence of her music, she began to relax and enjoy his presence. In their separate spaces, they worked in tandem as if they'd done this for years. The clink of his pen against the ink jar punctuated her notes every now and again. It didn't disturb her pace, but at times enhanced it like a harmony from an accompanying flute. It settled the tension from his presence and the other day's debacle.

The melancholy tune which had teased her last night, the one she'd been reluctant to sit down and write this morning, faded into the background as a new one came forward. It startled Marianne with its effervescence and she followed its lead, playing with a vigour she hadn't experienced since the last time she'd performed for Mrs Nichols. It wasn't the piece but Warren's presence creating the change. She didn't fight it and slid into the music, not like a cave to hide in, but as if it was a pool of cool water on a hot day.

A long time passed before Lady Ellington returned. Pollen from the last of the summer roses clung to her dark skirt as she carried them to the vase on top of the pianoforte. While she arranged the flowers, she looked back and forth between the two young people and smiled with a self-satisfaction Marianne didn't mind. When Marianne reached the end of the piece, Lady Ellington clapped.

'It's too lovely a day for you both to be inside for so long. Marianne, why don't you show Sir Warren the garden?' Lady Ellington suggested to Marianne's amazement.

The peace Marianne had enjoyed while playing ended. Why didn't Lady Ellington draw the curtains and lock them in the room together? It would be more effective.

'Yes, I need some exercise.' Warren stretched

over the back of the chair, the arch of his body more appealing than the buds in the vase.

We shouldn't be alone together...we can't be trusted.

She couldn't beg Lady Ellington to stay with them like a child afraid of the dark. Warren had been brave to come here unannounced. She could summon enough courage and self-control to walk with him in the garden, in broad daylight and in plain sight of the house. It wasn't as if she were dragging him to the orangery, as tempting an idea as it might be. No, it wasn't tempting but ridiculous and it was time to compose herself like a proper lady and not some hoyden. 'All right, then.'

She rose from the piano bench and led him outside. Lady Ellington's excuse for not coming followed after them. A stiff wind whipped through the garden, blowing dead leaves off of the fading summer vines and revealing more of the provocative statuary. Marianne regretted bringing him here to walk. She should have taken him to the front of the house. Perhaps he wouldn't notice the statues.

'Lady Ellington has some very unique garden

decorations,' Warren remarked as they passed a well-endowed satyr.

'The house used to belong to her brother, the prior Marquess of Falconbridge. These were his statues. For some reason, she's never got rid of them.'

'Maybe they remind her of him.' With a smile, he nodded to the naked Zeus entwined with a nymph.

'Given some of the stories she's told me about him, they probably do.' Marianne had never minded the garden decor before. Today, all the naked marble bodies in a variety of suggestive poses made the unspoken between her and Warren even louder. She still didn't know what to think of the kiss, or him. He hadn't groped her like other men, but it had still been secretive, with no promise of anything else except possible rumours. She kicked a small pebble with her boot. It didn't matter. There was no future with him or any respectable man and no reason for her to think of one.

'Your playing has had quite an effect on my story today. I couldn't write my war scene so I finished the feasting one instead. Sometimes critics accuse my novels of being too dark. I don't think they'll say the same about this one.' He laughed with an agility Marianne admired. 'I hope you don't mind the intrusion, but I needed to see you.'

'For me or my inspiration?' She stopped and faced him, needing the truth.

'Both.' He studied her, his green eyes intense like a field of fresh grass in the spring. 'I cut off my dealings with Rupert because of what he said to you.'

'You think there's more to be gained by associating with a woman like me than a man like him?' It didn't seem possible.

'Yes.' His honesty shook her expectations. Few people had ever been worried about losing her. Here was one who wouldn't let her run away. It scared her more than any rumour or scandal she'd ever faced and fuelled the hope which had been building inside her since their kiss. If they weren't standing in the centre of the garden, she might slide her hands over his broad shoulders and pull him down to her. She raised her hands anyway, resisting the inclination to cow before her worries and doubts. This morning, she'd thought he'd never want to see her again and here he was in front of her as though she were as important to him as the Prince.

He shifted closer to her as her hands settled on his shoulders, his body hard beneath her palms. He stared into her eyes with mesmerising intensity which drew them closer. She began to slide up on her toes as his arms encircled her, aching to taste him again, to restore the connection between them which had been broken the other day.

Then the squeak of a wheel sounded over the birds. She jumped back from Warren just as Walker came around the corner rolling a wheelbarrow full of dirt. He waved to them. Warren waved back without hesitation. Marianne wasn't as exuberant with her greeting.

'We always seem to attract an audience,' he joked, but she didn't laugh.

If they kept up these near misses it wouldn't be long before his decision to stand beside her was tested. She expected him to fail, almost everyone else had. It was time for them to exhibit more decorum, especially in Lady Ellington's garden. 'Walker isn't a gossip. Is Mr Hirst?'

He fiddled with the loose knot of his cravat, the gesture more telling than his words. 'I made it clear his ruining your reputation would ruin his. Besides, he saw nothing.'

'It doesn't matter. He guessed enough and it's all he or anyone needs to condemn me, and you too. You could lose patrons and people's support.' She didn't mention what she might lose. She didn't want to think about it.

'I sold books and earned money before people like the Cartwrights or even the Prince found me. I can do it again. I don't care what they think of me or what they might say.'

'Some day you will, just like the Smiths, and then I won't be as tempting to you.' She started for the house.

He caught her hand. 'You think you aren't worthy to be cared for, made to feel important and valuable, but you're wrong.'

She tried to pull away, but he wouldn't let go, his hand firm around hers. 'Experience has taught me different.'

'I'm not like them.' He drew her slowly back to him. She put up the weakest of resistance, moving step by step closer to him. She didn't want to fight him as she did the rest of the world, but believe in his affection. It was foolish, ridiculous, but her lonely heart didn't care. She wanted to lose herself in his desire for her. They stood so close her breasts brushed his chest with each of her deep breaths. He continued to hold her hand while his other smoothed the wisps of hair from her temples. 'You're a wonderful person and others are shallow and blind if they can't see it.'

He tilted his face down and she lifted her chin. His kiss jolted her like a carriage thrown off balance in a turn. She clutched his arms to steady herself, not against him, but from the old habit of retreating. Even if she'd wanted to run away from him, his light hand against the small of her back wouldn't allow it. She folded her body into his, lost in his heady heat. She reached her fingers up to touch the hair brushing his collar, the strands as soft beneath her fingertips as his mouth. He'd come here because he didn't want to be without her. In her answering kiss she reassured him she wouldn't bolt, but would stumble with him through whatever was burgeoning between them.

'Sir Warren.' Darby's voice cut through her joy.

As fast as Warren's kiss had united them, the butler's appearance sent them flying apart. Marianne wanted to scream in frustration. She and Warren should consider sending invitations to their next meeting. It would be more convenient for all involved.

'A message has come for you from Priorton Abbey,' Darby announced. 'You're needed at your publisher's in London right away.'

Darby's message delivered, he left the couple. Marianne wanted to stomp her foot at his pretend deference. He wasn't as tight-lipped as Walker and was probably whispering what he'd seen to Lady Ellington already. The Dowager Countess would clap her ring-covered hands in glee. The picture of it settled her anger for it was exactly what she hoped her friend would do. She could now tell Lord Falconbridge there was more to Marianne and Warren's arrangement than impetuous desire or skirting scandal. What exactly it was Marianne refused to say. She was too afraid to give voice to such a thing and kill it like a seedling planted before the threat of frost had passed.

'I have to go. If Mr Berkshire has sent for me,

it must be important,' he explained with notable regret.

'When will you return?' She didn't want him to leave. It was the rare person who returned to her.

'I don't know, it depends on what Mr Berkshire wants, but I'll make sure to be back in time for Lady Astley's musical evening. You will be there, won't you?'

'Yes.'

'Then I look forward to it.' He claimed her lips with a swift kiss, catching her off guard. She grasped his firm upper arms, not wanting to let go, his kiss more honest than any words. He broke from her and she wavered on her feet, unable to say anything before he touched her cheek longingly with his fingers, then turned and made for the house.

Snatches of his parting conversation with Lady Ellington carried out of the open sitting-room windows before it faded way.

Smoothing her hair and adjusting the wrinkled fichu over her chest, she returned to the house, trying not to skip back. He'd kissed her, again, and told her she was more precious to him than his brother-in-law. It hadn't happened in a darkened room, or while he was drunk, but in the open for everyone to see, eliminating doubts about his intentions, especially hers. If Darby hadn't interrupted them, who knew what other declarations he might have made.

Her cheeks burned as she caught sight of Lady Ellington waiting for her, a self-satisfied smile adorning her lips. It seems Darby had been quick to report to his mistress.

'Too bad Sir Warren was forced to leave so soon,' Lady Ellington lamented as Marianne stepped inside. 'It was quite nice of him to come to see you today.'

'It was.' Marianne leaned against the door jamb and stared at the desk where his papers had sat a short time ago. The surface was empty again, with no sign he'd been here, but she knew, the whole house did. He wanted her and she wanted him. She touched her swollen lips, his kiss still lingering there and with it the promise of what could happen when they met again. A passion for anything beside the pianoforte was dangerous, but it didn't mean she couldn't wield a little of its power. Perhaps it was time to play up her less musical assets. 'I've been thinking, maybe a new gown for the musical evening would be a good idea. Perhaps a blue one like you mentioned the other day?'

'You mean something like this?' Lady Ellington slid a ladies' magazine off of the table beside her and flipped it open. She held it out to Marianne, struggling as much as her young friend to refrain from showing too much enthusiasm. 'It would be stunning on you.'

Marianne leaned forward, her eyebrows rising at the cut of the neckline, not sure even the stiffest brocade could contain her. Tongues would wag if she wore something so daring, but never in her life had she wanted a man's consideration as she did Warren's and she would have it. A new dress, and the fondness created by his absence, would all but guarantee it. 'How fast do you think Madame Martine can sew the dress?'

Lady Ellington flipped closed the magazine and set it aside with a triumphant smile. 'As I've already sent her instructions to do it up based on your last measurements, I'd say very soon.'

'What was so important you had to summon me from Sussex?' Warren demanded as he strode into Mr Berkshire's London office, his legs complaining from the three-hour ride. Whatever it was, it had got his notice and was the only thing short of a fire at Priorton which could have separated him from Marianne and her glorious figure against his.

Mr Berkshire pushed himself up out of the leather chair behind his massive oak desk. He wasn't fat, but solidly built like a dockworker. Despite his size, he possessed the authority and self-assuredness of the aristocrats he flattered to secure their patronage for his authors. He also specialised in anonymous memoirs of wronged society mistresses. He had yet to betray a pen name while marketing salacious stories the public ate up. He held out a copy of the *Morning Post* to Warren. 'Read this.'

Warren took the newspaper and read the headline proclaiming the latest debate in Parliament for the Pains and Penalties Bill against Queen Charlotte. What the devil was he supposed to be reading? 'I assume you didn't bring me to London to discuss the proceedings against the Queen.'

Mr Berkshire pointed a stubby finger at the paper. 'Look at the piece about halfway down.'

Warren found the small article near the bottom, under one lamenting the rising price of wheat. Calling it an article was being generous. It was the latest tattle about a duke and his mistress. The next line made Warren start to sweat.

The famous novelist Sir W—has been enjoying the delights of the country and Lady P—n's vast estates. Even the dowager Countess of M's companion, a young lady of dubious background, whose notorious relation caused quite the scandal four years ago, has been snared by the Lothario's literary ways.

The moisture on his fingers smudged the ink and blurred the last few words. The *Morning Post* was a cut-rate rag with more gossip than news, but the salacious stories it published were as popular in London as they were in Sussex. It would only be a matter of time before this one found its way to the country, and Marianne and everyone else's attention.

'What have you been getting up to at Priorton?' Mr Berkshire asked as he took his seat.

'Nothing with Lady Preston.' Warren flung the paper down on the desk.

Mr Berkshire's bushy eyebrows rose. 'Then the rest is true?'

'It's not a dalliance.' It was a great deal more. With the memory of Marianne in his arms, new stories had begun to fill his mind during the hours he'd spent on the road. It had made the endless countryside pass without notice until the smoke of London had appeared in the distance, just like the craving to be near her had carried him from Priorton this morning. When he'd received her note crying off, he'd refused to let it stand or to allow the incident with Rupert to fester and undo all the progress they'd made. He'd gone to Welton Place, expecting to be turned away, not welcomed by both Lady Ellington and especially Marianne. Writing beside her, he'd felt the excitement and potential which used to fill him with each new story return. It had hurt him to leave her and the pleasure of her kiss, but for the first time in too long he felt like the old Warren, the one who could create not only tales, but every aspect of his own life.

'Whatever it is, it's not time spent writing. It's been a year since you've given me anything new,' Mr Berkshire reminded him, illustrating how much further Warren still had to go until he was his old self.

'The repairs to Priorton have interrupted me, but I assure you, you'll have something within the month.' If Mr Berkshire doubted Warren's ability to produce, his biggest ally might find himself another author to support.

Mr Berkshire thumped the top of his desk. 'I warned you not to buy the thing. Being lord of the manor is distracting you from your real purpose. Stay here in London and work in the peace of your town house.'

'No, I need the quiet of the country and Miss Domville. She's helping me, the way Leticia used to. The rest will soon be resolved.'

Mr Berkshire leaned forward on his burly arms and spoke with more caution than he usually displayed with Warren. 'If financial issues are hindering your writing, I can always help.'

Warren shook his head. 'I've never taken

money from you that I haven't earned, I won't do it now.'

'But you will earn it.' Mr Berkshire threw up his hands, unable to comprehend Warren's reluctance. Sometimes Warren didn't either, but it was who he was and he wasn't going to allow difficulty to make him change. He would fight through his troubles like he always had.

'When I do, you will pay it to me and not before.'

'Then hurry up with things. You know how fickle the public is. Wait too long and they'll forget you.'

'Not with pieces like this running in the paper.'

'Mr Steed is already taking the necessary steps to make sure the publisher of this fish wrap is silenced by the threat of a libel suit.' Mr Steed was one of the best solicitors in London. To be involved with him in a hearing was to have it in all the papers and to lose, expensively. 'Who do you think sold them the story?'

'It could have been Rupert.' He explained about their falling out. 'He's never shown this much initiative, but he has the most reason to hurt me and he needs the money.'

'Then you'd better make it clear to him that if he sells any more stories like this he'll have Mr Steed to deal with.'

'I'll see what I can do before I return to Sussex.' Warren didn't pity his brother-in-law. Rupert deserved every punishment he received.

'I think I'll come with you to the country. Get in a little hunting and see for myself what's going on there and soothe things over with Lord Preston. Can't have him turning his back on you. He's influential, it'll encourage others.' Mr Berkshire shifted back in his chair and hooked his thumbs in his waistcoat pocket.

'I don't need a chaperon,' Warren retorted. There'd be enough for him to deal with when he returned without Mr Berkshire hovering over him. Including finishing the book and explaining to Marianne why she was now in the gossip column. He'd promised her no scandal. For the second time in a week he'd failed to keep his promise. If he wanted her in his life, he'd have to win her before she found out about this. It was time to prove his faith in her and them, not because of his work, but because of his heart. He'd lost it to her and in doing so he'd regained something of the man he'd been before the tragedy of Leticia's death. His confidence in himself and his stories had returned with her tenderness and understanding. He wouldn't lose it or her.

Chapter Nine

Marianne entered Lady Astley's ballroom with a nauseating mixture of apprehension and anticipation. Everyone turned to view her, their eyes never rising above the low-cut neckline of her shimmering blue-silk gown. There was nothing vulgar about the dress, not the sleeves covering her upper arms, the length of the skirt or the silver trim beneath the bust and along the hem. However, it was far more revealing than what they'd come to expect from her. If they couldn't see her heart beating against her chest, she'd be stunned. She'd never once showed these people her fear of them. Tonight she wanted to grab Lady Ellington by her massive diamond bracelet and race back to the carriage.

As if sensing Marianne's apprehension, Lady

Ellington twined her arm in the younger woman's and drew her deeper into the room. It wasn't just for Marianne's benefit she did this, but for everyone who looked to her and the Falconbridge family to set the tone. Marianne was grateful for the solidarity, but it wasn't enough to stop the women from whispering behind fans or to put an end to the men's lurid looks. These people wouldn't snub her with Lady Ellington present. They'd find more snide and cutting ways to make their disapproval clear, to try and chip away at her like an artist she'd once seen in Paris sculpting a block of granite. She wouldn't let them, not with Warren beside her, encouraging her as he always did, assuming he was here.

She looked over the guests, trying to ignore their silent insults and sneers as she searched among the men for him. It had been three days since he'd left her at Welton Place. She worried he hadn't returned in time for tonight. Then her bravery would be wasted, especially if he'd forgotten her in the rush of London and his work.

I shouldn't be so quick to doubt him.

He had yet to let her down.

At last she spied him. He stood near a gilded

table with a stocky gentleman she didn't recognise. As if sensing her, he turned and his jaw dropped open. Instead of wanting to cover herself, she stood up straighter, pressing her shoulders back to give him a better view of her in the dress. He stroked her with his gaze, not just her ample chest, but her entire body. A potent thrill raced along her skin and the tips of her breasts hardened beneath her stays. This wasn't the first time she'd turned a man's head, but it was the first time she'd experienced the power of being alluring and understood why it had so obsessed Madame de Badeau. If they weren't in the middle of the classically decorated sitting room, she'd rush to close the distance between them.

Instead she stood as she always did at these gatherings, as if nothing anyone said or did could pierce her steadfast surety. Even if she was crumbling inside, they'd never know, nor would she reveal the excitement she experienced at Warren's quick stride as he made his way to her. Her heart beat so fast she could feel it in every gloved fingertip.

Warren bowed to Marianne, his pulse fluttering as fast as hers above his at last properly tied cravat. The darkness of his coat across his shoulders contrasted with the green waistcoat beneath his jacket which echoed the tone of his eyes. He wore his light hair swept back off of his forehead. It had been trimmed while he'd been in town so it no longer touched the edge of his white collar.

'Did you have a good trip to London?' Lady Ellington asked while Marianne struggled to reclaim her voice. It had been startled out of her by Warren's heated regard.

The question stiffened the corners of his smile and trouble clouded his eyes before it vanished. Marianne wondered what had happened in London. Perhaps something with his book? Whatever it was, it bothered him despite his effort to hide it.

'Very productive. In fact, I brought my publisher back with me. Allow me to introduce him.' He waved over the stocky man by the fireplace. 'Miss Domville, This is Mr William Berkshire. Mr Berkshire, this is the accomplished pianist I told you about.'

'Ah, I see.' He nodded appreciatively at Warren, who offered him a terse frown, alluding to something the two of them alone understood. She wondered what Warren had said to his publisher about her. It couldn't be the more salacious tales the bucks who visited Madame de Badeau's used to exchange. Warren wasn't so crude. It was something more disturbing, one she sensed had nothing to do with books. Perhaps Mr Berkshire had doubts about her ability to play or had balked at publishing her compositions. It could easily cause tension between the two men. 'Warren told me about your gift for music and your interest in publishing your compositions. Will you be playing tonight?'

'No, I'm not. There are very few people beside Sir Warren who are aware of my playing, or my compositions.'

'Well, if Sir Warren is as talented a judge of music as he is a writer, there'll be many who learn of your music once we're done with you.'

She smiled graciously at him and his unexpected compliment. At least he wasn't resisting Warren's efforts on Marianne's behalf. It fuelled the hope she'd nurtured since Warren had first made his offer and edged out her previous worries. Maybe she could at last create a new life and reputation for herself, one free of all the people eyeing them with disapproval while she commanded the famous author's attention.

'Mr Berkshire, no business tonight. Instead, you must tell me all the gossip from town,' Lady Ellington chided with her usual grace.

'Ah, well, there isn't much to tell,' Mr Berkshire blustered and again there was the knowing exchange between the publisher and Warren. It didn't last as Lady Ellington pulled Mr Berkshire far enough away from Marianne and Warren to give them privacy, but remained close enough so no one could accuse her of abandoning her charge.

'Did all go well in London?' she asked, eager to learn what was going on.

'Yes. There was some difficulty with a newspaper, but nothing Mr Berkshire's solicitor won't see to,' he murmured before fixing her with an admiration to make her toes curl. At home, she'd fretted over wearing the gown and at the last minute had considered changing it. She was glad she hadn't. The heat in his eyes was worth every disparaging look from the other women. He, not them, was the only one who mattered. 'You're stunning.'

Experience warned her to pry and discover what he was hiding behind his charm, but she didn't want to break the spell of his adoration. 'Careful, if you flatter me too much it will go to my head and I'll think myself too important to play for you.'

'You could never be so arrogant. You're too kind and enchanting.' He shifted a touch closer and dropped his voice. 'I missed you while I was in London. Writing wasn't the same without you.'

His breath caressed the tops of her breasts, stoking the fire building deep inside her at the nearness of him. His breathing matched hers and she was sure his pulse did too, both of their hearts beating together like two perfectly timed duet players. If they could be alone, they might move with one another like dancers, his solid body against hers, leading her through every movement of this growing affection and intimacy, one as intoxicating as it was new to her.

'I've missed you too.' The admission felt as revealing as her gown, but she didn't want to hold back from him. The last two nights, she'd nearly licked her lips raw with the reliving of their last kiss. She cursed the rules of propriety stopping her from falling into his arms now and experiencing again the thrill of his mouth against hers.

The butler struck a small gong from the front of the room, silencing everyone. 'It's time to take your seats for the performance.'

The room drained as the guests entered the ballroom where the pianoforte had been moved to the centre at the far end. Chairs gathered from all over the house stood in neat rows and ladies and gentleman filed in to fill them up. An attractive but little-known singer from Austria was to perform tonight, accompanied by a young male pianist. The entertainment wouldn't pass muster in London, but it was perfect to while away a dull autumn evening in the country.

'Shall we?' Warren offered her his elbow.

She laid her hand on his arm and accompanied him into the room, excited to at last be able touch him in the only way allowed. As they fell behind the crowd, she considered slipping off with him to somewhere where they could be alone. She didn't want to share him, not even with the singer. It was tempting, but she wasn't so daring. She couldn't openly defy convention, not even for Warren.

He guided them to the chairs in the back row. She didn't condemn his choice. By sitting behind everyone they'd be as alone as possible in the gathering. No one could turn their heads and frown at her, or watch them and speculate. It would drive them mad, except it wasn't them she wanted to tease, but Warren. She pushed back her shoulders, raising her breasts in the magnificent gown. The corner of her lips curled into a smile when she caught Warren admiring them. Desire wasn't just trouble, but a heady power and for the first time ever, she flirted with the allure of it. With Warren, she felt safe unveiling it.

He took her hand to help her sit and it was his turn to tease her. The pressure of his fingertips through the satin of her gloves reached inside her as did his nearness. She didn't want to let go of him or look away from the passionate smile gracing his fine lips. She wanted to tilt her face to his and feel his mouth on hers again, but with everyone around them shuffling into the rows, she was forced to let go and take her seat.

Lady Ellington and Mr Berkshire settled in on his other side as the singer and her pianist took their places. Most of the audience was here for something to do in the country as opposed to hearing the music, but they were polite and welcoming as the woman began her first song.

Marianne struggled to listen, more aware of Warren's steady breathing than the singer's arias. He was as tempting as the last sweet in a box and it took all her effort to avoid laying her hand on his thigh, pressing her fingers into the firmness of it and resting her head on his shoulder. She'd never wanted to be close to someone, to touch them and be touched by them the way she did with Warren.

The singer's voice rose, drawing Marianne's attention and she settled in to listen to the song. The performer was quite accomplished as was her dark-eyed pianist, a young man who exchanged more than one knowing glance with her. Marianne felt the connection between them as she did the one between her and Warren. His thigh pressed against hers thanks to the tight packing of the chairs and their knees bumped when he shifted in his seat. It was the most he could touch her without drawing either Lady Ellington's or Mr Berkshire's attention. Marianne didn't slide away from him or turn her legs, but left her thigh against his, twisting her foot to caress his heel with hers. He slid her a sly smile and she returned it without hesitation.

The song was in French, a tale of love and the fear it wouldn't be returned. Marianne understood more than the words and the melody carrying them. To need someone was to risk being hurt as she'd learned too many times in the past. She'd needed a mother and the woman had turned her back on her. She'd needed a family and the Nichols and Smiths had cared for her only as long as they'd been paid. She craved love and something more to look forward to than a life alone. Did Warren love her, or would his regard fade the moment he wrote 'the end'? She wasn't sure. Experience was a difficult thing to shake but it didn't fill her with dread as it had in the past. He was here beside her, in front of everyone. There must be something more to it than inspiration for a story and the prospect of it lifted her spirits as much as the song.

* * *

After a lengthy programme, the woman sang her final song. The guests clapped, the sound muffled by gloves and the bored uninterest of the men.

Lady Astley rose and, as was her custom, invited others to play. A few of the older gentlemen grumbled, but were silenced by their wives. The ladies found it preferable to listen to amateurs than to trudge home to another dark evening with family around the fire.

Miss Cartwright was the first to take up the invitation. Her eagerness to play had more to do with displaying her talents to any eligible gentleman than to amuse the guests. For all Miss Cartwright's other faults, her playing wasn't one of them. She executed a concerto with admirable skill instead of the painful pickings of so many other country ladies.

At the end, Miss Cartwright stood and curtsied to the crowd.

'You should play,' Warren whispered, the caress of his words across her shoulders as startling as his suggestion. 'Give them something else to talk about beside tired old rumours or the new ones they're inventing.'

'No, they don't deserve to hear it.' It had taken enough courage to come here in the low-cut gown. She wasn't going to waste what remained of it to play for these ingrates.

'Does anyone else wish to play?' Lady Astley asked her guests.

'Yes, Miss Domville.' Warren rose, giving everyone a genuine reason to finally turn around and look at them. He held out his hand to Marianne and she wanted to smack it away. How dare he make a spectacle of her after she'd told him she wouldn't play? Her music wasn't for these people, but for her and him.

Lady Astley exchanged a desperate look with Lady Cartwright as if hoping her friend might offer a suitably polite but firm refusal of Warren's suggestion.

He didn't give her the chance. 'Come, Miss Domville. The instrument awaits.'

His encouragement gave her strength. He wasn't doing this to humiliate her, but because he believed in her and her talent. He'd told her before he'd lend her the strength of his name, to stand beside her when she at last decided to make public her talent and he was keeping his word. It was time for her to be courageous and worthy of his faith in her and at last stand up to these people. She'd knock them out of their seats with her talent and prove she was more than they believed her to be.

She placed her hand in his, rose and went with him out of the row. She held her head high as Warren escorted her up the aisle between the chairs to the pianoforte. He stopped before the instrument and let go of her as she came around the bench. The turn made the blue silk of her dress flutter around her legs before she tucked it beneath her to sit. Whispers and the shuffle of feet against the hardwood floor filled the air above the audience as Marianne prepared to play. Warren didn't return to his seat, but stepped to the far end of the piano, his presence bolstering her confidence. She focused on him as she began, forgetting everyone else.

Beyond the pianoforte, the audience's expressions changed from scowling disapproval to slack-jawed astonishment. Warren hoped those moved by Marianne's music would be less inclined to assist Lady Cartwright in her attacks against Marianne, but he doubted it. Angels could come down from heaven and accompany Marianne with harps and it wouldn't change most of their opinions. Once the song ended, they'd clap away their amazement and return to their gossip and lies. Even if they did, Warren didn't fear for Marianne. She was at last facing them, showing her true self instead of allowing them to define her.

Her face was beautiful and serene as she played, her hair warm gold beneath the candlelight which sparkled in the diamonds gracing her earlobes and echoed in the silk of her dress. She'd worn the stunning creation for him, he was sure of it, revealing more of herself as she had through her music. The first sight of her tonight had nearly stunned all rational thought out of him, it still did. Her magnificent breasts pressed against the rich fabric as each movement of her arms up and down the keyboard made the supple flesh quiver. If he could accompany her home tonight, undo the long row of buttons along the back and take the fullness of her in his hands, he would, but he couldn't. At least not yet.

He picked at a small imperfection in the lacquer of the pianoforte. His time away from her, despite the pressing issues of the newspaper and Rupert, had made more acute how much he cared for her. He loved her. The piano case vibrated under his fingers with her playing as the realisation struck him. While he'd been in London, he'd missed her melodious voice, the sense of calm he experienced in her presence and the inspiration of her being. With her he could be himself in a way he hadn't been since the summer before he'd enlisted when he'd simply been the poor sixteen-year-old son of a country vicar, not a surgeon or a famous author. He was a better man because of her, not as haunted by his past, willing to let it go and embrace a future he couldn't have imagined a few weeks ago. His path would no longer be dictated solely by his career, or fear and guilt, but by the life he might lead with her beside him. He wanted her for longer than through the completion of his novel. It was what she wanted of him which concerned him.

Regret crept along Warren's spine like the vibrations of the piano beneath his fingertips. He reached into his pocket and crinkled the cut-out gossip article. He hadn't found his brother-in-law in London. His housekeeper had claimed she hadn't seen him for days and he hadn't answered one note or letter from Warren. Even the papers from Mr Steed with all their legal warnings had gone unanswered. The threat of him still lingered out there somewhere waiting to strike, but Warren would make sure it could do them no harm.

Marianne drew the enchanting piece to a close and threw Warren a glorious smile. In her radiance, all the challenges facing them faded away. He withdrew his hand from his pocket and laid it back on the piano case. He wouldn't show her the newspaper, not tonight. Let her enjoy this small triumph and her happiness. Tomorrow he'd speak with her and they'd figure out how to face the coming trouble together.

At the end of the piece, Marianne folded her hands in her lap. Silence hovered over the stunned guests until Lady Ellington, accompanied by Mr Berkshire, rose to their feet to applaud. With a mixture of enthusiasm and reluctance the other guests joined in, but they didn't stand. Lady Cartwright didn't so much as twitch. She sat in the front row, her face screwed up as tight as a book binding. Warren shifted around the piano to block Marianne from the woman's acid stare as she rose from the bench and dipped into a dignified curtsy.

'After such fine playing, there won't be anyone who wants to perform next,' Lord Astley announced before his wife could, as eager as most of the men for the music to end. There was hunting to discuss and they'd sat through enough pretty playing. 'Let's retire to the sitting room for some refreshments.'

Mr Berkshire and Lady Ellington threaded their way through the retreating guests to Marianne and Warren.

'Everything Sir Warren said about you was true and more,' Mr Berkshire exclaimed. 'Was that one of your works?'

'No.'

'Well, if you can write music with as much passion as you play it, we'll sell thousands of copies of your compositions.'

'Do you really think so?' She didn't reject the idea as she'd done when Warren had first proposed it—her daring tonight had given her a new confidence which made her glow. Warren admired it and hoped to see more of it. She would need it if things with the newspaper story grew worse.

'I do,' Mr Berkshire concurred. 'Especially if we can arrange for you to do a few performances.'

The hint of colour in her cheeks faded, along with some of her courage. 'Perform? In public?'

'There's plenty of time to discuss and arrange it all later,' Warren interrupted. He didn't want Mr Berkshire pressing her for more than she was ready to do and making her retreat into her reserved self again.

'Of course. We must enjoy the evening.' Lady Ellington waved Mr Berkshire towards the door with one glittering hand. 'Come and taste Lady's Astley's lemon curd. It's the only thing her cook doesn't ruin.'

Warren and Marianne were slow to follow. 'Well done, Marianne.'

'I can't believe I did it.' They'd spoken of Vienna once. He'd love to see her in the grand opera house there, her fine skin glowing under the candles, a young lady enjoying life instead of hiding from it.

'They noticed you tonight and for the right reason.' He longed for tomorrow when they'd be alone at Priorton Abbey and he could savour her lips and the press of her breasts against his chest. He should concern himself with all their other problems, but nothing, not his reputation as an author, his bills or the possibility of scandal could intrude on his moment.

He offered her his arm and they walked together to the sitting room as naturally as they had in the garden, even if everything they did was still dictated by the rules of propriety. Instead of joining the small groups of people gathered on the sofa or around the gaming tables, they wandered to a place near the French door leading to a balcony. More than once Warren fingered the cool brass door handle, wanting to push it open and slip with her into the night with nothing but the stars to watch them, but he didn't. He couldn't allow his eagerness to be with her to compromise her more than he feared he already had.

* * *

Marianne stood across from Warren, silently willing him to open the French doors and escort her outside. Despite the people chatting together in small circles or watching them from across the tops of their fans, she wanted to be alone with him. For the first time ever, she'd stood alone against her critics, not with Lady Ellington using her influence to defend her, or Sir Warren pressuring them, but with her own talent. When she'd played, she hadn't been here worried about ugly people and ugly words, but somewhere else. Warren had once said there was a world outside this one which didn't care about her or her scandals. Playing tonight had been the first tentative step towards finding it. 'Thank you, Warren, for encouraging me. I couldn't have done it without you.'

'You're the whole reason I came home.' He turned a bit so his hand which he held by his side was close to hers. Hidden from the others by her body, he pressed his fingers into her palm, his touch firm and welcome like a hot stone clasped between cold hands. 'I'm glad I could inspire you, the way you've inspired me.'

'It's as if I don't fear the world so much when I'm with you, as if I can at last live as I want to, with pride instead of being ashamed like they want me to be.'

'You can and you will.' He ran his thumb across her palm, his touch as natural as the chemise against her skin. She didn't want to pull away, but to draw him closer, to tug off her glove and experience more of his bare skin against hers, to be one with him. This wasn't the lust she'd feared sitting latent inside her and ready to spring out to ruin her, but a deeper connection. He'd made her believe in herself in a way not even Lady Ellington had done and there was freedom in it, freedom to be herself, to take pride in her accomplishments and to at last open herself up to the affection and connection she'd craved her entire life.

'Promise me, no matter what happens, you'll never allow them to make you believe you are anything but the beautiful, intelligent, talented and witty woman you are,' Warren demanded.

The haunted expression from his portrait flickered through his eyes and she tightened her fingers around his, concern undermining her bliss. 'Why, what might happen?'

He hesitated, pressing his lips together as if holding back words he debated speaking. 'Anything, you know as well as I do how cruel the world can be.'

'I do.' She'd stood up to her critics tonight, but it wouldn't be the last time she'd be forced to do so. The strength she'd drawn on to cross the room, to sit at the piano and reveal her talent would have to be called on again and again. The thought didn't weary her as it had in the past. With Warren beside her she could face anything and anyone, and at last achieve victory over every low opinion of her, including her own.

Chapter Ten

'It'll cost twice what I originally told you,' the foreman announced.

Warren stopped picking his way across the attic, his hope of seeing the roof finished without additional expense vanishing. 'What?'

'These supports are rotten.' The foreman scraped a beam with a small knife and the wood flaked like pastry. 'This section won't take the weight of the new slate and needs to be replaced.'

Warren would call the man a fraud, but he'd seen enough waterlogged hospital ships to know when wood was strong and when it wasn't. 'How much?'

The foreman screwed up one side of his mouth and rubbed his scraggly chin. 'Two hundred pounds.'

'Everything is two hundred pounds.' Warren stared at the exposed beams and the cobwebs hanging in the corners of the rafters. Sunlight through the narrow attic windows revealed the thick dust covering everything. 'Will this be the last of it?'

'No such thing in a house like this, sir.' The foreman chuckled. 'But it should see to the roof, keep water from damaging more once the bad weather sets in.'

Warren pinched the bridge of his nose, frustrated and exhausted, the peace and excitement of last night rubbed away beneath the pressure of this morning and this latest setback. A lack of sleep didn't help matters. He'd been up so many times pacing, Lancelot had growled at him as if to say he was disturbing his sleep. During his numerous trips up and down the front hall, the wood overhead creaking with the cold, the suits of armour silently watching him, he'd noticed how different the house was when Marianne was here. She brightened it, filling it with her presence and her music. She made his success, Priorton, everything richer and worth having.

If only he were worth having. She'd bloomed

under his belief in her last night, but in reality he hadn't deserved her thanks or her faith in him. He hadn't been honest with her about the newspaper, but today it would change. He'd greeted the sunrise ready to ride to Welton Place and tell her, to plan with her how they would handle the encroaching issue together before he'd been waylaid by the foreman. If she didn't learn of the gossip from him and see how determined he was to remain beside her until it passed, he'd lose her trust. It was time to be done with the man.

'Then make the repairs. Rain running down the stairs will only cost me more money.' Warren left the attic, dropping down each step of the narrow and curving upper staircase. When he reached the first floor, Turner, the butler, hurried up to him.

'Sir Warren, Lord Cartwright is here to see you.'

'What's he doing here?' The Baron had never deigned to visit him before, always summoning Warren to him as if he were the king. His coming to Warren so early in the day, especially after last night, made him uneasy

'He didn't say. He's waiting for you in the sitting room.'

'Thank you, Turner.' Warren made his way down the wide front staircase, in no mood to face the man this morning. He didn't like Lord Cartwright, especially not his wife, but tolerated them like he did so many other titled people because of their patronage. He was beginning to think he should abide by his own advice to not care what people thought of him. There were plenty of common men in England who purchased his novels, and if Mr Berkshire could see them printed in America and Europe as he planned, there'd soon be even more. With so many more fans of his books, he could at last dismiss people like the Cartwrights. He didn't like relying on anyone, especially not haughty lords with too many friends in the *ton* who thought nothing of looking down their pedigreed noses at him and Marianne.

Warren entered the sitting room. Lord Cartwright stood in the centre of it waiting for Warren, hat in his hand.

'Good morning and welcome to Priorton. What do you think of the repairs?' Warren motioned to the updated room with the newly polished panelling, white plaster, better furnishings and fresh curtains. It was a great change from the hideous shape it had been in when he'd purchased it.

'I can't say. I've never visited here before.' Lord Cartwright waved his hat at the room, rude in his uninterest.

'What brings you here today?' Warren planted his fists on his hips, bracing himself for what he guessed wasn't going to be polite chit-chat.

'I'm very disappointed in you, Sir Warren. I've been nothing but generous in supporting you and your little stories, pushing them on my friends and introducing you to the best families in the county.'

Warren's shoulders stiffened at Lord Cartwright's condescension. 'I thank you for your support, but I believe it was my own effort, more than anyone else's, which gained me entrance into last night's party, Lord Preston's and many others.'

'How dare you, a jumped-up tradesman, thumb your nose at my patronage and my family?' Lord Cartwright's grip on his hat tightened, twisting the felt brim. 'Last night, in front of everyone, you encourage Miss Domville, a woman of dubious background, to show up my daughter at the pianoforte.'

Warren ground his teeth at the insult before the truth in the man's accusation eased his jaw. The memory of Lady Cartwright shooting daggers at Marianne after she'd played came rushing back to him. Warren had encouraged Marianne to play and her superior talent had inadvertently eclipsed Miss Cartwright's. With the gossip circulating in the *Morning Post* threatening to reach them, assuming it already hadn't, Warren might have made things worse with his rashness. Despite his guilt where Marianne was concerned, he wouldn't stand here in his own home and take Lord Cartwright's insults. 'I may not have inherited Priorton, but at least I have the fortitude to work to maintain it, not to sit at the gambling tables like certain lords do and throw it all away on chance.'

Lord Cartwright's bulbous nose turned a deep shade of red as he scowled at the blatant reference to his gambling habit and the debt he was too proud, foolish and lazy to work to pay off.

'How dare you? First you allow your mistress to insult my daughter and then you insult me.'

'Miss Domville isn't my mistress,' Warren growled, ready to call Turner and have him escort Lord Cartwright out.

'You think I haven't read the news in the *Morning Post* about the two of you?'

Warren stiffened again. People had heard. It wouldn't be long before Marianne did too. He had to reach her, to tell her and make his determination to remain beside her through it all clear.

'You've become too grand for your own good,' Lord Cartwright spat out. 'I suggest you remember your place and who are your betters.'

'And I'd suggest you remember who my friends are. When I tell Lady Ellington about your snide comments about Miss Domville and she tells Lord Falconbridge, he may not be so generous in regards to your gambling debts next time. How much was it you lost to him last winter that he forgave?'

Lord Cartwright blanched, seeing his mistake as clearly as he'd pointed out Warren's. He smashed his hat down over his grey hair and stormed out of the room. A moment later, Warren heard the jingle of equipage as the carriage carried him and his rage off. Warren wished he could so easily walk away from their exchange. It wasn't just the loss of Lord Cartwright's patronage that concerned him, but Marianne.

He raced up the stairs towards his room to change into his riding clothes and hurry to Welton Place. At the top of the stairs, he paused as two men straining under a thick beam balanced on their shoulders crossed the hall. The weight of everything settled on Warren like the wood on the workmen's shoulders. He drew in a deep breath, craving even the faintest hint of Marianne's delicate perfume to settle him but there was nothing except sawdust.

Maybe I have reached for too much.

The noise of hammers pounding and chisels scraping used to fill him with pride. Today, it sounded like his hard-earned money being spent on a foolish dream, just like his father had done with the vicarage school. Warren could have bought something more modest in London, but the opportunity to purchase Priorton, like his meeting with Mr Berkshire ten years ago, was one he hadn't been able to resist. Through hard work he'd gained everything he'd ever dreamed of as a child, all the fantasies which had carried him through the darkest moments aboard ship and after his father's death. With the same tenacity, he'd won Marianne's heart. Nothing, not even a leaking roof, would make him choose begging to the Cartwrights over Marianne. He'd write more, sleep less if necessary, but he wouldn't give up on Priorton, or Marianne.

Marianne sat on a bench in the garden with her eyes closed and her face turned to the sun to enjoy its warmth. Despite spending half the night lying in bed thinking of Warren, she was exhilarated instead of exhausted this morning. The edginess which had haunted her all summer faded in the autumn cool and it was because of last night, because of Warren.

In the middle of the night, as she'd stared at the swirls of brocade in her bed canopy illuminated by the coals in the grate, she'd begun to imagine going to London in the spring, perhaps even travelling to Austria as Lady Ellington and Warren had suggested, except every time she pictured herself in the Vienna opera house enjoying a performance, it was Warren who was at her side. In the short time they'd been together, he'd encouraged her to step into the world instead of shying from it. Bit by bit she'd taken his advice until last night when she'd plunged into it at last. In doing so, she'd soared in a way she hadn't believed possible a few months ago. It was because of him and the way he gazed at her as though she was more precious to him than his writing.

She opened her eyes and fixed on the statue of Zeus embracing the nymph, admiring the sensuous lines of Zeus's marble fingers on the nymph's plump thighs, her billowing dress revealing every curve of her as she opened her mouth to kiss the god. When Warren had admired her in the dress, Marianne had felt like the nymph, revelling in his awe of her body instead of wanting to hide it away. The thrill of it rushed through her again and for the first time she felt like one of the other young ladies who became giddy over a beau and society and the future. Warren wanted her and it was no longer for inspiration, but something much deeper. It had been there in the clasp of his hand on hers last night and his every encouraging word. Warren believed in her, and it had strengthened her belief in herself and the possibility she might have at last what she'd always craved, but never thought she'd obtain—genuine love.

'Good morning, Miss Domville.' The familiar male voice made her cringe and burst her contentment.

She turned on the bench to see Lord Bolton standing behind her, hat cocked over his forehead, his charming smile oozing confidence and making her want to retch. 'What are you doing here?'

He settled his hands on his walking stick. With a lean body, forceful jaw and dark hair, he was too handsome for his own good. 'Is that any way to greet an old friend and admirer?'

She stood, pinning him with enough spite to wilt a rose. 'You were never an old friend.'

He stared at her breasts, a lascivious smile curling up one side of his too-perfect mouth. 'But I'm still an admirer.'

'Of my money. Surely you didn't travel all the way up from London for me to refuse you again?' She started off down the walk, determined to be rid of him, but in two strides of his long legs he was beside her.

'Apparently, I'm not the only one. I read an interesting story in the *Morning Post* about you and Sir Warren. Of course I didn't realise it was you until Lady Cartwright told me over tea this morning. It was all she could talk about, especially after his stunning performance with you at Lady Astley's musical.' His smile widened as she stopped so fast on the walk, pebbles shifted beneath her half-boots. 'I'm sorry I missed it, but I was delayed by a thrown horseshoe.'

'Too bad the horse didn't throw you.' She pulled back her shoulders, regaining her usual disdain for him, refusing to reveal any more shock or the anxiety creeping in beneath it. Warren had been in London. He must have heard the stories. Was this the silent unease he and Mr Berkshire had shared last night and the trouble with a newspaper he'd mentioned? If so, he shouldn't have kept it from her, but told her instead of leaving her to discover it from slime like Lord Bolton. 'Lady Cartwright should have more important things to discuss than me, especially since her daughter is without a husband after a very expensive Season Lord Cartwright can ill afford.'

'I'm not surprised Miss Cartwright failed to take. Her assets aren't as impressive as yours.' His licked his lips as he came to stand over her. 'My offer still stands. I'll make you a respectable wife and you'll free me of my debts. I need an heir and I'd like to leave him a little more than an over-mortgaged estate. You should accept me—what other decent man will have you?'

'Get out or I'll have Lord Falconbridge ruin what's left of your reputation.' She needed him gone as much as she needed to see Warren, to know if the rumours were true or another of Lord Bolton's plots to undermine her confidence. He'd been as ruthless as Madame de Badeau in trying to make her believe she needed him and the protection of his name. She hadn't believed it then, she wouldn't now, even while her faith in Warren was wavering.

He shrugged away her protest. 'You needn't bother threatening me with Lord Falconbridge's wrath. My debts have ruined my reputation as much as your sister did yours. As tainted by her as you are, 'I'm the best chance you have of regaining any respect and not ending up a spinster.'

She balled her hands at her side, struggling not to strike the smirk from his face. 'Get out.'

'If you're counting on Sir Warren to offer for you, then I recommend you don't. With the Cartwrights shunning him for his liaison with you, it won't be long before others do too. He'll give you up before he loses any more patrons, unless he thinks your money is worth the trouble. I do.' Lord Bolton twirled his walking stick as he strolled around her and made for the house. 'When Sir Warren makes a formal offer for you, I'll gladly step aside. Until then, I'll be at the Horse and Lion in the village should you change your mind.'

Marianne dropped down on to the cold stone bench in front of the fountain, the fight shocked out of her. She'd been brave last night, defied everyone and their petty expectations of her and the only thing it had gained her was more derision. She could imagine the Cartwrights sitting around the tea table, laughing about her with Lord Bolton and gobbling up his stories of her from her time with Madame de Badeau. He'd probably made up a few more to amuse his snickering hosts. It shouldn't matter, she shouldn't care. For a brief time at the piano last night, and for hours afterwards, she hadn't. She did today because it might cost her Warren.

She stared across the garden at the statue of Zeus, Lord Bolton's warning about Warren ringing in her ears. Warren hadn't declared for her and his association with her was at last costing him patrons. No, she shouldn't lose faith in him so easily. He'd stood by her last night and had always scoffed at all her previous fears over what their time together might do to him. He wouldn't abandon her simply because one or two families shunned him. He had the Prince for an admirer and who knew what other aristocrats in London. He didn't need the Cartwrights. He also didn't need her reputation placing their patronage at risk too.

She jumped up and paced in front of the statue, barely aware of the footsteps crunching over the gravel coming up from the house. She never should have come to rely on Warren. A month ago she wouldn't have cared if he never spoke to her again—this morning it terrified her. He might leave her like nearly everyone else she'd ever been close to had done.

'Is everything all right, miss?' Darby asked, appearing strangely out of place in the garden carrying a silver salver.

'Yes, thank you,' she rushed to answer and he was deferential enough not to pry. He'd leave that to Lady Ellington after he told her he'd noticed Marianne was distressed. For the first time, Marianne didn't mind. Down the walk, through the open French doors, the curtains billowed out with the fresh breeze, revealing the pianoforte. It didn't call to her like it had in the past. She didn't want to sit there alone, but be with someone to talk and figure out what was going on in her mind and her heart. She wished Lady Ellington was here instead of off paying calls. She needed to hear her say, as she had so many times in the past, all would be well.

'This arrived for you.' Darby held out the salver to reveal a letter from Theresa.

Marianne took it, relieved to see it was a friendly missive instead of something more sinister like a parting note from Warren. She'd ignored Theresa's other letters for the past couple of weeks, but she tore this one open, craving kindly words. She shouldn't have avoided her friend or allowed her malaise to make her dismiss the people who cared about her. She might have been reluctant to admit her need for them in the past, but she couldn't today, not with the possibility of Warren ending things facing her.

She read the letter. There was a friendly chiding about Marianne not coming to visit. She said if Marianne was worried about encountering Lady Menton she need not be since the woman had gone to visit her sister for a month. Marianne could come see Theresa whenever she wished though she hoped it would be soon. She pledged her unending friendship to Marianne before ending the letter.

Marianne folded it, guilty at the way she'd neglected her friend. If Theresa didn't survive her travails, and there were many women who didn't, Marianne would lose one of the few people who genuinely cared about her. Theresa, along with her husband, had stood with her as much as the Falconbridges, even against Mr Menton's parents. With her enemies mounting yet another attack, Marianne needed all the amiable smiles and pleasant conversation she could gather.

'Darby, please summon the carriage. I'm going to visit Mrs Menton.'

'Miss Domville isn't here,' the bland Welton Place butler informed Warren.

Warren stuffed down the urgency which had gripped him since Lord Cartwright's visit, determined to remain level headed. He must talk with Marianne before the news of the scandal did its damage. 'Where is she?'

'Visiting a friend.' Lady Ellington's regal voice carried out from behind the butler. The tall man stepped aside and allowed the Dowager to come forward. There was no hint of blame in her answer. She simply announced what she knew. 'Walk with me, Sir Warren, I wish to show you my Italian landscapes.'

She took his arm and Warren allowed her to lead him into the entrance hall despite his eagerness to set off to wherever Marianne was. They stopped at the bottom of the main stairs and she gestured to the stunning collection of

Italian landscape paintings hung three and four tall along the walls.

'I heard a very unsettling rumour while I was visiting friends today,' the Dowager announced as she stared up at her collection.

Warren stopped himself before he could adjust his cravat. 'Did it have to do with the column in the *Morning Post*?'

'Ah, I see you are aware of it.' She at last faced him, scrutinising him like captains used to do to their new sailors.

'Is Miss Domville?' His stomach dropped when the Dowager nodded and the large diamonds dangling from her ears brushed her cheeks.

'She had an unfortunate visit from an old suitor this morning who saw fit to inform her.'

Warren didn't know who the vile man was who'd delivered the news, but he wanted to thrash him. 'I apologise. It was never my intention to compromise Miss Domville or to make her a target for ridicule.'

'And now that she is, what do you intend to do about it? Miss Domville has not had an easy life and does not need yet another person failing her. I won't allow it and neither will Lord Falconbridge.'

If Warren had ever thought losing the Cartwrights' support would be unfortunate, he sensed it was nothing compared to garnering Lord Falconbridge's wrath. With his power and influence, the Marquess could ruin him in a way none of the other country families could dream possible. However, losing Marianne would be a greater punishment than anything Lord Falconbridge might conceive.

'I won't fail her, Lady Ellington,' he assured her, as vociferous in his declaration as Lady Ellington was in her duty to her young charge. 'I care very deeply for her and I only want to see her happy.'

Lady Ellington nodded sagely. 'Have you told her this?'

'It's why I'm here.' He opened his arms to the hallway. 'But she's not.'

She tilted her head, appraising him as if he were a new bauble to adorn her fingers. Then she straightened, the decision made. 'She's gone to visit Mrs Menton at Hallington Hall. It's an easy ride from here, just on the other side of Falconbridge Manor. Mrs Menton is very preoccupied with her baby, so I don't see how she'll pay much attention to Miss Domville.' Lady Ellington winked at him. 'Good day, Sir Warren.'

'Of course Lord Bolton is wrong,' Theresa reassured Marianne. She sat in a deep chair by the fire with Alexander, her infant son, perched on her slowly shrinking lap. The chubby-cheeked boy sucked his little fingers, his eyes wide as he listened to the ladies. Marriage and a baby had mellowed Theresa's high spirits since they'd met four years ago when Lady Falconbridge, the cousin who'd raised her, had brought her to one of Madame de Badeau's salons. It was Marianne's friendship with Theresa which had led her to betray her mother and reveal to Lord Falconbridge the plot to see Cecelia humiliated by Lord Strathmore.

'What if he's not?' Marianne stopped pacing across the flowered rug to peer out of the window. Below, the lawn slipped down from the back of the house to a copse of trees. Through their nearly bare branches the lake shimmered in the sun. 'The Astleys and the Prestons and who

knows what other patrons in London may abandon him. His work fuels everything he does, it's who he is. He won't let anything jeopardise it.'
Not even me.

'You must speak with Sir Warren. It's the only way to settle your fears.'

Fears. She hated them and how they dominated her life as much as she hated the uncertainty of waiting on Warren's response to the gossip. The entire situation felt too much like the week after she'd written to the Smiths asking to return to them. She'd waited every day for their answering letter, not even unpacking her things at Lady Ellington's, sure she'd soon be on her way to her old guardians. Their letter severing all ties with her had been a blow, one she feared Warren's reaction to gossip would be too. She wiped at her eyes, pushing away the tears building there. 'I don't know if I can face him.'

Theresa set Alexander in the cradle beside her chair. She approached her friend and laid her hands on her shoulders. Marianne didn't flinch from her touch, but was grateful for the gesture and the comfort it brought her. 'If he's placed this much effort in you, he isn't going to let you go so easily. Don't run from him, Marianne. He's good for you. A month ago you wouldn't have played for Sir Warren, or even Lady Astley's guests like you did.'

'And what has it gained me except more problems?' Marianne's shoulders sagged. 'I'm tired of fighting people.'

'It won't be for ever. Nothing lasts so long.'

'Then when will it end?' A lifetime of frustration made her clench her hands at her sides. 'When they've finally driven me from the countryside or Lady Ellington tires of constantly defending me?'

'Lady Ellington will always help you like she helped me and Adam marry, and Lord and Lady Falconbridge find each other again. She won't give up on you no matter what.'

It was difficult to believe, especially after Lord Falconbridge's warning the other day that Marianne's future here depended on Lady Ellington being right about Sir Warren's intentions. If he made his aunt choose between him and her, she felt certain she'd lose. 'And Sir Warren?'

'Give him a chance to surprise you. I think he will.'

Alexander began to fuss and rub his eyes.

The stout nurse in her starched apron appeared in the doorway. 'Time for Alexander's nap, Mrs Menton.'

'All right.' Theresa offered Marianne an apologetic look. 'I must feed him, to Lady Menton's horror. She thinks I should hire a wet nurse. Will you wait here for me?'

'No, I want to walk by the lake.' She was too agitated to sit still.

'All right, I'll come find you when I'm finished.'

Marianne picked her way downstairs, cautious in case Sir Walter was about. The baronet had been cordial enough to Marianne every other time she'd been here, but there'd been no mistaking his cool disapproval of Marianne's friendship with his daughter-in-law. It would turn to outright disdain if he'd read the newspaper and Marianne might find herself permanently banned from Hallington Hall, despite Theresa's protests.

To her relief, Marianne saw no one as she made her way through the house to the back sitting room. She stepped outside on to the stone portico and crossed it to the steps leading down to the lawn. She followed the path heading into the woods and to the lake beyond, the sense of isolation increasing as she moved further and further away from the house. A breeze blew through the trees, sending a shower of brown leaves fluttering to the ground. Marianne caught one, but the brittle thing crumbled beneath her grip like everything with Warren seemed to be doing. She tilted her hand and the pieces cascaded to the ground. If only she could release her concerns the same way, but nothing except a meeting with Warren would settle her. She wasn't sure she could face him and risk his turning away.

At last she reached the lake and stood at the shore. A stiff breeze blew across the wide expanse and drove it up to lap over the rocks dotting the sand. The surface reflected the clouds passing overhead and made her feel as lonely as the grey water.

I wish Warren was here.

A path followed the bank to a Grecian temple perched on an outcrop. Marianne followed it, then climbed the lichen-covered steps leading up to the main walkway under the temple dome.

The second floor of Hallington Hall appeared over the trees. The dark stone didn't stand out against the red and orange leaves as it had nearly four years ago when she'd stood here with Theresa to admire her friend's new home. Theresa was here because she had a husband, a child and peace. Marianne had nothing.

No, I might still have Warren.

She hoped Theresa was right about him not giving up on her. At one time she would have balked at needing him, but it was clear she did. Under his influence she'd begun to live as Lady Ellington had always encouraged. She wanted more of it, more time to see what existed beyond the pianoforte and the small world she'd created for herself at Welton Place. With him beside her, helping her to disregard everyone who wanted to pull her down, she could have it, assuming he wanted to remain with her. She wouldn't be surprised if he washed his hands of her and hurried to undo the damage his relationship with her might have caused.

She leaned against the cold stone building, not sure how she would stay sane with all this uncertainty nipping at her. A duck swam by, cutting a widening V across the surface. She must see Warren and settle things, one way or another. Even if meeting him meant the end of their relationship, their brief time together proved there existed gentlemen who might care for her. It should have been a comfort, but it wasn't. She didn't want any future gentleman. She wanted Warren.

Rustling from behind the temple caught her attention. She followed the curve of the building around to the other side and out of view of the house. She expected to see a rabbit or a deer in the underbrush. She was startled by the sight of Warren emerging from the woods atop a chestnut-coloured horse, Lancelot trotting beside him.

She moved, ready to run down the steps and throw her arms around him as he dismounted, but she didn't. She wasn't sure why he was here and she wasn't going to embarrass herself by clinging to him as he bade her adieu.

'I didn't think you one for riding,' she called out to him, summoning the old Marianne, the one adept at appearing aloof no matter what the situation. It was a much more difficult thing to accomplish today than in the past.

'I wouldn't be a proper baronet if I didn't.' He flipped the horse's reins over its head to dangle on the ground.

'Do you usually ride on the Menton lands?' She fingered the outline of the slim gold ring beneath her glove, as nervous as she was thrilled to see him.

'No.' He climbed the steps to her while Lancelot wandered off, sniffing the ground as he went. 'I did it to find you. Lady Ellington said you were here.'

He came for me.

She let go of her hands and let them drop to her sides. He hadn't told her what he wanted yet. 'You came to discuss the story in the *Morning Post*?'

'I'm sorry you had to find out about it from so dubious a source. I wanted to be the one to tell you.'

'Why? So you could at last admit our arrangement was a mistake, that I'm costing you patrons?' She ducked away to follow the curve of the building. She hated hearing the words spoken aloud, but she'd said them to avoid him doing it first and crushing her already fretting heart.

Warren's footsteps echoed in the dome of the building behind her. 'Marianne, wait.'

It was the same tone he'd used the day he'd burned his copy of *Lady Matilda's Trials*. He was asking her to listen to him, to let him make things right. She faced him, opening and closing her fists at her sides, willing to give him the chance.

He strode up to her, concern deepening the small furrow between his eyebrows. 'I'd never choose them over you. You're worth more to me than any of their praises or support. I need you in my life more than I need them.'

'As your muse.' Despite the earnestness in his voice, the doubt she'd carried for so long still haunted her.

'No, as the wonderful woman you are.' He reached out and caught her hands, his solid grip spreading through her like ripples over the surface of the lake

'What are you saying?'

'You captured me with the first note you played and every day we've been together since.'

He raised his hands to her cheeks, cupping her face as his words did her heart. 'Before you'd played for me, I'd lost my talent and despaired of ever being the man and writer I was before my sister died. You've helped me to unlock the stories which were holed up inside of me and to reclaim my faith in myself. I love you and I want you to be with me for ever, to be my wife.'

Her gasp of surprise was smothered by the touch of his lips to hers. His defiance of her expectations made her head whirl as much as his mouth against hers. Warren loved and cherished her, more than patrons or stories or reputations. He wanted her with him, scandalous past and all, and she would be his, free and trusting as she'd never been with anyone before.

Lancelot's loud barks as he raced past the Grecian temple and up the path interrupted their bliss. Warren broke from her and she wavered on her feet before his tight arms steadied her.

'Will you marry me, Marianne?' he asked.

'Yes.' She laid her cheek on his chest and played with the sloppily tied cravat beneath his chin. She didn't care who found them here. Let them see the two of them united against every trial and person determined to humble them. Their nastiness couldn't separate them.

'Come.' He took her by the hand to lead her to the horse.

'Where are we going?'

'For a ride.'

She resisted his gentle tug. 'I can't leave my friend.'

'I think she'll understand.' He motioned to the woods.

Theresa stood petting Lancelot beneath one of the few evergreen trees. She wiggled her fingers in goodbye with a smile as mischievous as one of Lady Ellington's, then faded back into the tree line. Lancelot raced to them with excited barks before bolting off into the woods.

Theresa had been right about Warren and so had Lady Ellington. They'd never allow her to forget it and she didn't mind. It was the most glorious thing anyone could ever hold over her.

Marianne laughed when he caught her about the waist and lifted her to sit sideways across the saddle. He gripped the leather in front of her thighs, the height of the horse and the strength of Warren overwhelming as he pulled himself up behind her. His legs were strong against hers as he tightened the reins between his hands and clicked the animal into motion.

The wind slid around them, tugging a few of her curls out of their pins as the horse carried them around the curve of the lake. At the far end, the path turned to lead them deeper into the woods. Lancelot bounded past them before veering off into the trees to chase a bird.

'I've never seen Lancelot so active.' Marianna tucked her windswept hair behind one ear, but it refused to remain there.

'Sometimes his instincts get the better of his laziness, especially when he's chasing something.'

Her instincts came alive under the pressure of Warren's chest against her shoulder, his thighs hard against her buttocks. She leaned against him, all the concerns of the last day, the Cartwrights, Lord Bolton and the past dissolving in his presence.

The path led out of the trees to follow the rolling hills. She'd never ridden this way across the Menton lands or even the edge of the Falconbridge estate. Her life was circumscribed by the dower house, Falconbridge Manor, Hallington Hall, the country families and the village. After today, she would at last break free of this small existence and its influence on her, but for now she was grateful for it. While they were here it was just the two of them, untarnished by anything or anyone.

They talked while they rode. She told him about the Protestant School and the jokes they used to play on Mrs Nichols at All Hollow's Eve. The darker memories of the lonely nights in the dormitory, or the lack of letters or gifts on her birthday or at Christmas didn't intrude to overwhelm her like they used to. The warmth of the spring sun on the flowers in the garden between the school walls and the house, and the friendship of two older girls who'd come to the school three years before she'd left were the most vivid memories today.

The same optimism filled Warren's description of his childhood at the vicarage. He laughed as he explained the pranks he and the other boys used to play on his father. His smile widened with his description of Christmas dinners with the boys who hadn't gone home for the holiday.

In his words, Marianne could almost smell the excitement of the season, and the aroma of the chestnuts and spiced pudding which had filled the vicarage during their small celebrations.

'Leticia and I used to play in the ruins of the Norman keep behind the village. My mother made her a princess dress out of one of our grandmother's old gowns. She'd stand in it on the old stone parapet, calling across the field to her imaginary prince to save her.' He surveyed the rolling hills of brown grass, neither his memory nor his smile darkening with anguish over his sister's passing. Like her he was too elated to be pulled down by past sorrow.

'What did you do while you were there?' Marianne laid her head on his chest and revelled in the rumbling of his voice in her ear. His happy childhood didn't make hers seem so stark, nor did she ruminate on what she hadn't had. Instead, she imagined their future children and the care and happiness they'd enjoy. They'd never doubt her love for them, or their parents' love for one another.

'I had a rusty breastplate my father had found in the attic and a wooden sword he'd carved for me out of an old plank. I used to pretend the rocks were dragons and I'd slay them and then I'd seize their imaginary treasure hoards.' Warren guided the horse down the hill which skirted the woods above Falconbridge manor. 'Some day, when the repairs to Priorton are done, I'll commission a dragon sculpture for the garden. It'll be a sleeping one I can lay between the shrubs so our children can pretend to wake it. Maybe I'll get a winged one too for near the cloister.'

'You don't have to wait. I'll buy them for you as a wedding gift along with a stone treasure chest for them to guard.'

'No, I won't take money from you to do it. I'll earn it myself, you'll see. In fact, I want your fortune placed in trust with Lord Falconbridge administering it. No funds are to be advanced from the trust unless you and he approve.'

'But why?' She pushed up from his chest, surprised by the determined set of his chin and his green eyes fixed on the road ahead. 'I want you to be able to use it for us, for Priorton. I don't want you to worry about patrons and sales.'

'No. I won't have anyone thinking I married

you for any other reason than love and I will continue to earn money with my talent just I always have, do you understand?'

'I do.' His success was important to him and she wouldn't undermine it.

'I love you, Marianne, you're the only treasure I need.' He swept his lips across hers, tempting her more than a dragon's stash of rubies or gold. He wasn't a fantasy or some imagined man hidden by the mist, but hard and hot flesh beneath her fingertips. Her insides melted under the pressure of his kiss and she reached up to lace her hands in his hair, to pull him closer and deeper into her.

The horse snorted and tossed its head, breaking their kiss.

'So much for our mighty steed.' Warren laughed as he guided the animal to where the trail ambled down through another forest. It rose again to follow the ridge behind Falconbridge Manor. Their sweet conversation continued until the roof of Welton Place peaked above the orange and yellow treetops.

Warren tugged the horse to a stop. 'I don't want to go back.'

Neither did Marianne. 'We don't have to. Turn here.'

He guided the horse to the path Marianne pointed to. It followed the slope of the hill beneath two sprawling oak trees until the red brick of the orangery came into view.

'What's this?' Warren asked, bringing the horse to a halt.

'Somewhere we won't be disturbed.'

He dismounted, then reached up for her. She held tight to his arms as he lifted her down, her skirt flaring out before his legs pinned the fabric against her thighs. She didn't let go, but studied him. The afternoon sunlight through the branches cut hard across his cheeks and played in the light hair at his temples. She ran her hand down the curve of his arm and entwined her fingers with his. She led Warren inside the orangery where the sun through the tall windows warded off the chill of the brick and the day. In this moment, she wanted to be more than his intended, but one with him.

'I see the Falconbridge family's taste in art extends to the decorative ones too.' He cleared his throat as he motioned to the gilded screen dividing the room.

Marianne closed the double doors and threw the lock. She didn't need any curious maids, or, heaven forbid, Darby, stumbling in on them. She came to stand in front of Warren and with her fingers turned his face from the erotic embroidered screen to her. 'Lady Ellington's brother used this place for trysts while keeping his regular mistress in the dower house. He was too cheap to pay for a London home.'

'And why are we here?' It was clear from his hard swallow he knew, but she appreciated him wanting her to make it clear. He wouldn't fall on her because of opportunity, but wait for her to guide them both. Today, she would be with Warren in all the ways a woman could be with a man without any interruptions. This wasn't wrong or licentious like her mother's old liaisons, but beautiful and made richer by his promise to love her for ever. 'To seal our betrothal.'

She unbuttoned her pelisse and dropped it to the floor as she slipped behind the tall screen to the windowless half of the orangery. Then she peered around the edge of it, cocking her finger at him to join her. He didn't hesitate, entering the shadows and embracing her with the same force as the embroidered Apollo taking Calliope. She followed his unrestrained passion, allowing it and hers to carry her beyond regrets, or second guesses. They couldn't wait, and she didn't want to. He loved her and the rest was all a formality.

Breaking from Warren's kiss but remaining within the circle of his arms, she leaned back and undid the small pearl buttons of her fichu. Slowly she slid it off her neck to reveal the tops of her breast before flicking it away to flutter to the floor. Warren's eyes were ablaze as he took in the length of her cleavage. He slipped his hand from around her waist and brought it up to cup one heavy mound through the fine muslin. Leaning down, he tasted her neck, his tongue making small circles on the skin as he worked his way to her décolletage. His breath against the moisture from his tongue made her shiver and her nipples peaked, the tightness of them increasing the desire for him building inside her. For the first time ever she understood what it was to want someone beyond reason and good sense. She'd never craved a man the way she did Warren, her legs weak with her need for him and the love he'd promised. It wasn't physical passion driving her forward, but the longing to finally end in his embrace the loneliness which had shadowed her for years.

As if hearing her desire, he placed his hands behind her and began to undo the long row of buttons. While his nimble fingers worked, she tasted the smooth skin of his neck, inhaling the rich cedar scent of him made more potent by the heat of the ride. His breath caressed her ear as he slipped each button free, exposing little by little the skin on her chest. There was too much between them, too many laces and linens, buttons and tapes. She wanted to feel his skin against hers, the weight of him on top of her, to be covered by his touch and his love.

When the last button finally came loose, the garment dropped before catching on the cups of the stays supporting her breasts. He shifted back from her and ran one finger along the edge of the cotton, across her skin to slip the dress free. She shivered as the muslin brushed her thighs as it dropped over her to puddle at her feet. He raised his eyebrows in admiration of her as he traced the curve of her hips and narrow waist beneath the stays. She didn't shrink from the wanting in his eyes, or knock his hand away, but stood strong in front of him. He didn't want her as some plaything to enjoy and toss away. He wanted her future, her talent and the friendship and support which had grown between them. She would give it and all of herself to him.

She tugged his coat from his torso, pushing it down to trap his arms before she rose up on her toes to press her lips to his. He tasted like fine port and she drank him in, languid under his influence. She drew back, clutching the wool, and he smiled playfully as she held him prisoner. At last she slid the coat the rest of the way off of his arms and tossed it aside to add more wrinkles to the ones already marring the wool. One by one, she undid the line of buttons on his waistcoat and soon it joined the other garments scattered around them. It didn't take her long to untie the loose knot of his cravat, her fingers as nimble with the linen as they were at the keyboard. She twisted the free ends around her hands and pulled slightly, drawing him down to her. With his body against hers, she felt the hardness of him through the stiff cotton of her stays and the chemise beneath. It urged her on, but she held back, not wanting to rush or appear like the hussy so many painted her to be. She was his alone and, after their marriage, every-one would know it.

She let go of one end of his cravat and pulled it off his neck. Then she shifted back out of his arms. He straightened to watch as she raised first one stocking-clad foot and then another to step out of the circle of her dress. Turning slowly, she exposed the laces of her stays. Glancing at him over her shoulder, she silently invited him to undo them. She would reveal everything to him, just as she'd done when she'd played her composition for him, laying bare not only her emotions but her whole being.

Warren ran his hands over her buttocks, than traced the line of the laces to her stays. Last night he'd feared he'd lost her. Today she offered him her entire self. He would be worthy of her, help her fight the rumours and work even harder to make a life for them. Row by row he slipped the laces free, letting the past and all his concerns fade with each empty eyelet. While they were together, nothing could trouble them.

At last the confining thing dropped away. He caught her chemise by the sides and drew it over her head. She turned to face him, unflinching in her nakedness, her gorgeous breasts tight and heavy above her flat stomach. He'd dreamed of seeing her like this so many times during the darkest nights in London, but not even his imagination could match reality. He reached out to caress the pointed tip of her breasts, his chest catching as they drew tighter with his touch. His fingertips dug into the generous flesh as he cupped the heavy mounds. She moaned as he took one pert nipple into his mouth to sweep it with his tongue. She tasted as good as fresh water after a long voyage, quenching the burning pain which had driven him on for too long. He'd worried about her turning away from him, but she embraced him, offering him everything as he'd given all of himself to her.

He trailed his fingers down the length of her stomach and slipped them between her thighs. She pressed her hips against his hand as he worked her pleasure, her body like the finest sand on a beach never touched by a man before. She was innocent and open, sensuous and inexperienced. He wanted to teach her and see her bloom beneath his touch. Her breathing quickened and her body tightened around his until he slid free, determined to be one with her when her pleasure came.

He leaned back to tug off his shirt, then pulled her to him again, delighting in the softness of her body against his as he claimed her mouth once more. While her tongue tasted his lips, her fingers stroked the skin of his chest, following the line of his torso to where his breeches encircled his narrow waist. He allowed her to explore his muscled body, her curiosity feeding his building need. She pulled free the fall from its buttons and he caught her hand. He stepped back to push down the buckskin and reveal himself and his desire for her.

Marianne swallowed at the sight and strength of Warren. For all the statues in the garden, nothing could have prepared her for the true majesty of a man. She wrapped her hand around his member and he tilted back his head and closed his eyes. He moaned as she stroked the hard shaft, revelling in her ability to bring him as much pleasure as he brought her. A chill slipped through the room and she let go, eager for the heat of his skin against hers. She pressed her body to his and his hot member against her stomach made her rise on her toes in delight. She wanted him as much as he wanted her and they tumbled together on to the wide sofa.

Thoughts fled from Marianne as Warren covered her, his chest hard against her softness. He settled between her thighs, his eager staff seeking entrance. She opened to him, gasping as he slid forward to claim her. He was slow and cautious, waiting until she could completely embrace him before stroking her with slow and even thrusts. They reached into her very heart as she clung to him, hands tight on the contours of his back. She'd never been so close to someone before, one with him in both body and heart, taking him deeper into herself and her life.

He slid his arms beneath her back to grip her shoulders and nuzzle her neck, his subtle groans against her skin the most stunning of music. As she began to lose herself in the flurry of their passion so did he, his thrusts growing faster and faster until he surged forward one final time, pushing her over the edge to cry out with him as they reached their pleasure together.

As the last of her quivers and his faded, Warren didn't withdraw from her, but continued to hold her tight. She'd been as much of a dream for him as Priorton or his writing. Like them she was his, completely and without hesitation. In her arms failure couldn't touch him for there was more to strive for now than money or freedom. He would be for her the one constant she could count on, the person who never left her, who believed in her as she believed in him. Together they would pursue their art and become more than their pasts. With her, he couldn't fail.

He slid off to hold her close and she rested one curving leg on his hip as he traced circles on the alabaster flesh. The filtered light from the front half of the room turned her glowing skin a gorgeous shade of cream. She stroked the line of light hair in the centre of his chest, her heavy breasts resting against his chest rising and falling with a long, contented sigh. He matched it with one of his own, catching the birds twittering outside and the peace and still of the room and their time together.

'I assume you enjoyed that.' He smiled against her temple, not regretting what they'd done. It was the sealing of their promise to one another and there was nothing sordid about it.

'Very much,' she purred, her contentment matching his.

'There'll be a great deal more of that after we're married.' Their day before the altar couldn't come fast enough for him. He wanted her at Priorton with him, her inspiration filling the house and his life.

'I hope so,' she answered with a wicked little laugh. 'Will you obtain a common licence?'

'No, we'll read the banns so everyone will hear about our marriage and how proud I am to make you my wife. I don't want anyone to think it a quick and clandestine affair.'

'It'll be difficult to wait three weeks to make afternoons like this a regular and blessed affair.' She ran her tongue over her upper lip, like one of his more sultry admirers, but the gesture was for him the man, not the famous author.

His member began to stiffen in anticipation and he cupped his hand behind her neck and drew her to him. 'We needn't wait.'

Chapter Eleven

Morning light filled the study as Warren collected his papers in preparation for the visit to the vicar. It had been difficult to leave Marianne and the pleasure of the orangery yesterday, to spend the night away from her, but the sooner he arranged for the banns, the sooner their life together could begin. He folded the note from Marianne outlining the details of her birth and parentage which the vicar would need for the licence. They'd agreed to continue with the lie of her mother being her sister. Their marriage would create enough talk without the added gossip of her true lineage.

Lancelot raised his head to the door and let out a small bark.

Rupert stood there, glaring at Warren the way

he did whenever he mentioned Leticia's death. 'I told you never to come back.' Warren marched up hard on him and grabbed him by the arm. 'Get out.'

Rupert's boots scratched and banged over the black and white tiles of the entry hall as Warren pulled him along.

'Not before I show you this.' Rupert jerked away, revealing more fortitude than he had during Leticia's trials. He shoved the piece of paper he was carrying in Warren's face.

Warren batted it aside. 'I'm no longer interested in anything involving you.'

'You should be. It's the stockholder agreement laying out all the assets of the company to be sold in case of debt or default. It outlines how you were the primary backer and placed Priorton Abbey as collateral in case the business failed. Everyone who invested in this venture was convinced you believed in it enough to stake your entire reputation and all your assets on its success. When the business fails, and it will, it's not me the investors will press to recoup their losses, but you.'

Warren snatched the paper out of Rupert's

hands and skimmed the print. Sweat began to pool in the small of his back as he read in black and white Priorton Abbey and all future profits from his books laid out as collateral for the business. His stomach clenched as it had the first time he'd cut into flesh, but he fought to stay on his feet and to not give in to the horror chewing out his insides. This couldn't be. It was a lie, like everything connected to Rupert.

Warren flung the paper in Rupert's face, refusing to be bested by this scum of a man. 'I never agreed to this. This is fraud. I'll see you in the Old Bailey for what you've done, not just to me, but to other innocent people.'

Rupert allowed the paper to flutter to the ground, leering at Warren in triumph. 'I'm not the one who'll be pilloried in the newspapers when the truth comes out. You deserve to suffer like all those dupes whose money I took. They have bags of it, but when I asked them for a pittance they made me grovel for it, just like you did.'

'If you wanted what they and I have, you should have worked for it. Instead you were too lazy, you always have been.'

'Spare me another of your lectures. You'll need all your strength to write and keep this pile of mouldering bricks over your head.'

Lancelot trotted to Warren's side. He didn't sit on his haunches like he normally did, but remained on all fours. The hairs on the back of his neck rose as he pointed at Rupert and growled. If the dog were an Irish Wolfhound, capable of ripping Rupert's throat out, he'd set the animal on the man, but he wasn't about to risk Lancelot being hurt for the piece of filth standing across from him. He dropped his hand on the dog's head and stroked it, steadying the animal and himself. 'I'll fight you on this and you'll lose.'

'No, I won't. When you resist the seizure of Priorton Abbey, it'll appear as if you're unwilling to pay back everyone who trusted in you. Your entire reputation, everything you strived to build these last ten years, will come crumbling down around you.'

Fear curled through Warren again. Rupert was right. Warren had watched society tear down the Duke of York for his scandal over the selling of commissions and he was one of *them*. They'd do worse to Warren, a man viewed by many as an upstart who'd invaded their ranks. They'd be glad to see him demoted, crushed beneath their heels into oblivion while they continued with their rounds of balls and gossip.

'I helped you, Rupert, I gave you money when no one else would, provided my blessing for your and Leticia's marriage and this is how you thank me?' Warren hissed, wanting to take a sword from the arms on the wall and run Rupert through.

'You never helped me, but tried to turn Leticia against me. She said I was crazy to think you didn't believe in me or I wasn't good enough for her, but I was right. I hate you now more than the day I married her, or the morning you let her die.'

Warren rammed his fist into Rupert's face and his brother-in-law crumpled to the floor. He gripped his nose, wailing in agony as Warren stood over him. 'You bastard. You will return every last pound you accepted from every investor or heaven help me I'll make sure you hang for forgery.'

Rupert smiled through the blood running

down his nose and dropping on the marble. 'I can't give it back. It's gone.'

'Then you'll find a way to work to repay it.'

Rupert pushed to his feet, wobbling on his toes, but never losing his nasty smirk. 'Not me, Warren, you. The day the debtors come to auction off your entire library, this house and all the rusty junk in it, I'll be here to watch. The morning your ship sets sail because you're forced back into the Navy to make a living, I'll be there on the wharf watching you. You'll regret the way you treated me.'

'I'll regret I didn't kill you.' He snatched a medieval dagger from the wall and held up the thin, sharp blade between them. Rupert's blackened eyes widened and he lost his arrogance as he scurried out of the house like a rat, fat drops of blood trailing him across the pebbled drive.

Warren dropped the knife and it clattered against the marble floor. His floor in the house he was about to lose, along with everything else he'd built. He snatched up the investment paper and read it, wanting to throw up the way he used to after surgery. How much money had Rupert taken and from whom? Warren couldn't fathom the trouble he was in, but it was large, like a wave at sea threatening to drown him.

He crumpled the paper between his sweaty hands. Everything was being cut out from under him, but he wouldn't allow it to be taken from him without a fight. He wouldn't go back to the Navy or lose everything he'd strived so hard to create. He had to get to London and Mr Berkshire. His solicitor, Mr Steed, and his barrister partner, Mr Dyer, were the best in London. They'd find a way to undo the damage and straighten out this mess before Rupert made it known. First he had to see Marianne and tell her before she found out about it from a more dubious source.

He hurried upstairs to change, pausing on the landing. The first floor was quiet since the workers had yet to arrive to begin their day. Beams, tools and cloths dusted with sawdust littered the hall and many of the adjoining rooms. The beauty of the house was hidden beneath the construction, as his life with Marianne was fast being eclipsed by Rupert's treachery.

He leaned on the hallway wall and rested his head against the cool plaster. The wood chips and their aroma of pine reminded him of a ship-yard he'd once visited while in the Navy. In the scent was the very real possibility Warren might be forced back into the stinking ships reeking of death and blood to keep himself, Marianne and his mother from starving. He wouldn't allow it to happen, but if too much was owed, if he couldn't triumph over Rupert, he might not have a choice. He must support his mother. Marianne was another matter.

He pushed away from the wall and wandered to his room with heavy steps. Marianne's wealth could save him, or he could end up squandering it in the fight against Rupert like his father had squandered all his income from the living, leaving his family with nothing. In the end, he might still be forced to re-enlist and then where would she be? Sitting at home with his mother like Leticia used to do, in near poverty, constantly worrying about whether he would return or be blown to bits. To see her life torn apart the way his, Leticia's and his mother's had been by his father's death wasn't what he wanted for Marianne or their future children. He couldn't risk visiting the horror or uncertainty of poverty on those he loved by rushing Marianne into marriage.

Warren tugged at his cravat as he entered his bedroom and began gathering up everything he'd need to make for London after he had visited Marianne. He had no idea what he'd say to her or how he'd make her see they must postpone the ceremony until things were settled one way or another, no matter how much time it took. With any luck, it wouldn't be long, but with no real knowledge of the situation he now found himself in, he couldn't say. As much as he loved her and wanted her beside him in this crisis, he wouldn't drag her down with his failure or have another scandal heaped on her because of him.

He stuffed the crinkled stock agreement in his satchel along with his notebooks then buckled it, tugging the leather to make it tight. She would resist, but he'd make her see it was for the best for both for them. He'd never relied on a woman or anyone else for financial support before and he wouldn't do so now, nor have everyone, including her, doubt the sincerity of his love by the convenient timing of their union. He hoped she would agree to wait for him.

The very real prospect she wouldn't seized him and he leaned hard on his hands against his dressing table. He stared at his reflection in the mirror, his face as ashen as after an amputation. His inability to provide for a wife and his family, to be like his father, was everything he hadn't wanted, the reason for resisting her allure during their first days together. He was nothing without Marianne, but if Rupert succeeded in ruining him, he'd be even less. She deserved happiness, not squalor or a husband stinking of blood and gunpowder. No, it wouldn't come to that, he wouldn't allow it.

He straightened, regaining control over himself and his fears as he hung the satchel strap over one shoulder. He loved her, but he wouldn't wed her as a failure. He would be for her the strong man who'd overcome this difficulty as he had every other one in his life, a man made worthy of her hand by the industry of his own.

'I wish we had time to go to London for the trousseau,' Lady Ellington good naturedly complained as they left the milliner's shop on the village high street, 'but with the wedding breakfast and so much else to plan, there isn't time.'

'It doesn't matter. I could be wed in my riding habit for all I care.' Marianne floated down the walk beside the Dowager, oblivious to the people wishing them good day as they passed. Not long ago, she'd thought the normal life of a young lady impossible. Today, she'd shopped for her trousseau, anticipating her union with Warren and all aspects of their life together. After telling Madame Martine the reason for their visit, Marianne was sure the news of her engagement would be all over the entire countryside by evening. It would be confirmed when the banns were read and then everyone who'd ever tried to pull her down would see they no longer had any hold on her. Even if they never stopped gossiping about her, she was done caring about what they said or thought. Her life with Warren was the only thing that mattered, the rest was simply noise.

'Miss Domville,' a voice called out over the passing wagons and the men laughing in front of the tobacconists. Down the walk Mr Hirst pushed through the promenading people in an effort to reach them. 'Miss Domville.'

'Come, we have more things to do today.' Marianne took Lady Ellington by the elbow and hustled her towards the coach. She wanted nothing to do with Mr Hirst or for his nasty, leering remarks to tarnish the happy day.

'Miss Domville, please wait, I must speak to you.' Mr Hirst jumped in front of them. His crooked and swollen nose beneath two black eyes and a bloodstained cravat was as startling as his insistence. 'It's urgent, about Warren.'

'Has there been an accident?' Panic seized Marianne. All her life so many pleasant times had been torn from her by people and circumstances outside of her control. Despite her elation over the engagement and Warren's love, it wasn't difficult to imagine something happening to end it all.

'Warren did this to me.' He pointed at his nose as if he expected pity.

'Then I'm sure you deserved it.' She pushed past him to reach the carriage where the tall footman stood, watching to decide if he should intervene or not.

'Wait, I've come to warn you. Warren only wants you for your money. His business venture is failing and he doesn't want to sell Priorton to pay back the investors. He needs your wealth to keep him out of debtors' prison.' He shoved a paper at her. 'This is the stock agreement, it outlines everything.'

Marianne stopped and Lady Ellington held up her hand for the footman to remain where he was. Marianne took the paper, covering her mouth with one hand as she read the script laying out Priorton Abbey as a guarantee against losses and the backing of the investments by Warren.

'You aren't the only wealthy woman he's tried to woo either.' Mr Hirst slid an old edition of the *Morning Post* over the stock agreement. 'Lady Preston has also been a great admirer of his work, in more ways than one. With her support and your wealth, he can save Priorton, pay back the investors and keep the scandal from reaching the papers.'

Above a none-too-subtle allusion to Warren's relationship with Marianne was also printed an alleged affair with a Lady P. It had to be Lady Preston.

Lord Bolton's warning came rushing back to her.

'He might phrase the contract in prettier terms, but in the end he's after your money and he'll woo you for it like he wooed society and the Prince to get his title and lands.'

No, she wouldn't allow scum like Lord Bolton or Mr Hirst to make her doubt Warren. Warren had visited Lady Preston's manor to read his work, but it had been at the invitation of her husband. As for his wooing her before the truth could come out, she'd been the one to lead Warren to the orangery and hurry their intimacy. He wanted the banns read and for them to take their time and for her fortune to be safeguarded against his use. He wouldn't have insisted on any of those things if he'd wanted to capture her before she could flee, or if his need for her money was as urgent as Mr Hirst implied.

'I don't believe or trust you, Mr Hirst. I suspect it was you who gave this story to the papers and it's you who wants to brand him a liar and darken his name.' She flung the *Morning Post* into the dirt, then motioned for the footman to keep Mr Hirst at bay while she climbed into the coach. Lady Ellington swiftly followed, settling into the opposite seat, lips drawn tight with her concern.

'I'm trying to help you!' Mr Hirst shouted as the footman closed the door. 'Whatever misfortune you suffer, you've brought it on yourself,'

Mr Hirst's further cries were muffled as the carriage set off, leaving the bruised man yelling in the street.

Marianne studied the wrinkled document in her hand, the ink smudging the cream tip of her glove.

'Well?' Lady Ellington asked.

She handed her the stock agreement. 'I'm not sure what to make of it. It appears genuine but I'm not convinced.'

She'd learned from Madame de Badeau how easily letters and signatures could be forged. It was how Madame de Badeau had tried to bring down Cecelia and Lord Falconbridge. Her incriminating letter had been a note, this was a legal document. It was difficult to fathom Mr Hirst being criminal enough to draw up something like this, but his accusations went against everything she knew about Warren. He was too honourable to swindle people, too intent on making his own way to be a cheat or a con.

'You must speak to Sir Warren at once,' Lady Ellington advised. 'I'm sure he'll explain everything.'

She was right, but it didn't calm her fears. It wasn't simply the document which concerned her, but what else it meant. 'If what Mr Hirst said about the business venture is true, it will soon be all over London. My presence as Warren's intended wife will increase the gossip and make him look worse. There'll be no hiding away from it, or stopping people from bringing up my past to smear him.'

'No, my dear, there won't,' Lady Ellington gravely concurred. 'As his wife, you will have to face it and support him through it all.'

Marianne rubbed at the ink stain on her glove, amazed how once again notoriety was being thrust on her through no fault of her own. She couldn't flinch or hide away from it this time. By wedding Warren, she'd have to endure whatever vicious criticism was hurled at them and more stories like the one in the newspaper, possibly worse ones. It was what she'd feared when he'd asked her to play for him and when he'd encouraged her to publish her music.

She stared out of the carriage window at the passing countryside. The quiet existence she'd always craved was about to end in a way she never could have imagined. Instead of terrifying her, or making her want to hide from society or run from Warren as it would have a short while ago, the prospect of it no longer troubled her. The strength she'd relied on to stand firm against Madame de Badeau and her male visitors, the determination which had helped her endure every disappointment from her girlhood until now, would help carry her and Warren through this crisis. She loved him and she would stand beside him and their future, whatever it might hold.

Chapter Twelve

'You wish to postpone the marriage?' Marianne whispered, the floor rocking beneath her as though she were still in the carriage.

Warren stood across the garden path from her, his words littering the gravel between them like old leaves. It reminded her of the morning Mrs Nichols had told her she'd soon be leaving the school. She'd been impassive, direct, as if Marianne leaving the only home she'd ever known were nothing more than a slight upsetting of plans. It was the same way Warren had delivered his news and it chilled her just as much.

'Only until this issue with Rupert can be settled. I must stop Rupert and make sure he doesn't get away with it.' Warren had explained everything to her, his brother-in-law's role in the affair, the risk to Priorton and Warren's innocence in the scheme.

'We needn't delay the wedding for him, or allow his treachery to ruin our plans. Besides, you'll need funds to fight him and I have those.' Her bottom lip quivered ever so slightly as she tried to speak like the brave woman she wanted to be.

'And I won't take them, nor will I rely on the riches of a wife to save me or Priorton.'

'I want you to have them, for everything of mine to be yours,' she cried, wincing at the desperation in her voice. He was pulling away and she was trying to cling to him, as her mother had clung to Lord Falconbridge. If he wanted to be free of her, she should comport herself with dignity and let him go, but she couldn't.

'No.' The word was as hard as his stance and she sensed nothing, not a rational argument or even tears, could make him change his mind.

A gentle breeze blew across the rose bushes behind her, but the hard-pruned and scraggily branches barely moved. She wished she were as untouched by the cold as they were, then Warren's words wouldn't be tearing her apart. 'Why are you pushing me away?'

Warren's chest burned at the stricken look which came over Marianne's delicate features. She appeared as his mother had the morning they'd lost Leticia, as though the world was ending. It killed him to cause her such pain, but he must. 'I won't allow you to risk your fortune or jeopardise your security because, like a fool, I trusted Rupert.'

'Liar. You don't want me because you've finally discovered how much my situation will reflect on you. Once the public sees you with a woman like me, they'll judge you much harsher than they would if it were the venture alone sinking you.' Marianne settled her shoulders, a mask of indifference sliding over her. She was retreating from him and returning to the self-preserving caution which had marked her first days at Priorton.

Desperation seized him as it had when he'd realised Leticia was dying. He couldn't allow her to slip away from him or to stop him from doing what he knew was the best for both of them. He might hate himself now as much as she did, but some day when this was behind them, they'd both see he'd done the right thing. He only had to convince her to keep faith in him and his plan. 'It isn't true. I love you too much to have your past and all the stories about you dragged through the papers and ballrooms because of me. Nor will I allow our marriage to be questioned and doubted by everyone until they weaken your belief in me.'

'It isn't them weakening it, but you. You spent so much time working to get me to rely on you, cajoling me to care for you, convincing me you loved me. Then, at the first whisper of trouble, you run away.'

'I'm not running. I still need you, nothing about that has changed, but we can't marry until I'm clear. Can't you understand?' He took her hand, but it was like holding one of Lancelot's paws. She was no longer the passionate woman who'd pulled him into the orangery and shared with him the most intimate parts of herself, and it was his fault. 'I won't drag us both into poverty.'

'You're not your father, Warren,' Marianne

said in an even voice, something of the caring woman coming back into her expression.

He dropped her hand, her words like a slap he deserved. 'I will be if I fail.'

Her lips thinned with her anger. 'Then go to London and save yourself. I no longer care.'

She whirled on her heel and made for the house.

'Marianne, wait,' he called after her, but this time his entreaty didn't stop her.

'No, I won't be humiliated by you or waste my life waiting. I'm finished with you,' she cried over her shoulder before disappearing inside.

Tears blurred Marianne's eyes as she rushed into the sitting room and slammed the French doors closed behind her. She turned the lock, determined to stop him from pursuing her. The rings at the top of the curtain panels rattled in protest as she jerked them together, darkening the sitting room and turning the silent pianoforte a deeper black. She staggered to the instrument and sat down on the bench. The two brass knobs on the key cover were cold against her skin as she tried to take hold of them, but she couldn't make her trembling hands co-operate. At last she gave up, glad she couldn't play. She feared the dark and forbidding notes which might come from her. She'd loved him and he'd pushed her away just like the Smiths, like her mother, like everyone she'd ever cared about. She'd trusted him with her heart and her body and he'd made her regret it.

Tears streamed down her cheeks as a new anguish emerged from her sorrow. She dropped her hands to her stomach. Nothing there felt different and it would be a week or more before she knew how terrible a mistake she'd made with him. If a child came from their lovemaking, not even Lord Bolton would have her and the repercussions would be far greater than anything she'd ever faced before.

She rose and began to pace across the rug, refusing to glance out of the single uncovered window to the view of the orangery. Its place as a sanctuary was over, just as Lady Ellington's house might soon be denied to her too. The Falconbridge family had been steadfast in their support of her when all the rumours had been unfounded. If they were proven true, through an illegitimate child, there'd be no reason for them not to cast her out. Lord Falconbridge had already warned Lady Ellington about Marianne and Warren.

She shuddered to think what lies she'd have to resort to like her mother had to protect herself and a baby. She'd vowed never to be like her, except she was. Fresh tears stung her eyes. In the end, no wonder Warren hadn't wanted her.

'Marianne, what's wrong?' Lady Ellington appeared in the sitting room doorway. 'I heard you and Sir Warren shouting at one another in the garden and Darby tells me he left in a hurry. What happened?'

Marianne faced her friend, afraid of seeing the care and concern etching her delicate features turn into loathing and disgust. They wouldn't if Marianne kept silent about the depth of her relationship with Warren, but all the pain tearing her apart wouldn't allow it.

'I've made a horrible mistake and you'll hate me for it.' She buried her face in her hands and dropped back down on the bench, wishing she could stop crying, but she couldn't.

'I could never hate you, my dear.' Lady Ellington hurried to her, taking her in her plump arms and pressing Marianne against her chest. She stroked her back in the motherly way Marianne had craved during so many dark times in her childhood. 'Now, tell me everything.'

Lady Ellington held Marianne as the details of Marianne's conversation and relationship with Warren came spilling out. She couldn't hold the words back as she confessed her intimacy with Warren and her fears of what might happen because of it. Lady Ellington listened without interrupting as all the loneliness, abandonment, helplessness and tragedy which had marked Marianne's twenty years filled her words.

When Marianne was done, she braced herself, expecting Lady Ellington to rail at her for being so foolish and surrendering to temptation. Instead, the woman shook her head as though considering a blight on her roses. 'This is troubling.'

'I'll understand if you don't want me here any more,' Marianne choked out. Of all the places she'd ever had to leave, this one would hurt the most. Lady Ellington had been the closest thing to a mother Marianne had ever experienced.

'There's no reason for you to go anywhere.'

'But what about Lord Falconbridge? I over-heard him say to you the other day my future here depended on there being no scandal with Warren.'

'That's not what he said at all, my dear. He was afraid if I was wrong about you and Sir War-ren, you'd be hurt and things might become even more difficult for you in this part of the world than they already are.' Lady Ellington laid her jewelled hand on Marianne's and clasped it tight. Her eyes, which were usually so full of mirth, were serious and determined. 'I would never throw you out, not for any reason. And don't you dare worry about Randall, he wouldn't ei-ther. No matter what happens you'll always be welcome here.'

'Why? Why do you keep standing beside me when everyone else walks away?' Marianne asked with no small amount of shame, for both her behaviour and her low opinion of Lord Fal-conbridge.

'Because I know what it's like to be unfairly judged by others, especially for things you haven't done. My brother Edgar was a greater womaniser than King Charles II. After I lost my husband,' Lady Ellington fingered her diamond bracelet, her voice catching before she continued, 'and I came to live with him, I couldn't even talk to a gentleman without everyone thinking we were lovers and I was as wanton as Edgar. Refusing to remarry made the rumours worse, but after my husband, I couldn't wed again without love. I certainly couldn't accept any of the fortune hunters chasing after me.

'Then, one summer, when I couldn't take much more of the vicious rumours, I considered a proposal from doddery old Lord Fontgrass, thinking it would end them. When I told Edgar, he rode to Lord Fontgrass's and told him he and his proposal could go to hell. Then he came to me and, in his oh, so delicate way, said he didn't care what I or anyone thought about me and I shouldn't either. I should live as I wanted and ignore everyone else. He was right.'

Marianne shook her head. 'It can't have been so easy.'

'It wasn't, but in time when everyone realised they couldn't hurt me, they lost interest in trying. I want the same thing for you.'

'I thought I had it until this morning, but I

don't.' Marianne's shoulders slumped with her sorrow. 'If there's a baby, everyone will know I'm no better than my mother and all their derision of me will at last be vindicated.'

'If there is a child, we will deal with it as we have every other issue.' Lady Ellington sat back and took Marianne by the chin and fixed her with a serious look. 'As for you being like your mother, you are nothing like her. You have a heart. She never did. You are caring and loyal to those you love, even Sir Warren. Don't give up on him or your future, Marianne. You'll regret it if you do.'

'But he doesn't want me.'

'He does. He loves you as much as you love him, I'm sure of it, but I fear he's in a difficult state right now and not thinking clearly. Like you, he's fought his battles alone for so long, he can't conceive of accepting help, but you must assist him whether he wants it or not.'

Marianne considered what she said and what Warren had told her. He hadn't called off the wedding, but asked her to wait. She'd taken it as a rejection and retreated into her old habits just like he had. If she didn't find some way to make him see his mistake, as Lady Ellington had helped her to recognise hers, she might lose him for good. She couldn't allow it or return to the lonely life she'd led before she'd met him. She did love him and she wouldn't lose him, but she would fight for their future, though she had no idea how. 'What can I do if he doesn't want my help?'

Lady Ellington shook her head, as at a loss for ideas as Marianne. 'We'll think of something, some way to assist him which won't damage his pride.'

Marianne leaned back against the piano, the sharp edge of the key cover pressing into her back. If he refused to take her money, perhaps she could speak with Mr Berkshire and arrange to purchase some of Warren's books. Maybe Lord Falconbridge could act on her behalf, but if Warren ever discovered the ruse, it would undermine his need to help himself. If only he'd written a new story, the one he'd craved when he'd first proposed their arrangement. Then he'd have his next novel and the funds it might raise.

Marianne sat up straight as the idea struck her. 'The book.'

'What book?' Lady Ellington asked as confused as Marianne was excited.

'*Lady Matilda's Trials*. It's still upstairs in my desk. It's the one he sent me after we first visited him at Priorton.' The one she'd made him burn because of her fears. It was his fears ruling them now and she wouldn't allow it, like she would no longer hide from her past and the gossip or life, but face it and live as she wished. Marianne didn't know how many people would see the truth behind Lady Matilda's story, but it was a chance she had to take. 'If I give Mr Berkshire the manuscript, Warren will have his next novel, his advance, and the chance to earn enough money to pay back the investors and the solicitors.'

Lady Ellington clutched Marianne's hands, gripped by the thrill of the scheme. 'Then we must go to London at once.'

'Well, Mr Steed, can we fight it?' Warren asked the solicitor. He sat in Mr Steed's Temple Bar offices as the illustrious solicitor read over the document. From a room on the lower floor a woman and a man screamed at one another.

Mr Dyer, the noted barrister, read over his partner's shoulder. The gentleman had a reputation for dealing with forgery cases. There were rumours Mr Dyer had gained his flair for uncovering forgers through his secret work with the Alien Office, rooting out criminals and spies, but they'd never been confirmed. Mr Berkshire paid them to keep copies of Warren's books from appearing under the names of other printers. Hopefully, they were as good at preventing Warren's name from being connected to fraud as they were at maintaining the integrity of his work.

'What do you think?' Mr Steed asked his colleague.

Warren tapped his foot, waiting for an answer. If Steed and Dyer couldn't help him, he was sunk.

'Looks like Fink's work. See the O there and the way he's spelled Lord Cartwright's name. For a forger, he can't spell worth a damn.' Mr Dyer perched his hands on his hips, drawing back the corners of his coat and emphasising his impressive height and stance. 'I'll speak with him, persuade him it's more lucrative and to his advantage to confess than to try and protect Mr Hirst. I'm sure he'll be eager to assist us. It's better than swinging for forgery.'

The man's and woman's yelling grew louder, adding to Warren's tension. 'And if Mr Fink won't give evidence against him?'

'If Mr Hirst has no other documents from you supporting his claim to an agreement, then you have a very sturdy case against him. Your reputation, which up to this point has been sterling, should help.'

Warren's reputation wasn't so sterling after his time in the country. Lord and Lady Cartwright would be all too willing to testify to his shortcomings if this issue did come to trial. He wasn't sure who else might come forward to join them, eager to get rid of this upstart in their ranks. He could well imagine Lady Preston joining the chorus of his critics, and Marianne.

Regret gripped him for what he'd done, but there was no time to entertain it.

'I also doubt Mr Hirst has the resources to fight this in court,' Mr Steed added, laying the stock agreement on the blotter of his pristine desk. 'Especially if, as you say, he's squandered the money.'

'He's probably squirrelled it away somewhere,' Mr Dyer speculated. 'He'll need it, especially since he's the one who approached the investors. Even though he's tied this to you, Sir Warren, those who lost money will remember him and sue him too. If nothing else, he will need an income to live off if he plans to leave England to escape any consequences.'

It was thin comfort. If even a part of the money existed, it would alleviate some of Warren's debt, but they still had no idea what the outstanding amount was. It might be staggering, more than whatever Rupert had hidden away, or Warren could raise without selling Priorton.

'And the court of public opinion? A trial could ruin me and everything I've worked so hard to build,' Warren reminded them.

'Then we must make sure it doesn't come to trial,' Mr Dyer said. 'We'll find a way for Mr Hirst to admit his guilt by convincing him there's no other route but to produce whatever money is left and then disappear. I understand Australia is quite charming for criminals.'

He laughed, but Warren could barely join him. He wished he had the barrister's confidence in the outcome of this issue, but he didn't. Every expectation he'd considered solid in the last few days had shifted beneath him like the sea in a storm. Priorton and his career were in danger and all his dreams of a life with Marianne were gone.

He pressed his fingertips together and stared at the tightly fitted floorboard between his boots. He'd acted like an ass with her, storming away like a stubborn child, determined not to need anyone's help but he did, especially hers. He dropped his hands and sat up. No, he'd been right to postpone the marriage. He'd promised her at the start of their relationship he wouldn't expose her to more scandal and he wouldn't, nor would he chain her to a man burdened with the risk of ruin. 'Do whatever you have to, but make sure this doesn't become public.'

'Don't worry, Sir Warren, we'll see to it justice is done,' Mr Dyer assured him before Warren took his leave.

He hailed a hack, ready to make for Mr Reed's house to discuss his finances. Together, they'd see what could be sold to raise money and what measures might be taken to save Priorton in case things were even worse than they'd imagined. A vehicle drew up to the kerb. Warren gave the driver directions then climbed inside, wrinkling his nose at the mouldy smell of the conveyance.

The brackish taste of cask water began to singe his tongue.

No, not this. I don't need this.

He pressed his fingers to his temples, trying to drive back the chilling memory of the scrape of saw against bone and the unending screams of his patients and the moans of the wounded. The rock of the carriage as it drove along made the memories worse, mimicking the roll and pitch of a ship. He opened his eyes, hoping the daylight would drive it all back, but the darkness of the hack and the mouldy stench of its seats made the visions worse.

He banged on the roof, bringing the vehicle to a halt. He staggered out, dragging in a large lungful of the foul London air. The sooty river stench was preferable to the damp and rot of the hack, but not as settling as Marianne and her fragrant flower perfume.

'Everything all right, sir?' the driver asked from atop his high seat.

Warren fished a coin out of his pocket and tossed it up to the man. 'I need to walk.'

He made off down the street, weaving through the teeming mass of people. One or two paused to study him and he prayed they wouldn't recognise him. He didn't have the stamina to smile and coddle their interest in him. Anonymity was what he craved and Marianne. He shouldn't have let her go or pushed her away. In doing so he'd destroyed everything he'd built between them, he'd caught it in the hardness of her stance and her sharp, dismissing words. She'd spent her life being rejected by people and in the end he'd proven himself no better than them.

He ducked into a nearby pub and elbowed his way through the patrons to the publican behind the counter. He thumped the top of the scarred wood. 'Brandy.'

The publican poured out a measure into a pewter glass and set it before Warren. Warren lifted the cool metal cup to his lips and threw back the burning liquid. It made his eyes water, but settled him the same way rum used to aboard ship when nothing else would ease his nerves after a battle. He motioned to the publican for another. After three more, he dropped four coins on the counter and left the dark and tobacco-filled pub for the bright and noisy London streets.

Panic didn't drive him on as it had in the hack. Like the desperate days at sea when the end of his maritime nightmare had been something out of sight over the horizon, a life with Marianne didn't seem as unfathomable as before. He more than anyone knew all hells eventually ended and when his did, he'd court her again. Regaining her trust would take more hard work than pulling in sails during a storm, but he'd do it. It was the one good thing he had to look forward to and he held on tight to it as he moved with the surge of people in the street. He'd achieved every goal he'd ever set himself to and he would win her heart again once things with Rupert were settled.

Chapter Thirteen

'Thank you for seeing me on such short notice, Mr Berkshire.' Marianne smiled at the publisher as she sat before his desk. Warren's manuscript rested on her lap, a potent reminder of the risk she was about to take and what it might gain her. 'Sir Warren would have brought this to you himself, but he's been delayed by some trouble with his brother-in-law.'

Mr Berkshire scrunched his thick eyebrows in confusion. 'We spoke before he went to see my solicitor and he told me he didn't have a completed manuscript.'

'He was being modest. He gave me this copy before he left the country and asked me to deliver it to you when I joined him in town.' She held the journal out across the desk, struggling to grip it despite the tremble in her arm. Once the story was in the publisher's hands it would only be a matter of time before it was out in the world for all to see. She hoped Warren had hidden the truth of Lady Matilda's inspiration as well as he'd claimed.

Mr Berkshire reached out and took the other end of the manuscript. He began to pull it back and she opened her fingers to let go.

'I'll be sure to get on the story at once,' Mr Berkshire assured her. 'I hope this wretched to do with his brother-in-law doesn't undermine his talent. It could end up costing Sir Warren a great deal more than his livelihood.'

She knew all too well about the cost to him and her. 'Then we must make sure that doesn't happen.'

Warren crumpled up a piece of paper and threw it aside to join the many others littering the floor. He dug his elbows into the desk and scraped his fingers through his hair, wanting to cry out in frustration. After leaving Mr Reed's more morose than buoyed, he'd come home to his narrow town house in Gough Square, determined to finish this manuscript. He'd sat here the entire night trying to work, hoping it would settle the demons plaguing him. It had only made things worse. He had nothing to show for his efforts except dark circles under his eyes and wasted sheets of paper. Another expense he didn't need.

He took a deep breath, trying to calm himself without giving in to the temptation of having a drink. Fuddling his mind wouldn't help him, but perseverance would. He'd written with the pitch and roll of the ship making him sick. He'd worked beneath a single candle with the smell of dust and blood surrounding him. He could work through this. He picked up his pen, dipped it in the inkwell and poised it over the paper. A drop of ink hit the surface, feathering out on the parchment, but still nothing came to him.

He tossed down his pen before the door opened and his mother entered.

'Warren, you must eat.' She carried in a tray of cheese, cold meat and bread and set it on the corner of his desk. He'd tried to leave his mother at Priorton, but she'd insisted on accompanying him to London. She was just as worried as he was over the Rupert affair.

Warren glanced at the food, then hunched over the paper to read what little he'd managed to complete. 'I'm not hungry.'

'You won't help anyone if you make yourself sick.'

She was right. He snatched up the bread, tore off a piece and ate it. Once it was in his mouth his stomach growled and he at last acknowledged his hunger. 'I hate it when you're practical.'

'I hate it when you're pig-headed, just like your father.'

'I'm not like him.' He refused to be, at least where providing for those he loved was concerned.

His mother studied him, her head tilted to one side. 'In most ways you aren't, but you have his determination to make something of yourself.'

'Except he never did.' Warren flicked a crumb off of his paper. It landed on the floor in front of Lancelot's nose and the dog licked it up.

'He would have if he'd been granted more time.' His mother crossed her hands in front of her, regaining the stalwart but serene stance of a vicar's wife. 'I know you blame him for leaving us like he did, but try and forgive him, Warren. He was a good father to you and Leticia while he was alive.'

'Yes, he was.' Warren reached down beside his chair to scratch Lancelot's back. She was right. He should remember the father who'd cleaned up the breastplate for him and encouraged his fantasies, instead of the one he'd cursed after his death. Like Warren, he'd had his ambitions, but not enough time on earth to pursue them. His dreams had been snatched from him by death, just like Warren's were being threatened by Rupert.

Lancelot stood up among the wads of papers surrounding him and stared at the door. He wagged his tale, appearing more animated than at any other time today.

'What is it, boy?'

The bang of the front knocker echoed through the town house.

'Perhaps it's Miss Domville,' his mother offered, optimistic as always.

Warren continued to stroke the dog's back.

'She isn't one for convention, but not even she is likely to appear at the home of a single gentleman.'

'I don't know. She might surprise you.'

He wished she would. It would bolster his belief in winning her back after everything was settled.

The butler's voice echoed through the hall, followed by Mr Berkshire's. Warren's shoulders sank. It wasn't Marianne.

'Congratulations, Warren, you've done it again,' Mr Berkshire enthused as he strode into the room. Lancelot bounded up to him and received a hearty back rub. 'Mrs Stevens, you have the most talented son.'

'I know and he's persistent with it, just like his father.' She smiled warmly at Warren before leaving the men to their business.

He didn't mind the comparison because it was true. His father had given him a reason to strive and succeed. Without it, he wouldn't have achieved everything he was fighting to hold on to.

'Has Mr Steed or Mr Dyer told you something

about the case?' Warren rose to greet his guest, hoping he had good news for him.

Mr Berkshire appeared stunned at the mention of the nasty business. 'No, this is about your new manuscript. I read it last night and I couldn't put it down. It's excellent. You've never written anything like it before. I think it'll outsell even your last story.'

'What new manuscript? I didn't send you one.'

'Modesty won't serve you this time.' Mr Berkshire helped himself to some of the brandy on the sideboard by the bookcase. '*Lady Matilda's Trials* is brilliant.'

Warren gaped at his friend as Berkshire sipped his drink. 'How did you get that manuscript?'

'Miss Domville brought it to me yesterday just as you told her to. It's magnificent and I want to get it into print at once.' He smacked his lips in appreciation of the fine liquor.

'Miss Domville gave you a manuscript?' It wasn't possible.

Mr Berkshire stopped mid-drink and eyed Warren over the top of the glass. 'Don't tell me she wrote it and is passing it off as yours, in which case I need to find the young lady at once.

She's quite a talent. Better than you.' He laughed before he threw back the drink.

'No, I wrote it.' Warren stared down at his scrawled handwriting marring the paper on his blotter. Marianne had given Mr Berkshire the novel, the one she'd made him burn. She'd come to his aid even after his rebuke of her the other day and she was here in London. It could only mean one thing. He hadn't lost her, despite his stupidity.

Berkshire set aside the empty glass. 'Well, I can't sit here all day congratulating you. I'll have my man send over the last half of your advance. With this book finally done, can I sign you up for another? Same terms as before? I can have Steed's clerk draw up the contract this afternoon.'

Warren shook himself out of his musing. 'No, I want twice as much for the next one.'

'All right, it's yours. I'll get the manuscript to the printer right away, strike while the iron is hot as they say. Maybe we can release it before there's any more trouble with your brother-in-law?'

As fast as Warren's spirits rose, they came

crashing back down. 'Are you sure you want to sign a contract with a man teetering on the verge of scandal?'

'You wouldn't be the first notorious author I've handled. Besides, might increase sales the way it did for Lady Caroline Lamb's awful tome.'

Warren tapped the top of his desk. 'If it doesn't destroy me first.'

Mr Berkshire scratched his stomach on the outside of his waistcoat. 'It's called a pen name, my boy. People use them all the time. You could too. Then, when people forget the scandal, we find a way to out you to the papers. We could make a fortune with the story.'

'You give people too much credit for short memories.' Once the scam became public Warren would be linked to the swindle for ever. There weren't enough pen names available to save him.

'Listen, Warren, I've been in publishing a long time and if there's one thing I've learned, there's no such thing as a smooth path. No matter what happens or what you've achieved, some problem will always arise. It's the one constant you can depend on and the entire reason I engaged

Mr Steed and Mr Dyer. The trick is to face each challenge and overcome it. Those who do, succeed, those who don't crumple under the pressure and quit.'

'I can see why they give up. It would be a hell of a lot easier.'

'But you won't. You never have. That's why I believed in you. Still do. Today it will be your brother-in-law, tomorrow something else. You'll get through this and your difficulties with the young lady. I have no doubt of it.'

With a nod, Berkshire took his leave.

Lancelot watched Warren from his place before the fire, mildly interested as always. Warren summoned the dog to his side and stroked the soft fur, the motion centring him and allowing him to think clearly for the first time since the sun had set the night before.

'Why you returned to London in the autumn is beyond me,' Lady St Onge complained as they sat in the morning room of Lady Ellington's Hyde Park town house taking tea.

'I told you, Miss Domville and I came to London to purchase the last of her wedding trousseau.' This was the lie they'd agreed upon before they'd left Welton Place to keep from announcing the indefinite postponement of the wedding. If all went well, Marianne and Warren would keep their date before the vicar. She prayed they did. Marianne had endured a great number of humiliations in her life. She didn't relish adding betrothed for less than a day to the long list. 'There's only so much we can secure in Sussex.'

'Too true,' Lady St Onge mumbled into her tea cup before taking a sip.

Marianne didn't touch her tea, allowing it to grow cold on the table in front of her. Despite giving the manuscript to Mr Berkshire yesterday, they'd heard nothing from Warren. His publisher must have told him of Marianne's visit by now.

'At least remove the door knocker so no one realises you're here,' Lady St Onge suggested. 'Otherwise, people will talk.'

'One would think you were old enough not to care what people think,' Lady Ellington observed as she blew the steam from her tea.

'We don't all have your years of learning to

ignore it, what with your brother and nephew.' Lady St Onge set down her cup with a rattle.

Marianne wondered if they shouldn't take the knocker off the door. It would stop her from spending the rest of the day waiting for it to hit the strike plate. When the morning post had come and gone without a word from Warren, Marianne had suggested they pay a call on him, but Lady Ellington had balked. The Dowager might be one of the first to defy a convention or two, but not this one and not in London. Despite Marianne's impatient protests, Lady Ellington was certain if Marianne waited Warren would come to her. She tried to believe he would, if only to keep from going mad while she waited.

Lady Ellington offered her cousin an impish smile. 'Don't be so sanctimonious, Rosemary. You chased after Edgar like half the ladies of the *ton*, despite, or should I say because of, his scandals.'

Lady St Onge grew redder beneath her rogue and adjusted the pin holding closed her high necked gown. 'What a ridiculous thing for you to say.'

Marianne caught the hint of a smile before

the grand dame smothered it. She'd have to be sure to ask Lady Ellington about it once they were alone. It was hard to imagine the prim old widow having any kind of amorous past. It was also difficult to not picture herself turning into a woman like Lady St Onge if their plan failed.

The thud of the front-door knocker echoed through the house and Marianne nearly knocked over the table with her knee as she twisted in her chair to try and see out of the front window. She exchanged a look with Lady Ellington, who raised her chin with pride. 'That will teach you to doubt me.'

'You don't even know who it is,' Marianne shot back, secretly wanting to be proven wrong.

'It's probably Lady Rexton,' Lady St Onge added with a purse of her wrinkled lips. 'She saw your carriage and now wants to chatter on about her youngest son. As if anyone cares about him tromping through the African jungle.'

The old lady's muttering didn't last as Darby opened the front door. A deep voice rolled through the entrance hall.

'I believe it is Sir Warren.' Lady Ellington threw Marianne an *I told you so* look.

'Even more reason why you should have removed the knocker.' Lady St Onge sniffed. 'Look at the riff-raff you're attracting.'

'Rosemary, you're speaking of Marianne's betrothed,' Lady Ellington reminded in a firm voice.

'Oh, yes, I'd forgotten. Sorry, my dear,' the cantankerous woman grudgingly apologised.

Marianne didn't care what Lady St Onge said. Warren was here. He'd come to see her, just like Lady Ellington had assured her he would. It was what he'd come here to say she worried about.

She rose, adjusting the lace fichu over her chest. She shouldn't get excited. He might be about to officially end the engagement, their time apart having reinforced his decision to avoid adding her scandals to his. She faced the door, holding her breath as Warren's steady footsteps carried down the hall.

At last he stepped into the room and she swallowed hard. He appeared as serious this morning as he had in the painting at Priorton, the brim of his hat clutched tight in his ink-blackened hands. Shadows darkened the skin beneath his eyes with a weariness she felt. She'd barely slept these last few nights and she doubted he had either. Whatever had happened during their time apart, it hadn't eased his burdens or made him happy. She didn't revel in his misery, for it was hers too and with only one cure.

'Sir Warren, welcome. Will you join us for tea?' Lady Ellington greeted, unflustered by his appearance or her cousin's disapproving grimace.

'I'd like an audience with Miss Domville, please?' He fixed on Marianne as though the other two ladies didn't exist. 'Alone.'

Marianne shifted her feet forward, eager to jump up and rush into his arms, but she forced herself to remain seated, determined to retain at least some of her dignity.

'Of course. Rosemary, please join me in the sitting room.' Lady Ellington took her cousin by the arm and drew her out of the chair.

'You can't leave her alone with a gentleman. It isn't proper,' Lady St Onge protested as Lady Ellington all but dragged her from the room and closed the door behind them.

Marianne rose and laced her hands in front of her, willing her shaky legs to support her.

'It seems I'm to be bold with a gentleman once again.'

A small smile split the severity of his lips, bringing a bit of light to his eyes. It heartened her and she dropped her hands to her side as the tension between them began to ease.

'I understand you've been bold not just with me, but with my publisher. Mr Berkshire said you gave him *Lady Matilda's Trials*.'

'I did.' She couldn't discern if he was happy or angry about her decision.

'Why?'

'It's your best work and you need the money from the sale of it to fight Mr Hirst.'

'And the fact it's your story?'

'If it helps you, then let everyone read it. I no longer care what they think.' She slipped the ring on and off her finger, waiting for his response, to learn where they stood. 'Was I right to do it?'

'You were.' He set his hat down on the chair beside him and came to stand over her like the day in the cloister when he'd tried so hard to make her see she was more than gossip or her past. Much more. 'I wanted to save myself through my own industry. You giving him the story means I will, but I couldn't have done it without you. I can't continue to do it if you aren't with me. I love you, Marianne, and if you'll still have me, I want you to be my wife.'

She closed the small distance between them and laid her hand on his cheek. His skin, cool from his time outside, warmed beneath her touch. 'Through richer or poorer?'

'Through it all.' He took her by the waist and pulled her to him, his fingers digging into her sides with an intensity which echoed in her heart. 'I'm sorry I was a stubborn fool. I love you.'

'I love you, too.'

He claimed her lips with a relief as palpable as hers. This was everything she'd wanted when she and Lady Ellington had climbed into the carriage and set out for London, and the coming true of every girlish dream. All would be well between them. She was as certain of it today as she had been when they'd made love in the orangery. Their future together had nearly been ruined by their fears and misunderstandings. Neither of them would ever allow such a thing to happen again.

* * *

Warren savoured Marianne's moist lips and her curving figure against his angles. He wrapped his arms around her, not ever wanting to let go. Her love for him had been stronger than his troubles and hers, and although so many things remained unsettled or uncertain, in her embrace it didn't matter. He broke from their kiss, pressed his forehead against hers and inhaled her rich peony scent.

'Thank you for understanding.' She always had, never once laughing at his dreams, or his weaknesses. With her he'd stopped to enjoy what he'd built for himself. He wanted to share it and all with her, but there were still obstacles facing them. 'My dealings with Rupert aren't over yet.'

'Then we'll fight him together. If only the common licence didn't force us to wait seven days. We could marry at once and put all this foolishness behind us.' She straightened his wrinkled cravat, her hands on his chest light yet heady.

'Perhaps we don't have to wait.' He took one of her hands and raised it to his mouth, pressing his lips to the pulse of her wrist and making her inhale sharply. 'The Cartwrights may not like me, but I have other friends among the peerage, including one in the Prince's employ. He might be able to intercede with the bishop on our behalf and gain us a special licence.'

'If he can't, Lady Ellington and Lord Falconbridge certainly can. It will be expensive,' she warned, but he didn't care.

'I'll pay any cost to be with you.' He lowered his face to hers, her mouth tantalisingly close to his when someone behind them cleared their throat. He groaned, wondering if on their wedding night they'd be interrupted by as many people as those who regularly intruded on their kisses. He would have to make sure their bedroom door had a lock. He didn't want anything, not servants or intrusive relatives, to interrupt their wedded bliss.

Marianne stepped out of his arms with a mirthful smile, she more than Warren finding amusement in the interruption. They turned to find Darby waiting for their attention.

'Sir Warren, this arrived for you from your town house. The messenger said you are to read it at once.'

Warren took the letter, noting the mark of Mr Steed and Mr Dyer. 'It's from the solicitor.'

He tore it open as the butler left them. He read over the missive, the calm Marianne's sacrifice for him had brought increasing with Mr Steed's words.

'What does he say?' Marianne peered over his arm to read the letter.

'Mr Dyer has some evidence he thinks will send Rupert running from his claims and out of our lives. We have to present it to him and we'll need your help to do it.'

'I'll do anything to ensure he and his lies are destroyed.'

'I don't see why this meeting is necessary,' Rupert sneered at Warren from across the study in Warren's town house. Mr Steed and Mr Dyer watched the exchange from where they sat beneath the far window. Warren hadn't introduced them and they hadn't revealed who they were or why they were here. Rupert seemed to wonder at it as well as he glanced back and forth at the gentlemen, waiting for them to speak. 'Everything we needed to discuss was done in the country.'

'No, there's a great deal more we have to talk about.' Warren rose and came around the desk. 'I want a list of all the investors and how much each of them gave you. I also want an accounting of the money you still have, no matter how small, and with it a tally of your possessions and valuables which can be sold to raise more.'

'I won't give you any of the information, but let you swing while every investor rushes to attack you,' Rupert answered with wicked delight, his satisfaction in his victory making Warren want to blacken his eyes an even deeper shade of purple than they already were. Instead he remained calm, refusing to sink to his brother-in-law's level. 'I want you to sell Priorton to pay them back and then be thrown in debtors' prison because it still isn't enough.'

'The only one who'll go to prison is you. As for going into debt, it isn't possible. While Priorton has cost me a great deal, I'm far from broke or without resources.' Warren strolled to the door connecting the study to the adjacent sitting room.

'Of course you are. You can barely afford to pay the workmen, much less the investors.'

'On the matter of my finances, you're gravely mistaken.' Warren opened the door. Marianne strode through, the diamond engagement ring gifted to her by Lady Ellington and adorning her finger glittering in the early morning light. He took her by the hand and raised it to his lips. The memory of everything they'd shared in the orangery, and her coming to him in London, settled the anger and disgust struggling to take control of him. All would be well. Together they would make sure of it. 'I believe you already know my betrothed. We will be married by special licence tomorrow.'

Rupert gaped at them as he grasped what the coming marriage meant, but he remained stubborn in his hate. 'So, once you're done spending your money, you'll waste hers and in the end you'll both be without a house or reputations. I'll see to it the press ruins you for swindling aristocrats, then aligning yourself with the notorious relation of a whore.'

Warren's arm stiffened and he stepped forward to strike him, but Marianne's restraining hand stopped him. No, he couldn't hit the snake. They still needed a small measure of his co-operation.

'My guardian, Lord Falconbridge, is a prudent man,' Marianne replied with confidence, peering down her elegant nose at Rupert as though he were a weed in Lady Ellington's rose bed. 'As we speak, he is arranging for my money to be placed in trust where I will have access to it, but creditors will not.'

'You can't save him,' Rupert insisted, desperation beginning to undermine his determination. 'All you can do is make things worse.'

'He isn't the one who'll need to be saved, but you. You're in more danger than you think,' she replied as if explaining to him the notes on a pianoforte.

'Mr Dyer, do you care to inform Mr Rupert why it is I've asked him to join us today?' Warren at last addressed the two men.

Rupert paled at the mention of the famous barrister's name.

Mr Dyer rose and approached Rupert, who had the sense to step cautiously back.

'Mr Hirst, I've reviewed the documents you provided Sir Warren and have been briefed on what transpired between the two of you in regards to your venture,' Mr Dyer began, with the authority of a man used to addressing magistrates and lowlifes. 'Despite your claims it was Sir Warren and not you who invented this scheme, there's nothing in your possession signed by Sir Warren to prove it. Nor is there anything in writing showing he agreed to the terms you included in the stock certificate, including placing Priorton Abbey up as collateral.'

'It doesn't matter what you believe. The investors believed it and they're the ones who will crucify him.' Rupert raised one shaking finger at Warren. 'Especially once it reaches the papers and I'll make sure it does.'

'No, you won't because you won't be here,' Mr Dyer explained. 'You will be on the next ship to Australia. You'll go there to make your life over. You're to have no more contact with my client, you're not to sell the story to the papers and, if you ever set foot in England again, I'll see to it you're prosecuted for forgery, the penalty for which is death. As you know, my reputation for prosecuting such cases is unmatched.'

'You have no proof.' Rupert's voice wavered

as doubt about his plan began to take hold in his feeble mind.

'You're wrong.' It was Mr Dyer's turn to go to the door. He opened it and waved in a man with a flick of his fingers. A moment later, a skinny printer with a greasy hat held between his dirty hands crept into the room.

At the sight of him, the red flush of hate in Rupert's face vanished.

'I believe you know Mr Fink,' Mr Dyer said. 'He's ready to give evidence against you in exchange for protection from prosecution. He'll testify how you employed him to draft the forged investment papers which you then presented to a number of titled men. Once he's done testifying, I'll place every investor on the stand and have them tell the magistrate how it was you, and not Sir Warren, who convinced them to invest in the scheme. It's not Sir Warren they and the papers will crucify, but you.'

Rupert slumped against Warren's desk, knocking over the dusting-powder shaker, his plan crumbling around him and threatening to bring down his life with it. Warren didn't pity him. The man was as terrible a scandal creator as he was a businessman and deserved every punishment he'd brought upon his balding head. Then Rupert straightened himself, finding a little more fight in his weak constitution. 'You think you've won, Warren, but you haven't. There are still the debts and you might be paying Mr Dyer now, but when you have no money left, he'll stop fighting for you like any other bloodsucking barrister.'

'I'd gladly work for free to see scum like you ruined,' Mr Dyer replied, 'especially since I know you still have the investors' money.'

Panic widened Rupert's watery eyes. 'I don't. I spent it. It's gone.'

'Some of it is, but not the bulk of it,' Mr Dyer contradicted. 'Yesterday, I visited a friend of mine who owns your bank. When I explained to him the situation, he was very co-operative in showing me your false account and the money you've squirrelled away. He's more than happy to turn the funds over to me and avoid him and his bank being entangled in a forgery trial.'

Rupert looked back and forth between Mr Dyer and Warren as though it taxed his mind to believe what was being said and to find some kind of response to it.

'It's over, Rupert,' Warren said in the same voice he'd used to tell him Leticia had passed. Today was just as tragic as then, but this time it was all Rupert's fault. He'd done this to himself and no one but he would suffer. 'Whatever you planned, it won't happen. Instead, you'll find yourself at the end of a rope.'

'Unless you co-operate with us now.' Mr Steed rose to join the conversation. He laid out a sheet of paper, picked the pen off Warren's desk and held it out to Rupert. 'Write out a list of every investor and what they're owed. Include a full accounting of your assets so we may see to their selling at once and resolve this matter. You're also to sign over your quarterly inheritance payment to me to cover any additional shortfalls in what is owed.'

'You'll leave me destitute,' Rupert wailed as though expecting sympathy after everything he'd done.

'I'll leave you to your own devices, not here in London, but in Australia,' Warren spat out, wanting him gone from his life, his house and even the country for good. 'You'll succeed or fail according to your own merits, which are badly lacking.'

'I won't go.'

'Then you force us to turn everything over to the magistrate.' Mr Steed returned the pen to its stand. 'And you will be hanged for forgery.'

Rupert lunged at the pen, snatching it and the paper up. 'All right, I'll do as you ask.'

Like one of Warren's father's reluctant students, Rupert wrote out the required information. Over the next half-hour, the solicitor and the barrister questioned him to make sure he'd told them everything. He crumpled under their scrutiny like a weathered fence, signing his name to every affidavit and legal document they placed in front of him.

At last, when the two men were satisfied, Mr Dyer approached Warren. 'We'll handle any remaining matters from here, including making sure Mr Hirst has packed his things and is on the ship when it departs.'

'Is this the end of it, then?' Warren asked in disbelief.

'It should be. I'll let you know as soon as the investors are repaid.'

'I'll cover any differences, no matter what the cost.' With his new novel in Mr Berkshire's hands, and the inspiration for the next story one of the few bright points to come from this experience, he didn't worry about affording the extra expense.

'They shouldn't be much. He took sums from some well-known men, but it appears they didn't believe in him enough to give him large amounts.'

'And the papers?'

'I doubt anyone will say anything to them. No aristocrat wants to reveal having been duped by a man like Mr Hirst.'

Marianne slid her hand in Warren's and gave it a squeeze. 'Come, there's nothing more for us to do here.'

She tugged him into the adjoining sitting room where Lancelot slept on the sofa, his head resting on one tufted arm. Warren stared at everything surrounding him, especially the painting of Priorton hanging on the wall above the dog. The last time he'd sat in here, he'd feared losing it all. Now it was safe and Marianne was at his side.

'We won and you don't look happy.' Marianne wrapped her arms around his waist and held him close. 'What's wrong?'

'Mr Berkshire gave me some advice yesterday. He said challenges never end, but how you deal with them matters.'

'Lady Ellington said something similar to me. They're both right.'

'I'm glad they are.' Contented happiness replaced his seriousness as he bent her into a kiss. They were together once more and nothing would ever come between them again.

Chapter Fourteen

'Come, my dear, I have a surprise waiting for you in the church,' Lady Ellington announced as she hustled Marianne out of the carriage.

Above them the spiked spire of St Martin in the Fields rose against the bright blue London sky. True to his word, Warren had spoken to his royal connection and had asked him to approach the bishop about the special licence. Thankfully, the bishop was a great admirer of Warren's work and had been more than happy to grant the licence, especially when presented with autographed copies of Warren's novels. The clergyman had even arranged to perform the ceremony himself at St Martin in the Fields. The hurried affair meant no banns, and no spectacle for Warren's fans, much to Mr Berkshire's lament. Having been denied a more public wedding, the publisher had insisted on inviting his most trusted newspaperman to the ceremony to publish the story in the morning paper. Marianne was glad. She wanted all of London to hear of their marriage and her love for Warren.

'But, Lady Ellington, you've done so much for me already.' Marianne followed Lady Ellington into the vestibule, holding up the hem of her blue dress to keep from tripping on it. There'd been no time for a new gown, so Marianne had chosen to wear the one from Lady Astley's. They'd added a chemisette to it to make it more appropriate for the church, otherwise nothing else about it had been altered for the solemn occasion. She hoped the sight of her in it struck Warren as powerfully as it had at the musical and made him look forward to their first night together as man and wife as much as she did.

Lady Ellington hustled Marianne to one side, out of sight of the altar and the gentlemen standing there. Then Theresa's voice rang out.

'Marianne, you're gorgeous,' Theresa gushed as she hugged her friend. 'I'm so happy the wedding is taking place before my confinement. I didn't want to miss your happy day.'

'But how did you know?' It was then she noticed Lord and Lady Falconbridge standing behind Theresa and her husband, Mr Menton. 'What are you all doing here?'

'I summoned them,' Lady Ellington explained, quite pleased with herself. 'I wanted those who care about you the most to be here on this important day.'

'We're so happy for you.' Lady Falconbridge opened her arms to embrace Marianne, hugging her as well as a woman so heavy with child could.

She didn't pull away, but wrapped her arms around the graceful woman's shoulders and returned the tight embrace. It wasn't awkward or embarrassing, but the most natural thing she could do. This was the family she'd always wanted, the one she'd craved during the long nights at the Protestant School and in London with Madame de Badeau. She thought she'd found it once with the Smiths, but they'd never cherished her like the Falconbridges, Theresa or Lady Ellington. These people would never leave her or abandon her no matter what and she loved them.

Overhead the bells began to peal and the elderly sexton appeared to announce it was time for the guests to be seated for the ceremony.

Lady Ellington drew Marianne to one side while everyone, except Lord Falconbridge, left to take their places in the pew. Lady Ellington laid her hands on Marianne's shoulders, her eyes glistening like her diamonds. 'It used to break my heart to see you try and look cheerful when news from Theresa about her husband used to arrive, or the melancholy way you watched Randall and Cecelia. Now look at you, glowing like an Advent candle.'

Lady Ellington wrapped her plump arms around Marianne and hugged her hard before stepping away to allow Lord Falconbridge to approach.

'Miss Domville, may I escort you up the aisle?' Lord Falconbridge offered Marianne his arm.

'Yes, you may.'

A few moments later, with everyone seated, Lord Falconbridge led Marianne to the top of the aisle. Mrs Stevens sat in the pew with Lady Ellington, the two of them beaming with pleasure at seeing their efforts to match the young people complete.

Warren stood at the altar with Mr Berkshire and the bishop. He wore a dark green coat which increased the intensity of his eyes as they focused on her. Beneath his chin, his cravat was better tied than usual, but still remained at a slightly haphazard angle. It matched the gaiety in his smile and the joy illuminating his face like the light coming in through the tall windows behind him. He shifted on his feet, revealing his anxiousness to take her hand. His exuberance almost made her let go of Lord Falconbridge and sprint up the aisle to meet him. Instead, she marched in a stately gait with Lord Falconbridge as the organ behind them played. Her heart raced beneath her gown. She'd thought everything lost only a short while ago, now they were together for what would soon be the rest of their lives. He loved her, despite all the stories and their mutual missteps. He was hers and she was his and neither of them would ever be alone again.

At last Lord Falconbridge handed her to Warren and took his place beside his wife in the pew. Marianne pressed her hand in Warren's and the ceremony began. She heard little of what the bishop said as he read the service. She'd watched

Theresa walk down the aisle to Mr Menton, been there the morning Lord Falconbridge had married Lady Falconbridge. Each time she'd been happy for her friends while silently despairing of ever seeing her own wedding day. At last it was her turn before the altar and not with some leech like Lord Bolton, but with Warren, a man who'd always encouraged her to be more than even she'd imagined. Where might she go now with him as her husband? The idea of performing as Mr Berkshire had suggested didn't terrify her, not when she imagined Warren standing with her on the stage as he stood beside her now. She'd help him to reach even greater heights with his writing, all the while enjoying with him the love and security of a home and a true place in the world.

The promise of their life together was strong in his lips against hers as the bishop instructed them to kiss and seal the vows they'd made to one another.

After the ceremony, they returned to Lady Ellington's for the wedding breakfast. It was a rousing affair with a great deal of laughter and a few ribald remarks. For all the excited celebration, Marianne couldn't wait to be alone with Warren.

At last the time came. His carriage whisked them off to his town house, and soon they were alone in his room, indulging in the first private moment of their life together.

Warren made a show of locking the door and dropping the iron key on the table beside it. 'I refuse to be disturbed.'

'I'm surprised Mr Berkshire didn't insist on sending the newspaper man home with us after inviting him to the breakfast.' Marianne laughed as Warren stood over her and took her in his arms. He was solid and firm against her and it made her heartbeat quicken.

'Speaking of Mr Berkshire, what were you and he discussing before we left?' he murmured as he nuzzled the skin of her neck, his fingers slipping beneath the chemisette to caress the tops of her breasts.

She could barely recall the publisher's words under the pressure of Warren's touch. 'He was telling me about his plans for my compositions. He has quite a few of them.'

'Such as?' He slid a small pearl button through a hole and slipped the fine silk from her chest.

'Where I will perform my first concert.' She swept her tongue along the skin of his neck above his cravat, inhaling his strong male scent. 'I was thinking at Madame de Badeau's old town house. I still own it as part of my inheritance. It will attract people's attention and increase sales.'

Warren straightened as he examined her with a curious tilt of his head. 'Aren't you worried about society's reaction to such a questionable venue?'

'Not at all. After all, there is some advantage to scandal.'

'Indeed, there is.' He dipped her into a deep kiss and everything else faded away.

* * * * *

If you enjoyed this story,
you won't want to miss these
other great reads from Georgie Lee

A TOO CONVENIENT MARRIAGE
THE CAPTAIN'S FROZEN DREAM
A DEBT PAID IN MARRIAGE
THE COURTESAN'S BOOK OF SECRETS
RESCUED FROM RUIN

MILLS & BOON®

Why shop at millsandboon.co.uk?

Each year, thousands of romance readers find their perfect read at millsandboon.co.uk. That's because we're passionate about bringing you the very best romantic fiction. Here are some of the advantages of shopping at www.millsandboon.co.uk:

* **Get new books first**—you'll be able to buy your favourite books one month before they hit the shops

* **Get exclusive discounts**—you'll also be able to buy our specially created monthly collections, with up to 50% off the RRP

* **Find your favourite authors**—latest news, interviews and new releases for all your favourite authors and series on our website, plus ideas for what to try next

* **Join in**—once you've bought your favourite books, don't forget to register with us to rate, review and join in the discussions

Visit **www.millsandboon.co.uk**
for all this and more today!

MILLS_WEB_LP